W9-BLG-734

YOU CAN RUN

YOU CAN RUN

A NOVEL

Karen Cleveland

Ballantine Books

New York

Published in the United States by Random House, an imprint and division of Penguin Random House LLC, New York.

BALLANTINE and the HOUSE colophon are registered trademarks of Penguin Random House LLC.

LIBRARY OF CONGRESS CATALOGING-IN-PUBLICATION DATA
Names: Cleveland, Karen, author.
Title: You can run: a novel / Karen Cleveland.
Description: New York: Ballantine Books, [2021] |
Identifiers: LCCN 2020056068 (print) | LCCN 2020056069 (ebook) |
ISBN 9780593357798 (hardcover) | ISBN 9780593357804 (ebook)
Classification: LCC PS3603.L484 Y68 2021 (print) |
LCC PS3603.L484 (ebook) | DDC 813/.6—dc23
LC record available at https://lccn.loc.gov/2020056068
LC ebook record available at https://lccn.loc.gov/2020056069

Printed in the United States of America on acid-free paper

randomhousebooks.com

9 8 7 6 5 4 3 2 1

FIRST EDITION

Title-page art: © iStockphoto.com

Book design by Dana Leigh Blanchette

FOR BARRY, JAMES, WILLIAM, AND EMMA

The secret to creativity is knowing how to hide your sources.

—*Unknown*

Always go too far, because that's where you'll find the truth.

—*Albert Camus*

YOU CAN RUN

CHAPTER ONE

The clock in the corner of my screen reads 10:59 A.M. I stare at the digits, willing them to change, and for time to pass a little bit quicker. The minutes just *after* eleven will pass at warp speed; they always do. But the ones before are endless, interminable.

A muted chime dings, the familiar sound of a new cable hitting my queue. My gaze shifts from the clock in the corner to the browser window, open to the cable-tracking system, Fortress. A list of cables arrayed like an email inbox, the new one at the top, in bold type.

From Damascus Station. *Request for Encryption of New Source, FALCON.*

I knew the cable was coming, just didn't know it'd be today. It's a quick recruitment, for sure. But this guy—the one we're now calling Falcon—he's been on the fast track since day one, no doubt about that. He's set to be the CIA's newest source, once I vet him and send the cable up the chain. Something I'll start working on in exactly thirty-one minutes.

I shift my gaze back down to the clock just in time to see it hit 11:00.

Control-Alt-Delete. The cable system disappears, replaced with a small version of the Agency seal set against a black background. I catch sight of my reflection in the screen, and it catches me off guard, how little it looks like *me*. Hair in desperate need of a cut—and a style. Dark circles that no amount of makeup or coffee can fade.

Not the way I always imagined I'd look at this point in my life, for sure. But I wouldn't trade it for anything. It took three years of hopes and tears and injections—and all our savings—to get here.

"Eleven o'clock already?" Jeremy asks from the cubicle across from mine, right on cue. Same question every day. Creatures of habit, both of us.

I stand and grab my tote bag, sling it over my arm. "Sure is."

"Enjoy your lunch, Jill." He smiles awkwardly, pushing his glasses up the bridge of his nose. From anyone else it might seem like a dig, a *why-on-earth-are-you-taking-a-lunch-break-at-eleven*, but not from Jeremy. From him it's just conversation.

Besides, eleven's lunchtime, no doubt about it. Four hours of work, half-hour lunch, four more hours until the end of the day. The perfect midpoint. And more important, the thirty-minute window during which I'm guaranteed to catch sight of Owen. After his morning nap, before the afternoon one. Eleven's the scheduled time for his second bottle of the day, and now a container of pureed veggies, too.

If you'd have told me six months ago I'd see a cable like that in my queue and skip out at precisely eleven to watch an infant eat mashed peas, I'd have laughed. *A baby won't change anything,* I'd have said. Turns out, he changed *everything*.

Fact of the matter is, this is the kind of cable a reports officer like me *lives* for. The chance to vet a source like Falcon, at a time like this.

He's a Syrian defense official attached to a covert biowarfare program, working deep in one of our darkest black holes. And biowarfare's the new hot topic, like terrorism after 9/11. We've seen the fear a pandemic sows, the hit it takes on an economy.

Our adversaries have seen it, too. And quite frankly, that terrifies us.

By all accounts, *everyone's* ramping up their biowarfare programs. But penetrations of these covert programs are sorely lacking. And we at the CIA are desperate for sources.

A. J. Graham's the one who's behind this recruitment. Our best case officer in Damascus. It's my job to double-check his work, make sure he didn't miss anything, that he hasn't been compromised, blackmailed. I'm a trained case officer myself, but I traded life in the field for a desk at headquarters when Drew and I learned we'd have to start IVF.

I wade through the sea of cubicles and out of the windowless vault, with its stark, bare walls and too-bright fluorescent lighting. Down the narrow hall now, my pace quick, and up two flights of stairs to ground level. I badge out through an electronic turnstile, passing the host of armed guards. Into the lobby, then out into the sunshine.

A blast of warm air hits me, magnified by having left the frigid AC. It's June, and it's got to be close to ninety already. I wonder if they took Owen out for a stroller ride before it got too hot; I hope so. I can probably squeeze in another before dinner.

The path leading to the parking garage is perfectly landscaped, flanked on either side by vibrant blooms, and right now it's almost empty. No one else is leaving at this hour, and I pass only a single person heading toward the building: a woman in a suit, an impenetrable briefcase clutched tight at her side. A briefer, no doubt, heading back from downtown.

My RAV4's on the top level of the parking garage, which,

oddly enough, is at ground level; the lower levels are built into a hill. I'm halfway down one of the middle rows, like always. I slide into the car and start the engine, crank the AC. Then I open my laptop on the seat next to me, power it on. While it's booting up, I turn on my cellphone, then take my lunch bag out of my tote, open it up. Looks like Drew packed us salads today, topped with leftover grilled chicken from last night. I take out the plastic containers and arrange them on the center console.

I have this process down by now, know the exact order to maximize these thirty precious minutes. As soon as the phone's ready, I switch on the mobile hotspot. Then I open up a browser on the laptop, navigate to Favorites, click on the one saved link. A flashy homepage appears almost instantly.

All Children's Learning Academy. Learning Through Play. Ages 6 weeks to 6 years. I use the touchpad to move the cursor to the upper right corner. *Parent Login.* Type in my username, password, hit return, and a new screen appears. *Infant Room.* I click the link below—*Live View*—and wait for the video feed to load.

It's a little strange, I know, eating lunch in my car. But personal electronic devices are prohibited inside the building, and I'd never access something personal like this from my work computer. And it's not like I'm missing out on much social interaction. Before maternity leave I ate lunch at my desk every day, worked straight through. Most everyone in the vault does. I do feel a bit guilty for actually *taking* my lunch break, but eight hours—ten with the commute—is too long not to see Owen. If there's one thing I've learned since he was born, it's that guilt is inescapable.

Black-and-white footage appears on the screen, a trio of boxes, three separate camera angles. The main play area, littered with toys; the cribs lined up in the napping section; the kitchen, with a row of identical high chairs. Everything except the diaper-changing station.

I focus on the kitchen. There are two babies side by side in the row of high chairs, but neither is Owen. I look in his crib—empty—and scan the others, but there's just a single baby still sleeping, one with a thick head of dark hair, completely unlike Owen's blond fuzz.

Play area next. A handful of babies crawling around, one mouthing a plastic toy, another two strapped into low bouncy chairs. No sign of Owen. He must be getting a diaper change.

I glance at the clock in the corner of the screen. 11:07. Still plenty of time. I reach for the salad container on the console, pry off the lid, pour on the vinaigrette that Drew carefully packed in a separate little container—

A shrill ring from my phone startles me. I reach for it, check the illuminated screen. *Unknown.* Probably some sort of spam—

I press the green button and hold the phone to my ear. "Hello?"

"We have your son."

The voice is deep, robotic, devoid of inflection. An electronically altered voice, the kind I've heard in horror films.

We have your son.

Panic grips me. This isn't real. This *can't* be real.

Everything's calm in that room. Normal. Not like someone burst in there and nabbed a child—

"Who are you?" I ask.

"Breathe a word of this to anyone and you'll never see your son again."

It's a scam. It has to be. I've read about this, seen it on the news. A parent receives a call like this, their child's abducted or in trouble, and they panic, clear out their bank accounts, hand over everything. And all the while, the kid's going about his day, safe at school or home or whatever.

I get it now. I get why they run straight to the bank. Because this is *terrifying*.

I stare at the video feed, the side of the play area that leads to the diaper-changing station. He's going to be in that frame any minute now, clean diaper, ready for his bottle. He has to be.

"You have three minutes to verify this information."

I hear a mechanical *click,* followed by a string of short beeps. I pull the phone from my ear and glance at the screen. *Call ended.*

I focus on the laptop again, the video feed. Still no Owen.

The clock in the corner of the screen reads 11:08.

I unlock my phone with shaking hands, pull up the speed dial, find the entry. *Daycare.*

One ring—

"All Children's Learning Academy, this is Mackenzie speaking."

Mackenzie. The maddeningly peppy, eager-to-please receptionist.

"I'm—uh . . ." What do I say? "I'm calling to check on my son. Owen Smith, in the infant room." I eye the clock in the corner of the screen. 11:09.

"Mrs. Smith, hello!"

I've told her numerous times it's still Jill Bailey, that I don't plan to join the hordes of Jill Smiths of the world, but it goes in one ear and out the other.

"What can I help you with?"

"I don't see him. On the video feed. I just . . . I want to make sure . . ." What can I say? Can I say I want to make sure he's there? Or is that "breathing a word," saying too much?

"Don't worry, Mrs. Smith. Your brother picked him up."

My heart feels like someone's squeezing it, like I can't breathe. "What?"

"Your brother, Ty. He's bringing Owen to his six-month checkup. Remember? You called this morning. Told us about that meeting you couldn't get out of—"

Oh my God. This isn't happening.

"Mrs. Smith?"

Her voice sounds distant.

Ty's in Singapore this week. And he's never picked up Owen, not once. He's listed as an emergency contact because the daycare center required five, but surely they should have asked for photo ID before handing my infant son to a stranger, shouldn't they? Isn't that what the policy says? Wasn't it one of the features they touted when Drew and I toured the center, the ones that assured us our son would be safe here?

"Mrs. Smith, is everything all right?"

11:10.

Breathe a word of this to anyone and you'll never see your son again.

"Yes, thank you."

I press end and stare at the phone. My background's a picture of Owen, a huge grin on his face, two tiny teeth visible.

Someone has my son.

I don't know whether to cry or scream. I stare at his picture, that smile—

Another shrill ring, and Owen's face disappears, replaced with a single word. *Unknown.*

I press the green button, and I'm met with silence.

"Is he okay?" I ask, my voice sounding choked.

"He's fine, now. And he will continue to be, if you do as we say." The voice is the same, heavy and flat and mechanical. Chilling.

How is this happening?

Why is this happening?

"What do you want?"

Money? Oh God, we don't have enough, do we? Three rounds of IVF left us completely broke. *Worse* than broke, with that second mortgage—

But it is not about money, is it? The fact that I work at the CIA, that I'm sitting in my car in the Langley parking garage at this very moment, it's not a coincidence.

They want something from me. They're going to ask me to do something horrible. Treasonous. Something that will irreparably harm our country, or get someone killed—

"There's a new report in your queue. About Falcon. You're going to approve it."

I wait, heart thumping. "And?"

"And your son will be returned."

That's it? That can't be it.

"Do it now, Jill."

"Okay." I fumble for my bag, knocking over the salad container, scattering lettuce leaves and chicken on the front passenger seat.

"I'm going to disconnect. Come back to your car when you're done."

"Okay."

As soon as I'm in that building, I'll go to security, get help—

"One last thing. Put the phone in your pocket, bring it with you. If you say anything you shouldn't, if you do anything you shouldn't, we'll know. And Owen will be gone, forever."

CHAPTER TWO

The call disconnects, and for a moment I just sit there, phone in my hand, staring at the image of my son's smiling face.

This is a nightmare, isn't it? I'm going to wake up, and he's going to be safe in his crib, fast asleep. This isn't real.

But it is.

They have my baby.

Do it now, Jill.

I push open the car door and step out into the warm humid air, phone clenched tight in my fist. I sling my tote over my shoulder, slam the door shut, start walking down the row of cars, sliding the phone into the front pocket of my pants—

Pants. I'm wearing pants today. I have pockets. More often than not, in the summer I wear skirts or dresses. What if I didn't have pockets today?

Or do they *know* I have pockets? Are they watching me? Did they see me leave my house, drop Owen at daycare?

Of course they'd watch me. If they're going to do *this*, take my son, they've probably been watching us for days, or weeks.

They came up with a story that fooled Mackenzie. They knew

my brother's name, knew he was one of our emergency contacts. Called All Children's, pretending to be me—

How many are involved? A *woman* made the call. And a *man* walked in, pretending to be my brother, walked out of there with my son—

The thought of a stranger carrying Owen, walking to a car, turns my stomach. Does that man have a car seat? Did he strap Owen in tightly enough?

Why am I obsessing over a car seat? *My son's been kidnapped.* I can't think clearly.

I'm off the top deck of the garage now, back onto the walkway, and I'm intensely aware of the phone in my pocket. Smart move, telling me to bring it. I'm sure they've hacked in. That they're tracking my movements through GPS. Using the microphone to listen to everything I say, everything around me. The very reasons we're not permitted to bring phones into the building.

A couple of lone individuals are walking away from the building, toward me. A harried-looking woman who offers a smile as she passes. I'm too spooked to smile back.

Then a young guy in a suit, a briefcase at his side, avoiding eye contact. Preoccupied, self-important? Or is it something else? Is he monitoring me, reporting back to someone?

Is *she*?

I spin my head around, but her back is to me, and so is his.

Does it matter?

They're tracking me, listening to me, one way or another.

And one way or another, *they have Owen.*

Owen. Is he safe right now? Is he scared? The thought makes me sick. Drew and I have never even left him with a sitter. No one but the two of us, and the teachers at the daycare center, the same ones he's been with since he was three months old. How's he reacting to a stranger?

I reach the bank of doors, pull one open. Step into the lobby, feel the blast of cool air. There are the turnstiles up ahead, and guards in uniform. Three of them I can see. I'm suddenly frozen.

One step, then another.

Should I say something? I could, right now.

But the phone in my pocket—they're listening, aren't they?

I take a breath, deep but not too deep. Trying to appear calm, like everything's normal.

More steps forward, an even pace, slow and steady, until I reach the turnstiles. I don't make eye contact with the guards, don't look in their direction.

I hold my badge to the reader, enter my PIN, and the barrier drops. I walk through, still forcing myself not to look at the guards.

One foot in front of the other, eyes straight ahead. Every sense is on alert, waiting for the sound of footsteps behind me, for the touch of a hand on my shoulder, for the sound of a voice: *Come with me, please.*

But there's nothing. I'm through the turnstiles now, eyes still straight ahead. I reach the bank of elevators, glance around. No one there. Relief washes over me.

I press the down button and focus intently on the numbers above the elevator doors until one arrives. I step in, the only passenger, and travel down to the basement. Step out, hang a left—

"Jill!"

I spin around. It's that new reports officer from Iran Division, someone whose name is escaping me.

"I'm going to send you a cable later today," he says. "Reissuing COVCOM for Hawkeye. Just need your approval since he runs in the same circles as Buffalo—"

"Okay," I say quickly, turning my back to him, continuing on. He shouldn't be talking about covert communications in the hallway. *Or* using sources' crypts. Especially not when there's a phone in my pocket, transmitting everything.

I pick up my pace. I can feel him watching me go, a question on his face, my abruptness unsettling. But *they* don't see it. All they can do is listen.

I reach the vault door and hold my badge to the reader. The lock disengages with a click, and I push the heavy door open. The phone in my pocket feels like a time bomb.

Once, a few years ago, I accidentally brought my phone into the building, buried in my tote bag. Realized when I sat down at my desk, pulled out my lunch bag, caught sight of it. I immediately brought it down to security, turned myself in. Received a written warning, a black mark on my record. One isn't so bad; accidents happen. Two and it can affect your chances of promotions, or competitive assignments. After that your very employment can be at risk.

I walk down the aisle to my cubicle—

"Back already?" Jeremy asks as I approach, brows knitting together in confusion. There's a half-eaten sandwich in front of him. Peanut butter and jelly, by the looks of it. An open bag of Fritos, and a can of Coke.

I freeze. What am I supposed to say?

"Video feed wasn't working." I slide into my chair, avoiding eye contact.

Jeremy carefully places the remnants of his sandwich back into a Ziploc bag, folds up the bag of Fritos as quietly as he can. Like he doesn't want to eat in front of me unless we're eating together, each in our own cubicle, absorbed in our own work, like we used to.

Jeremy. I trust him. I could write a note about Owen, tell him I need help. I eye the pad of paper on my desk, the pen.

And then a voice rings in my head:

Owen will be gone, forever.

What if Jeremy doesn't get it, asks a question aloud? Or what if he goes quietly for help, but someone else says something they shouldn't?

My right hand finds the mouse in front of me. I move it, and the screen turns from black to blue, with a box in the center. *Username, Password.* I click, follow the prompts, and then the screen springs to life. There's Fortress, open, just like I left it. The new cable's at the top, in bold. I double-click, and then I skim.

It's what I expected, what I've known for some time is coming. Cables like this, encryptions of new sources, they don't just come out of the blue. A.J.'s been developing this source for months. Everything's documented here, the ops tests, the polygraph, the source's background. There are copies of his credentials in accompanying cables, separated for operational security. Photographs, fingerprints.

These are the big cables, the ones that are few and far between, that take the most time. Making sure the case officer has checked all the boxes, done all the requisite vetting. Making sure he or she isn't under pressure in the field, being blackmailed. That's the point of my job, really. I'm supposed to be the impartial one. Unbiased, unpressured, uncorrupted.

A.J. wrote the cable; Vaughn Craig, the Chief of Station in Damascus, signed off. Now it's on to me. After that, it goes to the Chief of Operations for our division—COPS, as he's known—and then on to the Agency's Director of Operations, Langston West. A newly streamlined process, designed by West himself, to expedite the onboarding of new assets. To simplify and streamline a time-consuming and overly bureaucratic process.

I'm not sure COPS even reads the cables, at least not closely. In his view, once the Chief of Station and I have signed off, it's good to go. I'm thorough, and I care, and everyone around here knows it. I doubt the Director of Operations gives it more than a cursory look, either. Syria isn't in his wheelhouse; he's a Russia guy all the way, known for wrapping up Russian spies, refusing to swap them, always looking for opportunities to take a hard-line approach against *that* particular adversary.

The last thing in the world I should do is approve this cable.

I close my eyes and try to focus, try to figure this out, but all I see in my mind's eye is Owen. Is he scared right now? Is he hurt?

Breathe a word of this to anyone and you'll never see your son again.

I scroll to the bottom of the screen, the notes section.

"Fully approved with no amendments," I type. I wonder if my phone's picking up the click of my keys, if they know what I'm doing, what I'm typing.

"Welcome to the family, FALCON." My standard comment, whenever I approve a new source. Usually I feel a burst of adrenaline when I type it. Anticipation. Now I just feel sick to my stomach.

I move the cursor to the Approve button. Hover there.

If this is what they want me to do, if this is what it takes to get Owen back—

I can fix it later. I *will* fix it later. Once Owen's safe. This action, sending this cable forward, it's fixable. Nothing else is going to happen today. It'll take COPS and the Director of Operations a day, at least, to get to it. I'll come clean before that, for sure.

Right now I need to do what they say.

I click, and the cable disappears from my queue, just as expected.

Almost like it never happened.

I let out a breath I didn't know I was holding.

Now what?

Owen.

I lock my computer again, stand up so abruptly my chair rolls back into my cubicle wall.

Jeremy looks over. "Everything okay, Jill?"

His half-eaten lunch is pushed to the back of his desk, against the corkboard where he's tacked a dozen snapshots of his beloved Great Dane, Max.

"I'm just going to head back to my car," I say. "I left my keys inside." I attempt a lighthearted laugh, but it sounds oddly shrill.

He nods slowly, and I walk away from our cubicles without another word.

Once out of the vault, I hurry down the hall, head lowered. The last thing I need is anyone approaching me in the halls, saying anything they shouldn't, taking up precious seconds of my time.

I take the stairs to the lobby, two at a time, hand resting on the front of my pants pocket as I go. Badge out through the turnstiles—

A high-pitched beep, long and steady. From *my* turnstile. I freeze. Then I look up, panicked, at the nearest guard.

Do they know what I've done? Could they have put some sort of alert on my badge, to stop me?

How am I going to explain the phone—

"Go on," the guard says, disinterested, waving me forward. "That one's been on the fritz lately."

Relief washes through me, leaves me weak.

What I'm doing is wrong. But I'll fix it. I'll make this right, just as soon as I have Owen.

I force a smile and a nod, and I keep walking, never looking back.

———

I slide inside my car and shut the door behind me, reach immediately for my phone. No missed calls, no texts, just the background shot of Owen staring back at me, those chubby pink cheeks, that drooly grin. And the time. 11:33 A.M.

Without the engine running, without the AC blasting, it's unnervingly silent. I stare at the phone, willing it to ring.

Come back to your car when you're done.

That means he'll call back, right?

What if he doesn't call back?

I have no way to get in touch with the man who has my son.

I set the phone down on the center console and reach for the laptop, still open on the passenger seat, stray lettuce leaves and chunks of chicken around it, a river of vinaigrette pooling in the seams of the leather.

I pull up the video feed and scan the room. Ariella's in the kitchen, cleaning the counters. The high chairs are empty.

A couple of babies are asleep in cribs, but not Owen.

And the play area—there are babies crawling, banging toys, one chewing on a board book. Lyla's sitting in the rocker with another baby on her lap. None of them are Owen.

Oh God.

They're not going to return him, are they? Not for what I did, for such a small thing. They'll ask for more, won't they? More, and more, and more—

I should call Drew. The police. *Someone.*

Breathe a word of this to anyone and you'll never see your son again—

I feel like I'm going to vomit. I have this overwhelming desire to go to sleep and wake up when this is all over, but *when* will it be over? How will this ever end?

I messed up, didn't I? I had an opportunity, in that building. I should have gone straight to security, come clean, gotten the authorities involved. The FBI could be out there right now, looking for Owen, and instead, I'm sitting here alone in my car, while my baby is God knows where—

A shrill ring.

I grab the phone.

Unknown.

I press the green button. "Hello?"

Nothing. No sound on the other end.

"Hello?" I ask again, panicked.

"Good work, Jill."

It's the same voice, the deep robotic one.

He knows. He knows I did what he asked me to do.

"Owen. Where's Owen? You said—"

"He's back at daycare."

I spin toward the laptop, scan each of the camera feeds again. Ariella in the kitchen, alone. Those same babies sleeping in their cribs. Still no sign of Owen in the play area. "He's not—"

I stop short. *There he is.*

Mackenzie's walking into the room, and Owen's in her arms, bright-eyed and smiling and perfectly content.

My Owen. He's back.

A choked cry escapes my lips, and my eyes fill. I can't take my eyes off him.

"We keep our promises."

I watch him on the screen, my vision blurred by tears. Mackenzie hands him to Lyla, who walks him over to the kitchen, places him in a high chair, secures the strap around his waist. She turns to get food, and he bangs his hands on the tray happily.

"Go get him, Jill."

There's a click, and three beeps, and the line disconnects.

I drop the phone and start the ignition. I don't close the laptop, don't want to take my eyes off the screen, off Owen.

Go get him.

I don't have to be told twice. There's nothing I want to do more right now than hold Owen in my own arms, to know for absolute sure that he's safe and healthy and this nightmare is over.

I peel out of the parking lot, desperate to get to him as quickly as possible. Before they come back, ask for more. Before the rug is pulled out from beneath me.

The video feed on the laptop freezes, signal lost. The mobile hotspot isn't strong enough.

Ten above the speed limit, fifteen. My eyes keep darting to the rearview mirror, watching for police cars.

It's a thirteen-minute drive to the daycare center.

I make it in nine.

I pull into one of the spaces closest to the front door, throw the car into park, run into the building.

Mackenzie's at the front desk, staring. "Mrs. Smith? Is everything all right?"

"I just want to see Owen." I say it too loud, too intense.

"Of course," she says, looking at me like I'm crazy. "I'll be right back with him." She stands, disappears down the hall, and I watch her go—

He did the same thing, didn't he? The man who took my son. He stood right here in this lobby, had a conversation with Mackenzie, waited while she walked down that hall, walked back again with my son in her arms.

My eyes find the camera in the corner of the ceiling, facing the front door. CCTV, security footage. A small green light, illuminated. Whoever did this, they'd be on there—

Footsteps. Mackenzie rounds the corner, and snuggled in her arms is Owen. He gives me a gummy grin and flaps his arms.

A sob escapes. I rush forward, take him into my own arms. *Owen.* My baby. He's soft and warm and—

And he smells like cologne. Men's cologne, and not Drew's. A kind that's unfamiliar.

A shiver runs through me.

"Are you taking him home, Mrs. Smith?"

"Yes," I whisper.

"Have a great afternoon! We'll see you both back here tomorrow."

I walk outside to the car, squinting into the sunlight, looking around, certain someone's watching us. But I see no one.

I strap him into his car seat, pull the belt secure. Hand him his stuffed elephant, the one he always clutches in the car. He looks up at me with wide, innocent eyes. He seems perfectly normal, like nothing ever happened.

I slide into the driver's seat, buckle in. My whole body feels weak, and spent. I watch his reflection in the rearview mirror; he's rear-facing, but there's a mirror strapped to the backseat.

I have him. He's safe.

I start the engine and back out of the parking space, much slower this time. Out of the parking lot, then left onto the main road, under the speed limit this time—

The phone rings.

Unknown.

This isn't over, is it?

I reach for the phone, eyes still on the road. "Hello?"

"Hello, Jill. I trust you're happy to see Owen?"

I glance around again, searching for someone, anyone. On the sidewalk, on the road, inside a car. But I see no one. The street's practically empty.

Where are they?

And what do they want?

There's a yellow light ahead, and I move my foot to the brake, begin slowing to a stop. "What now?" I ask.

They're going to ask for more. They think they have me now, that I'm compromised, that I'll do whatever they ask. They don't know that I'm going to come clean—

"Now, nothing. You did what we asked. We want nothing more from you."

Nothing?

I come to a stop at the red light.

I don't believe it. It doesn't make sense. And it leaves me completely unsettled.

"As long as you stay quiet, as long as you don't breathe a word of this, you'll never see us or hear from us again."

There it is, there's the kicker. *As long as you stay quiet.* Because I'm not going to stay quiet. Now that Owen's safe, I can admit what I did, make things right—

"But if this ever comes out, we'll be back. We'll take your son. And we'll kill him."

CHAPTER THREE

A horn blares behind me, blasting through the fog in my brain. The traffic light in front of me is green. I set down the phone—the caller has disconnected, Owen's grinning face is back on the screen—and my gaze darts to the rearview mirror. A car behind me, the driver clearly muttering a string of profanities. I raise my hand in an apologetic wave and press down on the gas, the car lurching forward.

Owen gurgles happily in the backseat.

Owen.

These people just threatened to kill my son if I come clean—and I *have* to come clean.

They'll be back. I might have Owen, but this isn't over. Not even close.

Witness protection. Surely there's something like that available to us. We'll disappear, Drew and Owen and me. The Agency will give us new names, new identities. We'll start over somewhere, just the three of us—

My parents. Drew's parents. Our siblings. Oh God, we wouldn't be able to see them again.

I tighten my hands on the steering wheel.

And our jobs—what would happen to our jobs? With new identities, our résumés would be blank, our educations worthless. Drew wouldn't be a member of the bar, wouldn't be able to practice law. How would we make ends meet? How would we pay our mortgages, our student loan debt, our car payments?

But it would just be temporary. Until we figure out who took Owen, who's threatening us. Once they're arrested, locked away, then we'd be free to return to our lives.

Would we, though?

Because it's not a couple of individuals behind this, or a small band of criminals, is it? It's a foreign intelligence service. A *government*. An adversary.

I glance at Owen in the rearview mirror, feeling sick to my stomach.

That's the only thing that makes sense. This is all centered around Falcon. Making sure I don't dig into his background, making sure he becomes a CIA source.

Most likely scenario? He's a dangle. A planted double agent. He's not *actually* a disillusioned Syrian defense official, doesn't *actually* want to assist the U.S. Someone's just making it look that way, and they knew that once I started digging around, I'd learn the truth.

I've done it before, several times in fact, discovered prospective sources weren't who they claimed to be. It's started with a thread, a piece of information that didn't check out. An address that didn't exist, or a degree that was never earned, and it's unraveled from there. And thank goodness it *has*. It's saved us from being duped by an adversary, fed false information—or worse. Having our officers targeted, or our technology used against us. We don't always know what the end game is, but this much is clear: nothing good comes from trusting a double agent.

And this one's sophisticated. This is someone who knows how we operate, how we vet sources. Someone who knew about *me*.

My name's out there, on the dark web. One of those intelligence leaks, years ago. Security notified me once. I never worried much about it; Jill Bailey's a fairly common name, and all it says is that I'm a reports officer, working Syria.

But these people, they knew I was working *Falcon*. That sort of information should *never* fall into the hands of an adversary. The whole point of having a headquarters-based reports officer is to prevent a scenario like this. And they knew *exactly* when the cable arrived in my queue. They knew before it happened; they already had Owen by the time it was sent.

A chill runs through me. These people are aggressive, and they're *good*.

Who's behind it? Syria makes the most sense, if the dangle's a Syrian guy. Syria's an adversary, for sure: a state sponsor of terrorism, a human rights violator, and a friend to our enemies. But are the Syrian intelligence services sophisticated enough to pull this off? In that respect it seems more like China, or Russia. Or what about a dark horse, a service that's sophisticated, but flying just under the radar? Iran, Ukraine?

Numerous intelligence services are operating in Syria; the country's practically overrun with proxy wars. It's a battleground for the U.S. and Russia, for Iran and Saudi Arabia. Israel's active there, and Turkey, and Qatar, and the list goes on.

My head is starting to ache. There's no way to know *who*.

What about *why*?

My first thought is COVCOM. Our covert communications system, the way we communicate with our sources. Foreign intelligence services are desperate to get their hands on it, to infiltrate it. What better way to ferret out spies? What better way to find *our* case officers operating in their country, and neutralize them?

But double-agent operations—they could serve any number of purposes. Could be to plant false information, something that would somehow benefit the country running the source. Could be to learn more about how we operate. Could be to identify our officers, or to target them, kill them, like what happened years ago in Khost, Afghanistan.

Here's the thing that doesn't make sense. They *had* me. I approved that cable, went back to my car, and waited for their call. They didn't have to return Owen right away. They could have asked for more. Names of assets, of case officers. Information from our most sensitive compartmented reports. *Anything.* As much as I don't want to admit it, there's a good chance I'd have done it, given it to them. That's how terrified I was, how desperate.

But they didn't ask.

Why?

Ten minutes later I pull into the driveway of our home in Vienna, Virginia. It's a small place, a boxlike little ranch built in the sixties, with a giant backyard, tons of huge trees. When we bought, the neighborhood was all older ranches; now, at least a third have been torn down, new McMansions erected in their place.

I unstrap Owen and carry him inside, past the American flag hanging out front, flapping gently in the breeze. I set him down on the floor in the living room, on his brightly colored foam mat, the one that's there to cushion him from the inevitable topples. He sits well on his own—the newest skill he's mastered—but sometimes he reaches too far for a toy and loses his balance. I move some of his favorite toys close to him. Stackable cups, a shape sorter. Then I perch on the edge of the couch and watch him.

He's safe. He's *here*, at home, playing contentedly.

Everything seems chillingly normal.

But nothing's normal, and it never will be again.

Owen's oblivious to it all, banging the blue plastic cup against the play mat, babbling happily. He's *fine*. Happy, healthy. But my God, how close did I come to losing him?

How close am I *still* to losing him?

I stand abruptly, walk into the kitchen. Wash my hands, scrubbing too hard, the water hot, like I can somehow wash away this cloud hanging over us.

I set to work preparing a bottle, because it's something to do, because he was without one earlier, wasn't he? I gather him into my arms, give him the bottle. He takes it hungrily.

He falls asleep in my arms, and I carry him to his room, lay him down carefully in his crib. He sighs and rolls over onto his belly, his eyes never opening.

I stand near the crib and look around his room. The rocker that belonged to my grandma, and then my mom. The shelf full of books: treasured favorites from my own childhood, and Drew's; gifts we opened at our baby shower; books we spent years collecting on our own for the baby we longed to have. The framed photographs of Owen as a newborn. The plaque on the wall with his tiny footprints molded into clay.

We're going to have to leave all of this, aren't we? Leave our home, start over from scratch.

If it's a hostile foreign intelligence service behind this . . . My God, how will it ever end? How will it ever be safe to come home again?

I leave Owen's room and walk through the rest of the house. The kitchen and bathroom, in desperate need of updating. The guest room that's been overtaken with big plastic toys. The dining room table that doubles as Drew's home office. All of the things that irked me about the house. Now they just seem homey. And fleeting.

Now I realize how desperately I'll miss it all.

My phone rings, startling me. Screen says *703*, nothing more. A call from Langley.

"Hello?"

"Jill, it's Jeremy. Hey, Violet just came by, looking for you. I wasn't sure what to tell her. You said you just went back to the car to get your keys . . ." He trails off, the question clear: *Where in the world are you?*

I just took off, didn't I? I was so preoccupied with going to get Owen it never occurred to me to tell my boss that I was leaving.

"Daycare called," I say, the first lie that pops into my head. "Owen's sick. I went to pick him up."

"Oh."

"I meant to call Violet, totally forgot. Would you mind letting her know? And tell her I'm sorry. . . ."

She had warned me I'd burn through sick leave like crazy this first year. Her kids are older now, but she remembers these days. It's the perfect excuse.

"Sure," Jeremy says. And then, after a pause: "Hope Owen feels better."

"Thanks, buddy."

I set the phone down on the kitchen counter and stare at it. Did *they* hear that call? They must have, right?

That was why I lied, wasn't it?

A white lie, a necessary lie. Just to get me by until it's safe to come clean, until I'm out of their earshot, until they're not listening.

Are they *watching*, too? I glance around furtively. The bookshelves in the living room, the television mounted on the wall—it's a smart TV. Those can be hijacked, just as surely as a phone.

My home—this place that's supposed to be a haven—isn't safe.

Drew comes home at five with a bag of Chipotle. He gives me a peck on the cheek, his stubble scratchy against my skin, then tousles Owen's blond fuzz. He deposits the food on the kitchen table, pulls his cellphone from his back pocket and places that on the table, too, then collapses into a chair.

"Rough day?" I ask, because it seems like what I'm supposed to say.

Because they're listening.

He pulls off his loosened necktie, tosses it over onto the counter. "Leo's on a warpath lately." Leo's one of the partners, the tough one. "He's going to start cracking down on this." Drew gestures toward the table in front of him, and I know exactly what he means, even without him saying it. Drew and a few other associates try to make it home for dinner with their families, then work at home long into the night. He rarely sees the inside of a courtroom; his work is tedious and solitary, and it can be done from *anywhere*. But Leo hates it.

Any other day, this would get me spun up. But now? Now it seems so very minor. Still, though, *they're listening*. "That's ridiculous. You put in just as many hours as anyone else there."

"More," he mutters, standing up and making his way to the sink. He rolls up his sleeves and washes his hands.

It's true. He's a hard worker, always has been. Contract law, that's his specialty, with a focus on the international. Worked out well early in our relationship: When I was posted in Turkey, he did a stint in his firm's Ankara office. When I was in China, he secured an assignment in Beijing. It wasn't easy for him; foreign languages don't come easily for him, the way they do for me. But he worked at it, persevered. I know, though, that he was relieved when I gave up the field postings once and for all. He's never felt the same longing for those days that I have.

I strap Owen into his high chair and open a jar of pureed carrots while Drew grabs forks and doles out the burrito bowls.

"How was your day?" he asks, taking a bite from his bowl. I eye his phone, on the table. Mine's nearby, too, because it always is, because I can't do anything out of the ordinary right now.

And then there's the television, watching, listening.

"Oh, fine," I say quickly, offering Owen a spoonful of carrots. "You know, the usual."

I set down Owen's spoon and pick up my fork, avoiding eye contact with Drew.

"Busy?" he asks.

"Sort of."

"I feel like I'm pulling teeth here, honey."

I shrug and take another bite.

"Owen have a good day?"

Owen. My chest tightens. "I picked him up early. He was sick." I don't even know why I say it. Because I already said it once, to Jeremy?

Drew turns toward Owen, his brows knitted with concern. He presses the back of his hand against Owen's forehead. "Fever?"

"A touch." It's unnerving how easily the lies are flowing. "Feels okay now. Looks okay."

"Maybe one of those twenty-four-hour bugs?"

"Maybe."

I take another bite of my burrito bowl.

"That means he can't go back tomorrow, doesn't it?"

It does. Twenty-four hours, fever-free. That's the rule.

But all I can think about are those words: *Go back.* I can't imagine bringing Owen back there. *Ever.* That place let a stranger take him away.

"I can stay home with him," Drew says. "Leo might have a fit, but you picked him up today. . . ."

"That'd be great," I murmur. And I stare at my food, because what little appetite I had is gone, completely. Tomorrow I need to go to work, and I need to come clean, and set this all in motion—

"Jill, is everything okay?" Drew's watching me with concern.

Of course it's not okay. Our son was kidnapped today. The people that did it, they've threatened to come back. They *will* come back, unless I stay quiet, and I can't stay quiet.

We'll have to leave everything we know, everything we love, for God knows how long. Our lives are about to change forever.

And I can't say a word of that right now.

I force a smile at my husband, and then I lie. "Everything's fine."

I spend the rest of the evening waiting for an opportunity to tell Drew the truth. Bath time for Owen seems like a possibility, at first. We're away from the television, the faucet's running noisily, my phone's still in the kitchen. But Drew's phone is in his back pocket. And he's wearing his smartwatch—I'd forgotten all about the smartwatch. They could be listening through that, too.

Then it's on to reading Owen books, putting him to bed. The usual bedtime routine, and one we do together each evening; neither of us wants to miss out on more time with Owen than we have to. But it's another missed opportunity. Drew's phone and watch are still on him.

As soon as Owen's asleep, Drew heads to the dining room table, gets back to work. I head into the kitchen. There's no dinner cleanup tonight, no bottles to prepare for tomorrow. I stand there awkwardly, because usually I zone out in front of the TV after this, and the last thing I want to do is sit there staring straight into their cameras.

I go to bed early and lie awake, staring at the ceiling fan. My phone's plugged into the charger on my nightstand, because that's where it always is, and I can't change my routine. Drew's will be charging on his own nightstand, anyway.

He comes to bed three hours later, and sure enough, plugs in his phone. "You still awake?" he asks.

"Yeah."

He scoots closer, curls his body around mine. "Good."

Could I whisper something? I could get out of bed, find some paper, write him a note. But what if he asks where I'm going? What if I bring it back and he says, *What's that?* Or what if they see it? I don't know what sort of cameras they've planted, or *where.*

His hands start running the length of my body, and I tense.

"What's wrong?" he murmurs.

"Nothing," I say, loud enough for them to hear.

His hands start roaming again, and I shift away from him.

"Owen's asleep," he says. "I'm done with work . . ." He trails off, leaves the rest of the thought unspoken: *Why in the world not?*

Because it's not just *us* here.

"Not tonight," I say.

He rolls away from me, and I can hear his disappointment in the silence that follows.

If he knew, he'd understand. But it's not worth the risk, telling him right now. I'll come clean at work first. And then we'll have security. People to watch over us, get us resettled in a protection program. Once they're around, I'll tell him everything.

Tomorrow I'll tell him everything.

———

When I get to my desk the next morning, the first thing I do is search for the cable, the one I approved yesterday. COPS approved it, too, and now it's waiting for the Director of Operations to sign off. It hasn't even gone all the way through the chain here at headquarters, hasn't been sent back to Damascus Station.

Next I pull up the accompanying cable, the addendum with the stripped-out details. There's Falcon's real name, Junaid Abdul Al-Noury. His fingerprints. And photographs. I stare at the headshot. About my age, round face, thick bushy brows, even thicker beard. Wide-set eyes, intense, almost a hazel tone. I linger on those, trying to read him. *Who are you? What do you want?*

Only a select handful in the Agency will know his true name. A slightly larger cadre will be aware of his crypt. But most analysts and policymakers will know him only as *a clandestine source with firsthand access,* blindly trusting that he's been properly vetted. To the general public, he'll be invisible; his reporting, the truth.

I close that cable, and the previous one is still up on my screen. It's highlighted green, a status update. *Approved with no modifications by DO Langston West.* Falcon's officially a source.

I still have time to make this right. Just not as much as I'd anticipated. Falcon's now eligible for COVCOM. It'll take time for A.J. to set up a meeting, to deliver the COVCOM. But I don't have time to waste.

I lock my computer and head for Violet's office. Take a deep breath, knock twice.

"Come in," she calls.

That sick feeling's back. I open the door and step inside, closing it behind me.

"Have a seat, Jill. I just need to finish this." She's typing away, barely glancing in my direction, focusing on her screen. Her blond hair is perfectly blown out, as usual, and she's in a black sheath dress today. Always something black; ironic for someone who shares her name with such a vibrant color.

I sit down across from her and wait. My heart is thumping. I cross my legs, then uncross them. Listen to the sound of her fingers flying across the keyboard.

A moment later she looks up. "Sorry to keep you waiting." She rests her arms on the desk, clasps her hands, sighs. "It's Brent."

Brent's not the most competent member of the team, to put it mildly.

"He's just approving one cable after another." She shakes her head. "No research whatsoever."

It's not something a boss should be saying about one employee to another, but we all know it's true.

"That's terrible," I say, my voice flat. Because she's about to have a way bigger problem on her hands than slacker Brent.

"Not everyone's as conscientious as you, that's for sure." She smiles at me. "Now, what can I do for you, Jill?"

Not everyone's as conscientious as you.

Her words stop me. What Brent does every day—cursory checks, hitting the Approve button—really isn't all that different than what I did, is it? I didn't do the research I should have. I approved the cable without fully vetting the source, verifying the information. People like Brent do it all the time, and it's *laziness,* not treason.

Then again, chances are that most of the sources we're approving are legitimate, genuine. I *know* there's something up with Falcon—

"Jill?" Violet says.

But it wasn't just me; this doesn't fall all on my shoulders. A.J. wrote the cable, the Chief of Station approved it. COPS did, too, and DO West. *It wasn't just me.*

"How's Owen feeling? Jeremy said he was sick?"

"He's okay. Drew's home with him today."

"This first year, it's tough. My kids were always getting sick. Being around all those other babies . . ."

I nod. My hands are clenched tightly in my lap.

She cocks her head to the side, watches me closely. "Are you doing okay, Jill?"

My eyes well with tears. I don't trust my voice to speak.

"Listen, it gets easier. It does." She smiles kindly.

I need to say something. I need to tell her exactly what happened—

There's a chime from her computer, and she looks at her screen. "Oh come *on*," she mutters. She double-clicks on something, then starts typing furiously.

"Sorry, Jill," she murmurs, without looking up from the screen. "I'm trying to find a place for Brent. Another division, something with minimal responsibilities. Somewhere he's not a *liability*."

I nod. My voice feels frozen. I came in here to talk, but the words won't come. I'm not really considering staying quiet, am I? I can't do that. These people, the ones who took my son, they'll be back. They know I'll do their bidding. They'll ask me to do something else, something worse. I'll be a liability to the Agency, to my country. *And this will never end.*

There's a rap at the door, and it opens a crack. The group chief's standing there, Violet's boss. "Need you in the conference room in five, Violet. The cybersecurity folks dropped the ball. *Again.*" He rolls his eyes, offers me the briefest of smiles, and shuts the door.

"If only every division was as competent as ours," she says with a smile. "Now, what is it we can do for you, Jill?"

Dropped the ball. Again.

It happens; of course it does. *Mistakes* happen.

I've been thinking all along that once I come clean, once we get a security detail, we're safe. But the truth is I have no idea if we'll be safe. I don't know who will be watching over us, how competent they are.

I'm about to put Owen's safety in the hands of a stranger. His *life*.

"Jill?"

Owen's safe if I stay quiet. And his safety—it's what's most important to me. I'll keep this secret because it will protect my son—

Until they come back.

And they will. Because I'm a liability now, aren't I?

Unless—

Suddenly I know what I need to do.

I straighten myself in the chair, look Violet in the eye. "I'd like to resign."

CHAPTER FOUR

"You'd like to *what*?" Violet says.

"Resign."

It's an impulsive decision, one I haven't thought through, not in the least. But once the words are out of my mouth, they seem right.

It's a way out, isn't it? I'm staying quiet, protecting Owen, but I'm not leaving myself open to more manipulation. I'm getting out.

Violet leans back in her chair. "Oh, Jill. You can't be serious."

"I am."

They said I could go on with my life. That they wouldn't ask for anything else. They didn't say I had to stay employed; they said we're done. I have to trust that's the truth.

And it's not like I have any way of getting in touch with them, asking if it's okay.

"Is it Owen?" she asks.

I nod, because it *is* Owen, just not the way she thinks.

"Look, I remember being in your shoes," she says. "Feeling like it was impossible to juggle it all."

She looks sympathetic, and that's a good thing. I learned long ago that sympathy has a way of making people blind to what they *should* be feeling. Like in this case, suspicion.

"But, Jill, you're doing *great*. You're my best officer. I can't afford to lose you."

"I'm sorry, Violet."

"I can shift around some accounts, lighten your load—"

I shake my head.

"Or we could cut your hours back to part-time?"

"No."

She's got it completely wrong, and she's so convinced she has me figured out. Truth is, as much as I miss Owen during the day, I've never seen myself as a stay-at-home mom. I love my career too much.

Loved my career. I just decided to leave it.

"Is there *anything* I can do to change your mind?" she asks.

It's not too late. I can go back on this decision, *stay* here, continue doing this job that I love—

Only I can't.

I can't keep working here, not when I can't uphold my oath. And not when the very act of continuing to work here means they might come back, do this again.

"No. This is the right decision. For me, for my family."

This is what I need to do to keep Owen safe.

"Then I hope it *is* the right decision, Jill," Violet says. "I hope it is."

When I walk in the front door at five, the scent of garlic and onion permeates the air. I deposit my bag on the bench in the hall, step out of my heels. "Hi," I call.

"Hi, honey," Drew says from the kitchen. I walk over, and he's checking the oven, Owen on his hip.

"Smells delicious." I give him a peck on the lips, take Owen into my arms.

"How was your day?"

I cuddle Owen close, kiss the top of his head, avoid eye contact with Drew. "Okay."

Drew turns to the counter, pulls the stopper out of an open bottle of Cab, pours two glasses. "Just okay?" He hands me one of the glasses.

I take a long sip. Owen's squirming, so I walk over to the living room, set him down on his foam play mat. Then I straighten, look Drew in the eye. "I resigned today."

"*What?*"

"I quit."

"What are you talking about?"

What am I supposed to say? People don't just quit their jobs, end their careers, without talking it over with their spouses.

But at the same time, *they're listening*. Watching. This is more for them than for Drew. I'll come clean to Drew later. *They* are what matters right now.

"Look, you know I've been unhappy at work since Owen was born—"

"You *have*?"

"Drew—"

"I mean, I know you miss him. But you love your career."

A pang of regret courses through me. I *do* love my career. *Did*.

And I *wasn't* unhappy. I just wished there were more hours in the day.

I watch Owen bang one plastic cup against another. "He's sick *again,* Drew. I just don't think that daycare center is the best environment for him."

"So we can move him to another."

"They're all the same."

He stares at me. "Why didn't we talk about this, Jill?"

I take another sip of wine. "It was impulsive."

That, at least, is the truth.

"Did something happen?" he asks.

"What?" I reach down and remove one of the plastic cups from Owen's hands, pretending I didn't hear the question and avoiding eye contact all at once.

"Did something happen at work?"

"I told you, it's Owen. Sick. *Again.* And just . . . everything."

Owen lets out a high-pitched babble, drawing our attention.

"Now you can take one of those transfers out of the area, like you've been wanting," I say. "Get away from Leo—"

"What about the house?"

"What about it? It's too small for us. We never intended to stay here this long. You've seen what houses are selling for—"

"To knock them down!"

"So what?"

He stares at me like I've sprouted two heads. And I don't blame him. As much as the house frustrates me, *I'm* the one who has always insisted we stay. I said it was because the longer we held out, the more our lot would be worth. But he and I both know I hated the thought of someone bulldozing the place where we created so many sweet memories.

But what does it matter now? This house isn't safe anymore. We can't stay here.

"What will you do for work?" he asks.

"I don't know."

"You don't *know?*"

"We'll figure it out."

What *will* I do for work? CIA job skills aren't the most trans-ferable. And nothing could be as interesting, or as rewarding.

Besides, how could I possibly put Owen back into daycare?

"Maybe I'll stay home for a bit," I say. "Take care of Owen."

"And how will we afford *that*?"

"We'll get a lot for this house. And we won't be paying an arm and a leg for daycare."

When I say it out loud, it actually sounds possible.

Owen starts fussing, and I reach down and pick him up, shift him onto my hip. As I do, I catch sight of the television. Are they watching? Surely they're listening.

"Look, I did this, Drew, whether it was a good move or not. Work with me here."

He downs the last of his wine, turns his back to me to refill his glass. I watch his shoulders; they look tense.

"I can't," he finally says, turning to face me. "I can't work with you, when this isn't *you*, Jill. Quitting your job—and doing it *impulsively,* like this. My God, it takes you a week to decide on a pair of *shoes* to buy."

The words catch me off guard. Probably because they're true. It *is* out of character for me to do something like this.

"Something else is going on," he says, his eyes boring into mine.

"It isn't." I hold his gaze—his expression's full of suspicion—and think of how different this afternoon could have been. If I'd have come clean, I'd have arrived home with a security detail, wouldn't I? I'd be hurriedly packing up suitcases, explaining as I went, while he stood there listening, shell-shocked.

He doesn't know how good he has it right now. But he will.

"We don't keep secrets from each other, do we?" His voice has an edge.

"Of course not." This is temporary. I'll tell him, soon enough.

"Because we promised never to do that, right?" Now it's betrayal I'm hearing.

Guilt bubbles up inside me. He's my spouse, my partner. He and Owen are *everything* to me, and the last thing I want to do is jeopardize the trust we've built. But he'll understand, when all is said and done.

He's giving me an even gaze, a searching one, like he's trying to see the truth in my eyes. But here's the thing: I've been trained to lie. I may work behind a desk now, but I didn't always. I worked in the field, and I learned from the best. I know how to lie, and I know how to do it convincingly.

I shoot him an indignant look, one tinged with anger.

"Drew, for God's sake. I'm your wife. You can trust me."

By the time we've finished dinner, Drew seems to be warming to the idea of moving. In truth, I am, too, if only to escape from this house, start fresh somewhere else. They'll leave us alone, won't they? I mean, I can't know that for sure, but it doesn't seem like they have a reason to approach me again.

I clean Owen's face and hands and set him back on his play mat while Drew clears the table. As I'm transferring the leftovers into a glass container, Drew runs some hot water in the sink, splashes in dish soap. He unlatches his watch, sets it on the counter, and plunges the pan into the suds.

His watch is off. *Finally.*

I turn to the counter, spot his phone. Perfect. I make a point to straighten a pile of mail, then pick up the rest of the counter: a stray pacifier, a pen and a pad of paper, Drew's phone. I deposit it all on the opposite end of the counter, behind a loaf of sandwich bread. If anyone was watching, hopefully it just looked like I was cleaning. It isn't much, but it's something.

Now I just need to get him alone. Quickly.

"We should go for a walk," I say. "It's beautiful out."

"That's a good idea."

The TV picked that up, right? Our phones, his watch—they're all transmitting that audio.

He's almost done with the pan. Then he's going to put his watch back on, isn't he? Grab his phone?

"Let's go now," I say.

"Now?" He puts the clean pan on the drying rack, empties the sink. Dries his hands—

I walk over, wrap my arms around him, and he pulls me close. "Well, this is nice," he says with a smile, giving me a kiss.

I kiss him back, then reach for his hand. "Come on. Let's take that walk."

He glances toward the spot on the counter where he'd left his phone, bare now. His brow furrows. He looks around—

I give his hand the smallest of pulls—

He shrugs, and follows.

It's a perfect summer evening. Warm, but not too hot. Not too humid, either. The lawns are full and green, trees are rustling softly in the breeze, the sun is inching lower in the sky. Drew's pushing the stroller; Owen's quiet and content, absorbing the surroundings.

There's no one else around. No phones, no smartwatches, nothing.

We can talk, finally.

"Drew, about today," I begin.

He looks over expectantly, waiting for me to go on.

I struggle to find the right words. *Any* words.

He needs to know. This is our son we're talking about. Our lives.

"Drew, something happened."

He turns toward me. I can feel it, even if my own eyes are still facing straight ahead. "What?"

"Today . . ." Every word seems wrong. Dangerous. *Difficult.*

Why am I having such a hard time getting this out?

Because of that warning. Because they told me if I breathe a word, they'll take Owen again, and they'll kill him.

But it's not just that. It's that I decided the best way to keep Owen safe is to stay quiet. *What if Drew doesn't agree?*

Truth is, I don't know how he'll react. I don't know if he'll insist we go to the authorities. He's a lawyer; he tends to see things in black and white. And this . . . this is gray.

"Honey?" He steers the stroller around an uneven section of sidewalk.

I shake my head. "I can't."

In the stroller, Owen gurgles happily. Drew is quiet. I watch a little girl approach on the sidewalk, on a bike with training wheels, pink streamers fluttering from the handlebars, her father walking just behind. He lifts a hand in greeting as our paths cross.

"Look, I know you can't give me details," Drew finally says. "We've been together long enough. I get it. But I just wish you'd told me that you weren't happy. That you were considering resigning."

He sounds hurt, and it feels like a crack in our marriage. Because I'd never have kept something like that from him. I've always been honest with him, always shared how I'm feeling, because I trust him, and because he always knows what to say to make me feel better.

In the distance I can hear the happy shrieks of kids at play. I look down at the stroller, at my son, watching the birds and the trees.

Right now, it's almost like it never happened. Life is normal, or close to it, and certainly far more normal than if we'd had to go into hiding, leave our lives behind. If anyone ever questioned what I did, approving that cable, I could always play it off as a slipup, a mistake.

No one will ever have to know the truth.

"I should have told you," I say softly. "But I just couldn't."

I stay home the next day with Owen, and I don't let him out of my sight all day, not even for a minute. I keep waiting for the other shoe to drop. For my phone to ring, *Unknown* to flash across the screen. For someone to come to the door.

But there's nothing. It's quiet.

The day after that, Drew stays home with Owen while I go back to work, after I lied and said Owen spiked a temp again. I hate lying to Drew, but I can't possibly send Owen back to All Children's. How could I, after what they did, letting him leave with a stranger? Surely Drew would agree.

The first thing I do, again, is check the Falcon case. There's an update from Damascus Station: A.J. met with Falcon this morning, gave him COVCOM.

The words leave me with a tight feeling in my chest. This was preventable.

But at what cost?

Today's my last day in the office; I'm using personal leave to finish out the mandatory final two weeks. Violet wasn't happy, but when I explained I didn't feel comfortable leaving Owen at daycare any longer, she relented. She reassigned my accounts, all the assets I'm responsible for following. Gave most of them to Jeremy, including Falcon. I hate that the case is assigned to him, but they'd have no reason to harass him. They got what they wanted: Falcon's a source.

I clear out my desk, turn in my badge, say my goodbyes. It all feels surreal. I thought for sure I'd be here until retirement. Never had the slightest interest in leaving. And now? Now I'm walking out on my dream career.

"Let's stay in touch," I tell Jeremy. It's hardest saying goodbye to him.

"Definitely."

"But let's actually do it."

He smiles. "I'll find you on Facebook."

We exchange an awkward hug, and then I take my cardboard file box full of personal belongings, and I walk out of the building for the last time, away from the career I love.

That evening Jeremy sends me a friend request on Facebook, just as he promised. I confirm it and browse his profile. A bunch of pictures of Max. A few videos, which are actually pretty funny. The dog bounds to the door, sliding on the wood floor and barking like crazy, when anyone rings the bell. I've seen it myself in person; each year Jeremy hosts a Labor Day cookout for the team. I won't be invited again, will I?

I open up the window to send him a message, then close it. I don't know what to say.

The next week is a whirlwind. Drew gets approved for a transfer within his firm. Fort Lauderdale, Florida. We pack up the house, get ready to leave our old life behind. I'm tense the whole time, but there's no contact from *Unknown*, no blowback for resigning.

One week after my last day of work, I file the paperwork to

legally change my name. I finally become Jill Smith. Anonymity no longer seems like a bad thing.

We buy a new house in Fort Lauderdale in a gated community. In Drew's name only; I convince him the mortgage application process will be smoother that way, with me out of work.

While he's signing the paperwork, I pick up new cellphones, with new local phone numbers, and a new smartwatch, the latest model. I stop in a Starbucks and set up new email accounts, then on to the bank to open new accounts. Drew's confused by all the changes, asks again if something happened at work, even quips that we're acting like we're on the run, but I tell him he's being ridiculous, that it's just the perfect time for a fresh start. I call on every tactic I learned in CIA training, use every trick to convincingly lie, and I think he buys it. Frankly, I think *he's* ready for a fresh start, too. Excited about it. He's been anxious to escape Leo's orbit for years.

I never thought I'd lie to Drew. Never thought I'd keep a huge secret from him. I feel almost overcome with guilt every time I look at him. I have to keep reminding myself that it's *our family* I'm protecting with my lies. He loves Owen as much as I do; he'd *want* me to keep our son safe, at any cost.

I know our trail isn't invisible, not even close. But it's a step in the right direction.

In any case, I hope that if they ever *do* come looking for us, we'll be harder to find.

It takes a week for our belongings to arrive. I arranged for storage pods, had them held in a warehouse briefly before delivery, figured it was harder to track those than a moving truck.

Again, not perfect. But better than nothing.

Everything's in the new house now. Furniture's in place, cardboard boxes are stacked in each room, movers are gone. In the nursery, I pull a clean fitted sheet over the crib mattress, smooth it out. Dig the diapers and wipes from a box, set them on the shelf of the changing table. In another box I find Owen's favorite books, *Goodnight Moon* and *The Very Hungry Caterpillar,* the ones we read every night at bedtime, and place them on top of the bookcase. Then I look around. There's still so much work to be done, but I feel such a sense of satisfaction, and relief. This could have turned out so very differently.

I pick up Owen and walk with Drew into the fenced backyard. There are palm trees in the corners, and a lake is just barely visible, beyond some other houses. The sun is setting, and the sky is streaked with brilliant pink. I point out an egret to Owen, in amongst the cattails on the banks of the lake. I don't remember the last time I felt this relaxed. Certainly not since that day my life changed forever.

Once we're back inside, Drew opens the bottle of pinot noir the previous owners left on the counter for us. He pours some into two paper cups, all that we can find. We toast with a smile. There's a warm feeling flowing through me. I did it; I got us out of this mess.

We're safe. *We're free.*

One day I'll tell Drew everything. They'll never know, and surely he'll agree that I made the right decision for our family.

Owen starts fussing, and Drew picks him up. "Hey, did you find his elephant?"

The favorite stuffed toy, the one that was inadvertently packed away, sorely missed. "Totally forgot. Let me go back and look."

I head down the hall to Owen's room and scan the labels on the boxes, wondering which one might hold the toy, when something in the crib catches my eye.

A piece of paper, folded, lies in the center of the mattress.

I know it wasn't there before.

I walk closer, filled with trepidation, with fear, but it's almost like I'm being pulled by some invisible force, like I have to see what it is.

I pick it up, my hand trembling, and open it.

Block letters, black marker.

YOU CAN RUN, BUT YOU CAN'T HIDE.

FOUR YEARS LATER

CHAPTER FIVE

I never breathed a word. Four years, and not one single word.

Once I found that note, any thoughts of coming clean to Drew went right out the window. It wasn't worth the risk. All they asked of me was to keep quiet. Keep quiet, and Owen would be safe. Why would I risk telling anyone?

Besides, Drew was happy. Content. What would it do to him to let him know someone's watching us, listening to us, *threatening* us? I hated living that way. I didn't want to put him through it.

Those first months were rough. We'd left everything behind. Our home, all our friends. And for what?

We had run, but they were right: we couldn't hide. They found us before the boxes were even unpacked. They made their way into our house, into Owen's *bedroom*. There was no way to escape.

So there was only one option: stay quiet.

Gradually, I stopped thinking as much about the phones, the smart TVs, the watches. Stopped being so intimately aware that someone might be listening to anything we said, might be watching. I had to, or I'd have gone crazy. This was the new reality, and as much as I hated it, I knew I couldn't change it. It was the price I had to pay for keeping my son safe.

We settled into life in Florida, and *I* settled into a life I never envisioned. I couldn't bring myself to send Owen back to a day-care center, not after what had happened. So I fell into the role of stay-at-home mom. Not something I ever wanted, ever thought in a million years I'd do.

Owen grew, and when he was about a year and a half, we had another child, a little girl. Mia. It happened naturally, much to our shock. We were making ends meet, but I don't know how we'd have afforded more rounds of IVF. I don't know if we'd have tried, either. As delighted as I was with the news, I was equal parts terrified. They'd already come after one of my children, threatened to come back. If they *did* ever come back, now it would be for *two*.

Life got more expensive with Mia, and I ended up taking a part-time job teaching at a private language institute downtown. Not something I sought out. But it was the only thing I found that provided the income we needed with a schedule that worked for our family: two evenings a week and all day on Sundays. Drew made sure to be home early on Mondays and Wednesdays, and we crammed all our family outings into our Saturdays. It was what we needed.

I teach Mandarin and Turkish to small classes of students, mostly ambitious young professionals, a few restless seniors. It was tough at first: I had left the career I loved to stand in front of a whiteboard and explain verb conjugation and fix pronunciation errors. But it grew on me, fast. Soon I actually started to look forward to work. It was nice to feel like I was doing something valuable again. That I was helping to prepare these young people for a lifetime of adventure, of possibilities—the kind of life I once had.

I miss my career. My old life, before *they* entered it. But I've come to realize the pain is dulled if I don't think about it. So I try not to. I stay away from the news, anything about international affairs or intelligence. I've taken up painting, and I throw myself into it. Watercolors, mostly. I find that when I'm focused on how light hits a subject, or the way two colors blend together, it's *all* that fills my mind.

Most of all, I try not to think about Falcon. He still creeps back into my thoughts occasionally, and every time he does, I feel overcome with guilt. I tell myself that if I weren't so conscientious, if I were more like Brent, I might have missed whatever it was they didn't want me to discover, anyway. And that it wasn't just me. It wasn't a single point of failure. It was on A.J., and the Chief of Station, and COPS, and even the Director of Operations.

But none of that assuages my guilt. Guilt is the price to pay for what I did.

Four years, and I never heard another word from them. Never saw any indication they were paying attention to us. Surely they'd moved on. And so I tried to do the same. I tried to stop looking over my shoulder, stop being on the lookout for someone watching us, following us. Tried to make new friends, even though in the back of my mind I knew we might have to leave them. Tried to feel safe again.

But I never, ever forgot about them.

It's noon on Friday, which means it's grocery time.

I've picked Owen up from morning preschool and we're at the Publix a few blocks from home. The kids are sitting side by side in one of the carts shaped like a race car, complete with two steering wheels.

Mia's convinced, as always, that she's driving the cart, and is taking her responsibility incredibly seriously. She's leaning forward, jiggling the wheel intensely. Owen's leaning back, head down. He has a book on his lap, one with hidden pictures.

The two kids couldn't be more different. He's as serious as she is spunky, as reserved as she is exuberant. He loves to read; she loves to climb. They even *look* different: his hair is still blond, albeit darker than when he was a baby, and straight. Hers is dark, full of wild curls.

"Owen," Mia chides, looking over at him. It comes out sounding like *Oh-ie*. "Pay *attention*."

I suppress a smile. She might be a year and a half younger, but you'd never know it, the way they interact.

He lifts one hand to the wheel, never taking his eyes off the book. "I just found the toothbrush, Mommy."

"You have to *drive*, Owen," she says, and she jiggles the wheel extra hard to prove her point.

"It's okay, Mia," I say gently. "*You* can drive, and Owen can do his hidden pictures."

"But there are *two* wheels," she says. She turns and shoots me a look that's like a flash of what life will be like when she's a teenager.

"Let's take a right here," I tell her, suppressing a smile, and she spins back around, yanks the wheel hard to the left. I turn right and head for the baby carrots.

"Found the comb, Mommy," Owen says.

"Owen, *drive*," Mia says, exasperated.

I reach for a bag of carrots and check the date. Ten days; that'll do. I place the bag in the cart—

There's a woman, staring at us. She's behind the table of tomatoes.

I'm used to people watching us when we're at the grocery store. Older folks, mostly. Inevitably they smile, make some remark about how it goes so fast, and I should enjoy these moments.

But this woman, she's not smiling. She's just watching.

She's younger than me, late twenties maybe, or early thirties. Statuesque, with short black hair worn natural and full, and a distinctive air of confidence, like she knows exactly how striking she is.

I smile, but her face doesn't change. Instead, she looks down, puts a carton of cherry tomatoes in her basket, and turns away.

I stare after her.

"Mommy!"

I realize Mia's standing in her seat, body twisted toward me, trying to get my attention. "Sit down, please, honey."

"Can we get pears?" Her tone makes it clear she's asked more than once. I didn't hear a word.

"Mommy, I can't find the teddy bear," Owen says.

"Pears. Sure," I murmur, watching the woman walk off.

"Mommy, the *teddy bear*," Owen says.

"The *pears*," Mia says.

The woman's out of sight now.

"I asked first," Owen says.

"No, *I* did."

"I hear you both," I say, refocusing, starting to walk. "I'm heading toward the pears. And Owen—" I give the book a quick glance, "look for the teddy bear down in the corner, near the comb."

She's quiet; he's quiet. I reach for a bag of pears, then look in the direction the woman disappeared. I'm completely unsettled.

By the time we head for checkout, the cart is loaded. Milk, eggs, bread, the other usual staples, the impulse buys the kids want. Owen's finished his hidden-pictures book, Mia's resting her head on the side of the cart, ready for naptime. Everything's normal.

That woman—it was probably nothing. Or maybe she wasn't even staring at us. It was my imagination, ghosts of the past haunting my thoughts, creeping back in when I least expect it.

We're safe here.

I pay for the groceries, head outside to the parking lot. Mia's fast asleep now, and even Owen's yawning. I get to the car, lift Mia in first, then Owen, buckle them into their car seats. Then it's on to the groceries. I load everything into the trunk, push the empty cart into the corral just beside the car, open the driver's-side door and slide in—

I go still.

There's a white sedan idling alone in the next row over, flanked on either side by a half dozen empty spaces, facing us.

There's a woman in the driver's seat, her head turned toward us. She's wearing dark shades now, but I recognize her. Same one from the produce aisle.

Fear returns with a vengeance. It wasn't paranoia before.

This woman's watching us.

They're back, aren't they?

CHAPTER SIX

*C*onfront her.

It's my first instinct. She's got to be one of *them,* those people who took Owen, who've made me spend years looking over my shoulder, feeling watched. And I've never had the opportunity to confront them, to tell them to leave us alone, to assure them I haven't said a word, and never will.

But that instinct, it's wrong. A remnant from a previous life. Maybe it would have worked if it were just me. But it's *not* just me. Owen and Mia are in the backseat. Am I really going to stop and get out of my car and talk to this person who's a threat to us *while my kids are in the backseat*? Of course not.

I pull my eyes away from the woman and look in the rearview mirror. Mia, fast asleep, head tilted to the side, a peaceful expression on her face. And Owen, awake, but with heavy eyelids. He smiles at me through the mirror, that sweet, shy smile of his.

I start the ignition and look over at the white sedan. Still idling there, the woman still facing our direction. I wait, my own car idling, and debate. I could leave the lot in either direction: left, toward that car, or right, away.

I choose left.

I pull out of the space and drive slowly past the sedan. Florida plates; I commit the string of letters and numbers to memory.

The woman turns her head as we drive by, watches us go.

The car doesn't follow—I watch it in the rearview mirror—but still I run a surveillance detection route on the way home. Skills I learned on the Farm, haven't used in a decade. A winding path, with stops. Gas, first; I top off the tank, and by the time I pull away, Owen's asleep. Starbucks drive-through next, for a tall drip I don't want. The whole time, I'm eyeing the mirrors, committing every car around me to memory, making sure I don't catch sight of that white sedan again, making sure no one else is tailing me. The last thing I want to do is lead them home.

But it's futile, isn't it? They know where we live. They've been inside our home.

I reach our neighborhood thirty-five minutes later, Popsicles no doubt a melted mess, my mind spinning. Why are they back? Just to keep an eye on me? To scare me? I haven't said a word.

Our street is quiet. No one's following me. No one's around. I pull into the garage and close the door behind me. Then I sit in the silence, trembling, feeling like a different person than when I set out from the house just a few hours before.

I carry the kids inside—they're both still asleep—and lay them in their beds, then unload the groceries and put them away. I feel like I'm in a daze. For the first time in ages, I wonder if they're listening. If they're watching, right here, right now.

The kids wake from their naps and the afternoon is as normal as can be. They play with toys, and out on the swing set, and don't seem to notice that I hover closer than usual, watching our surroundings, looking for eyes that might be watching *us*.

Later, they sit in the family room and watch a half hour of *Sesame Street* while I get dinner ready. A casserole, chicken and rice. I feel an unexpected sense of longing for those takeout dinners we used to have in our Vienna home. For that *life* we used to have, when I had my career, when I wasn't being watched.

Drew walks in at five-thirty, greets me with the usual peck on the lips. "How was your day?" he asks, loosening his tie, then removing it completely, laying it on the counter.

In my mind I see that woman. Watching us in the produce section, her gaze intense. Then in the parking lot, behind those dark sunglasses, her head turned toward us.

"Fine." I avoid eye contact, reach for the oven mitt. "Yours?"

"Long. Had that deposition today."

"That's right. How'd it go?" I open the oven and reach for the casserole, squinting through the wave of steam that escapes.

"Could've been better." He shrugs. "But could have been worse."

I nod and focus on the food. Remove the foil from the pan, pull out a knife, stick it in the middle of the casserole. Looks done.

He rolls up his sleeves, starts washing his hands. "Kids have a good day?"

Again I see that woman in my mind. My stomach twists. But the kids were oblivious, weren't they? "I think so."

Dinner's quieter than usual tonight. I'm usually the one driving the conversation, encouraging the kids to tell Drew about their day, asking leading questions. Asking Drew about *his* day, which invariably is more interesting than my own. But today I'm finding it hard to focus. *Or* eat. I have no appetite; I'm barely touching my food. I catch Drew watching me with concern.

When the plates are cleared and the kids are back to playing with toys, Drew pulls me aside in the kitchen, out of the kids' sight, and asks quietly, "What's wrong, Jill?"

"Nothing." It sounds like a lie.

"Something's on your mind."

What am I supposed to say? I reach for the plates in the sink and begin loading them into the dishwasher. "Just feeling a little off."

I can feel his eyes on me. "You sure that's all?"

I reach for the utensils at the bottom of the sink, transfer them into the dishwasher. "That's all."

He takes the kids up for baths, and I finish loading the dishwasher, then give the table and the counters a quick wipe, and look around. Clean, just full of the usual clutter.

I can hear the water running upstairs in the bath. Normally, I'd make my way up, help out. But today I head into the study. Drew's space, really. Law books fill the shelves of the maple bookcase; his diplomas and awards line the walls. My own are in boxes in the attic, a remnant of another life. My retreat is the patio, where I have my easel and my watercolors.

I sit down at the desk that feels foreign to me, open up the laptop. I eye the Google homepage.

I haven't done this, ever. I've stayed completely away from any news from the region. I haven't wanted to know.

But now? Now I feel like I need to know.

I roll the chair forward. My fingers hover over the keyboard, and then I type.

Syria.

Return.

The results populate immediately, and I click on the first link—Wikipedia—and start scanning. Situation isn't much different than four years ago, really. Instability, volatility. The country's still a battleground for the world's proxy wars. Everyone's got a dog in the fight: the U.S., Russia, Saudi Arabia, Turkey, Iran, and the list goes on. It's a tinderbox.

I can hear splashing upstairs in the tub. Mia's giggles.

I dig deeper. News sites. More on the proxy wars, the countries that are competing against each other, using Syria for their own purposes. A few articles mentioning Syria's nuclear ambitions, and the fledgling biological weapons program.

Biowarfare. I can't help but think of Falcon.

There's one byline that keeps popping up, one reporter who seems to have the most detailed information about Syria, the most scoops. The most access; the articles are full of attributions to unnamed government officials.

Alex Charles, *Washington Post*.

I navigate to the homepage of the *Post,* search for the name Alex Charles. His most recent article appears on my screen. Dated yesterday, about none other than Syria's biowarfare program. I'm on the third paragraph when I read a sentence that makes my heart seize.

A single clandestine source has emerged as a primary source of U.S. information.

I read the rest of the article—seems to just be a rehash of other information I've read—and close the article, then the *Post*'s site. The background's a picture of Owen and Mia at Disney World, in front of Cinderella's castle, big grins on their faces. I stare at their faces, my mind spinning.

Single clandestine source.

Falcon?

It's possible, isn't it? Possible we never recruited anyone else with that same level of access, or never retained them.

Falcon might be our primary source of information on Syria's biowarfare program.

I pull up the browser window again and google the name Alex Charles. I click on the first result, Twitter. The icon's a black-and-white picture of a typewriter. The most recent entry:

Working on something big. The people deserve to know the truth.

I hear a creak on the stairs, Drew walking down. The kids must be in bed. I better go say good night before they're asleep.

I close the browser window and shut the laptop. Then I head out of the study, completely unsettled.

The people deserve to know the truth.

I awake the next morning to light streaming through the blinds. Drew's side of the bed is empty, just an indentation in the sheets. I can hear kitchen noise downstairs, and a kids' show on television. I stretch my arms—

And then yesterday comes flooding back into my thoughts.

That woman, watching us at the store.

That article by Alex Charles. *Single clandestine source.*

And his tweet: *Working on something big.*

Maybe *that's* why they're back. Maybe this Alex Charles is sniffing around the Syrian biowarfare program, getting too close to Falcon.

Maybe they want to make sure I'm not one of those unnamed government officials.

I get out of bed, somewhat reassured by the thought. Because I'm *not.*

When I come downstairs, the kids are watching *Sesame Street* in their PJs and Drew's standing over the skillet, spatula in hand, making pancakes. He gives me a kiss and hands me a mug of steaming coffee. "Heard you get up," he says with a smile.

I take the mug into the family room and sit down carefully between the kids, lean over and give each of them a kiss. "Morning, kiddos."

"Morning, Mommy," Owen says. Mia's too absorbed in the television to respond.

I sip my coffee and stare, unseeing, at the television. My mind is still churning, and I just keep coming back to this: I haven't broken their rules.

And why *would* I? If I came clean now, told the authorities what I know, what I *did,* I'm guaranteeing myself jail time. I can't stay silent about something like this for four years and expect not to face consequences. *Of course* I'm going to stay quiet. They'll see that. They have nothing to worry about.

After everyone's dressed for the day, bellies full of pancakes, Drew heads to Home Depot and I bring the kids to the park near the library. It's surprisingly empty for a beautiful Saturday.

Mia's in pigtails and rainbow-striped leggings. Owen's in his favorite Superman shirt, the one with a little cape attached to the back. I watch them scamper up the ladder of the play set, dart through tunnels, down a slide.

They climb up a different ladder this time, cross a bridge, toward another slide. I trail behind them, down below, keep an eye on their progress.

Down the twisty slide again, laughing gleefully. They clamber up the ladder and slide down again, Mia first, then Owen. He bounces up off the bottom of the slide and runs over to me. "Mommy, can I go on the monkey bars?"

I glance over at Mia, who's halfway up the ladder. "Sure."

I lift him up to the monkey bars and he grabs on, hangs awkwardly for a few moments, then lets go, darts off toward the swings.

Mia's at the top of the play set, crawling through a tunnel toward the higher, straighter slide, the one with one side partially open to the ground below. I walk over and stand below it, just in case. I'm always afraid she'll lean over and fall out.

"Look at me, Mommy!" There's a huge smile on her face.

"Be careful, honey."

I look over toward the swings, where Owen's rather unsuccessfully pumping his legs. I wish they could just play together, do the same thing at the same time, but it never ends up working that way, not for long anyway. And it's stressful, trying to keep them both in my line of sight at all times, trying to keep them both safe.

She takes her time sitting down at the top of the slide, then stares down the length of it like she's working up the nerve to start sliding.

I glance back toward the swings, but Owen's hopped off, and he's running toward the rock wall. "Owen, wait for me before you climb."

He obeys, stands still near the wall, and Mia finally slides down the slide. I meet her at the bottom with a big smile, and she runs toward the seesaw as I head to the rock wall. I stand below Owen while he climbs, ready to help if he falls—

Mia bursts into tears. I reach up and lift Owen down, set him carefully on the ground, then rush toward her. She's bumped her chin on the seesaw. I bend down to her level, examine her chin. No blood, nothing too bad. I put my arms around her, pull her close, but she continues to wail, so finally I pick her up, let her bury her head in my shoulder, let her sobs subside. I turn around and look toward the rock wall—

Owen's not there.

I scan the play set, the slides, the bridge. Nothing.

The tunnels: I look at each one, wait for Owen to come out the other side—

Still nothing. My eyes dart around the playground, panic rising.

"Owen!"

I don't see him.

"Owen!" Louder this time, more desperate.

"There," Mia says. She points, and there's Owen, off to the

right, beyond the playground equipment, at the edge of the soccer field.

There's a dark-haired woman beside him, bending down at the waist, talking to him. As soon as my gaze lands on her, she straightens, and looks directly at me.

It's *her*, the woman from the grocery store.

"Owen!"

I rush over, heart pounding, Mia tight on my hip. The woman just watches me, impassive. And Owen doesn't move.

As soon as I'm close enough to touch him, I pull him to me, behind my leg, shielding him from her.

"Who are you?" I demand. "And what do you want?"

She watches me, expressionless, emotionless, like she's taking it all in.

"I'm Alex Charles," she finally says. "And I want to talk about Falcon."

I stare at her, my heart still pounding.

She's Alex Charles?

It's a reporter who's watching us, not *them*—

She said *Falcon*. The realization hits me like a slap. How does *she* know an asset's crypt? That information is classified. A journalist should *never* know that information.

I was right about one thing. Alex Charles is sniffing around, getting close to a story. But *he's* a she, and she knows way more than I would have thought.

And she's *here*, talking to *me*.

Oh my God.

"We're leaving," I say. I grab Owen's hand and start walking.

He's jogging to keep up. "Wait, Mommy, I didn't say goodbye." He twists at the waist, raises his little hand in a wave. I pull him along and grip Mia tighter.

My heart is pounding.

What if *they're* watching? I need it crystal clear that I'm *not* talking to her, that I don't want her near me.

I walk as fast as I can, Owen running beside me, desperate to put as much distance as I can between this woman and myself.

She can dig around all she wants, but she's not getting anything from me—I haven't been at the Agency in four years.

And about Falcon—How does she know I have anything to do with Falcon?

What does she know?

"I'll be at the Starbucks on Shore Drive tomorrow at ten," she calls after me.

I don't turn, don't slow, but I hear every word, and she knows it.

"If you don't show, I'm going to press with the story I have."

ONE WEEK EARLIER

CHAPTER SEVEN

Alex

The encrypted message comes in through ClandestineTips, the *Post*'s new platform for anonymous leads. Our own version of WhatsApp. More secure than anything on the market, apparently. I sat through a training a few months ago when they rolled it out. Didn't understand all the technical crap. Still don't. Here's what I do know: Tipsters are guaranteed anonymity. They choose a handle, and their IP addresses are masked. We can chat privately. And there's absolutely no way for me—or anyone else, for that matter— to find out *who* I'm conversing with.

This one comes directly to my inbox. Most of the tips end up in the general inbox, but users have the option to send to a specific reporter. Every day I get a handful sent straight to me. Usually they're addressed to Mr. Charles. Wouldn't be, if my byline said Alexandra. Or if I used a picture on my *Post* profile, or on Twitter. But I've been around this business long enough to know life's a hell of a lot easier as an Alex.

I glance at the framed picture on my desk, beside the computer. My mom, Imani. Different newsroom, different era. She's about the age I am now. Shorter than me, hair long and relaxed. But otherwise she looks a lot like I do. High cheekbones. Angular features. She was able to trace her roots back to Senegal. I like to think mine are there, too.

I open this tip at lunchtime. I'm at my desk at the *Post*, sandwich from the deli across the street open in front of me. Pastrami on rye, my favorite. Only reason I'm checking the inbox is because the office is so obnoxiously loud at the moment. Phones ringing, twenty-four-hour news blasting, someone laughing too damn loud.

> To: Alex Charles
> From: Afriend123
> Message: Ninety percent of US human intelligence on Syria's biological weapons program comes from a single clandestine source.

It's the figure that catches my attention. I've been doing this long enough to know that figures mean facts. It's the figures that separate the legitimate tips from the garbage. And let's be honest here, most of them are garbage. But this one . . .

This one has a figure.

I take another bite of my sandwich and chew slowly, eyeing that number. Ninety percent. Then I place the sandwich back on the paper wrapper, wipe my hands on a napkin. Fingers on the keyboard:

> To: Afriend123
> From: Alex Charles
> Message: Thank you for the tip. How do you know this information?

I press return and hear a ding. Sent. I stare at the screen. The user might be online now. Might respond immediately.

Nothing.

My eyes drift back up to that figure. Ninety percent. I feel a familiar itch of excitement.

Abruptly I reach for my phone and scroll through the contacts. Doesn't take long to find the entry I want. CIA Public Affairs. I tap the number and the call connects.

"Public Affairs, this is Kassie."

"Kassie, it's Alex Charles, at the *Post*." I've dealt with Kassie before. Not that it really matters *who* I'm dealing with. They're all the same.

"Hi, Alex." Her voice is guarded. Strained. It's clear she wishes it *wasn't* me. That it was anyone else, really.

"I'm working on a story. Just wondering if you could verify something for me."

"Certainly."

That was a reluctant "certainly" if I ever heard one. "Does ninety percent of your human intelligence on Syrian biological weapons come from a single source?"

The expected beat of silence. And then: "The CIA cannot discuss sources and methods."

Standard response. Public Affairs is usually a dead end. But it's a box I need to check, nonetheless.

"We'll make note of your interest," she adds tightly. "Certain folks here are *always* interested in what you're working on, Alex."

I roll my eyes. Some other journalists are intimidated by that sort of statement. Take it as a warning of sorts. But I'm not easily intimidated. Maybe because I grew up here, in a newsroom. Sitting in a chair in my mom's office, doing my homework, while she made just these kinds of calls. Received her fair share of veiled threats. Ones that never materialized into anything.

"Worth it to get to the truth," she used to say. And it's a mantra I've always believed. Always put into practice. I've never backed down from a tough story. Not the one about illegal wiretapping on military bases overseas. Or the one about the CIA's arms transfer that fell into terrorist hands. Uncovering wrongdoing in the military and intelligence services—that's my thing. And it's something a hell of a lot of journalists don't want to touch. My best stories have been the ones others were afraid to write.

"Please do," I say, saccharine sweet. "And if you think of anything else, you know how to find me."

I press the end button and look at my phone. The background's a mountain, one of those stock photos preloaded on the phone. Used to be more personal. A lot of things used to be different.

I open up the contacts again. Scroll until I find the name I need. Hana Ito. I choose the work number—she won't have her cell on her—and place the call.

"This is Hana," comes her voice, as the call connects.

"Hana, it's Alex." My number comes up as *Unknown*. Lots of people I know might not pick up otherwise.

"Alex," she says. "What do you want?"

"Got a question for you." With most of my Agency contacts, I'd have to beat around the bush until I had them on their cell. You never know who's listening in on calls. But not Hana. She's a senior analyst, works counterintelligence. Has her own office, not a cubicle like most of the rank and file. And as she's explained to me before, no one's monitoring her calls, because the information she deals with is too highly classified.

"Do you have anything for me?"

She's nothing if not direct. Got to respect that. Probably why we get along.

I'm not exactly a people person, like a lot of journalists are. But I'm a damn good reporter. I know how to make a deal.

"No," I say. "Nothing now. But I'll owe you."

"Nope. Sorry, Alex. Call me if you have something I can use."

She disconnects, and I pull the phone from my ear. Can't even be disappointed about this one. Hana's only ever given me information if I've given *her* a lead first. She's as eager and ambitious an analyst as they come. If I tip her off to a big story before it breaks, she gets a jump on putting together classified analysis on the topic. Her own version of a scoop. She told me once she's had more articles in the President's Daily Brief than any other counterintelligence analyst. I believe it.

There's a peal of laughter from the other side of the room. I glance over—can't see a thing—then back down at my phone.

I scroll through my contacts again until I find the next name I'm looking for. Beau Barnett. Hana's my best source on the analytic side of the CIA; Beau's the best on the operational side. Still looking for someone in Science and Technology. That'd be the trifecta. The big three. The heads of those directorates are known in the press as the Gang of Three. They wrote a string of stinging op-eds a couple years back, decrying roadblocks in the intelligence process, things like budget cuts and the need to attribute everything to a specific source.

Welcome to my world, I remember thinking. And it struck me more than ever before just how similar the fields are. Journalism and intelligence. We're all just trying to find the truth.

I met Beau in Baghdad years ago, and we overlapped again in Lebanon. He's a CIA case officer, now in management ranks. Senior guy, well connected. But down to earth as can be. Back in the U.S. now, but he did a stint in Damascus. He would know, for sure. I try his cell first.

"Beau, it's Alex," I say when he picks up.

"Alex. How the hell are you?"

"Doing well, old friend. You?"

"Oh, you know. Headquarters rotation, so I'm fairly miserable."

I laugh. "There's gotta be something good about it. Catching up with old friends?"

"Are you suggesting we catch up?"

"Yeah. Let's grab a drink at—"

"What do you need, Alex?" I can hear the smile in his voice.

"Better to discuss it in person."

"You know I can't answer your questions."

"And you know I wasn't supposed to give you leads." I'd never say more than that on the phone, but he knows exactly what I mean. He owes me.

He sighs. "Brewster's at five?"

"See you there," I say with a smile.

I'm going to pump him for info, and he knows it. But when we were abroad, he did the same thing. Pumped *me* for info, about my sources. I never gave names, but I'd give him leads. In exchange for information *I* needed, of course. Nothing overtly classified, but useful tidbits nonetheless. It was a mutually beneficial relationship.

In the end, we're after the same thing, really. Sources. People with access to information, who are willing to provide it: for money, or to do the right thing, or for some other motive. He always saw my sources as ripe for recruitment. I wouldn't be surprised in the least if he recruited a few.

I look at the computer screen again. That tip. *Ninety percent.* Then, abruptly, I roll my chair back into the aisle. "Hey, Damian," I call out down the row of cubicles. That new woman two cubes down shoots me an annoyed look.

Damian rolls his chair out into the aisle. "Yeah?"

"ClandestineTips. Got to be *some* way to figure out who sent a message, right?"

"You sat through that training, didn't you?"

"Yeah, but—"

"But nothing." He shakes his head. "Text-only messages are untraceable."

I know it's true. I heard the presentation. But if there's anyone who'd know a work-around, it's Damian. Our resident tech expert.

"Text-only?" I ask.

"You weren't paying attention, were you?"

"I got the gist of it."

He gives me a skeptical look. "Only loophole is when there's an attachment. A file, a picture, whatever. *Then* it's traceable . . . with some work."

Damn. No attachment in this one. "Okay, thanks."

"No problem."

He slides back toward his desk, and I roll back to my own.

I look at the tip again, on my screen. Four attempts to run it down so far, and I've hit three dead ends.

But one path is still open. Still a possibility.

One is all it takes. One scrap of key information, one favor, one lucky break. It's all I need.

And I'll be damned if I don't make it happen.

I get to Brewster's ten minutes early. It's dark inside, and I blink to force my eyes to adjust. It's a relaxed place. A favorite of the *Post* journalists. Old worn bar, plain tables and chairs. Unpretentious, with cheap drinks.

Beau's already here. At a table in the back, a pint in front of him. I walk toward him. He's ex-military. Still favors army green, and anything that's tight across his biceps. Always looks in need of a shave. He half stands as I approach. I slide in across from him. A server, a young guy with a bored expression, approaches before we've even had the chance to say hello.

"Get you anything?" the server asks.

I nod toward Beau's pint. "I'll have what he's having."

"You got it." The server heads off.

"Good to see you, old friend," I say to Beau.

"You haven't changed a bit, Alex."

I guess that's supposed to be a compliment? "Well, it hasn't been *that* long."

"Long enough for *some* things to change." He nods toward my left hand. "Trouble in paradise?"

Damn. How did he notice that already?

I look down at it. I can still see the indentation in my skin, a shade lighter than the surrounding skin. Or maybe it's just my imagination. "I'll talk if you do."

"What do you want to know?"

"I got a tip."

His eyebrows arch.

I lean forward. "Ninety percent of human intelligence on Syria's biowarfare program comes from a single source?"

Beau's a straight shooter. That's why we're friends, I think. That and the fact that he's more loyal to the truth than to any agency. He gave me key information on that story I broke about CIA arms transfers. And he did it because it was the right thing to do.

He gives me an inscrutable look. One I can't read. Then he takes a sip from his glass, his eyes never leaving mine. "Ninety percent, huh?"

The server returns. Slides a pint of beer in front of me. Some of it sloshes over the sides. I wait until he's gone to speak. "Sound about right?"

"Who's calculating these figures? Some analyst with too much

time on his hands? There's no way I'd know exactly what percent—"

"But there's one key source?"

He takes another drink. A long one, two gulps. Wipes his
mouth with the back of his hand. "It's tough there. Hard to operate. And a program like that? Pretty damn restricted."

I fight to keep my face impassive. "Who's the source?"

He gives a quick, firm shake of his head.

"Crypt?" The encryption, the name they give the source. I
know the lingo from my time in the field.

"Come on, Alex. You know better than to ask that."

I do, but it doesn't hurt to try. "That's a huge amount, Beau.
What if we lost the source?"

"We sure as hell better not."

"*Ninety* percent?"

"Look, when we get a good source, we run with it. What are
we supposed to do? *Not* take the info?"

"Get some other sources."

"Easier said than done. Good sources are damn near impossible to find. You know it as well as I do. Now"—he nods toward
my left hand—"your turn."

"We found out we weren't on the same page. About kids."

The words taste bitter. It sounds like we were irresponsible.
Like we didn't talk about the issue before we got married. We *did*
talk about the issue. He just changed his mind. And I didn't.

"Sorry, Alex."

I shrug like it's no big deal, when it *is* a big deal. A huge deal.

"Divorced, then?"

"Separated." *Technically* separated. He's filed already, but it's
not official yet.

"Maybe you'll be able to work things out?"

"Not really a middle ground here, is there?"

"Guess not."

We each take a sip from our glasses. There's nothing really left to say about it, is there? That's the point Miles and I reached, too. Not a damn thing left to say. I'm not having kids I don't want, and he's not missing out on something he *does* want.

"About this source," Beau says, and I'm relieved he's changing the subject, turning it back to something I *want* to talk about. "Who gave you the tip?"

"You know I can't say."

"You don't know, do you?"

I shrug.

"Make sure the info's good before you run with it."

"I know how to do my job, Beau," I snap. I couldn't run with it even if I wanted to. It's an anonymous tip I can't fully verify. The *Post* has standards, thankfully.

"Just sayin'," he says, holding up his hands in mock surrender. "Could be someone making shit up."

I smile. "Or I could have myself an insider."

I step into my loft an hour later. Couldn't be more different than Brewster's.

Everything's modern. Sleek, streamlined. And *neutral*.

I love the loft, always have. But I sure as hell miss the color.

We redecorated six months ago. Back when it was still *our* loft, before it was *my* loft. I wanted some pops of color. A bright wall, a bright rug, *something*. He wanted neutral.

We went with neutral.

He got his way a lot there, at the end. Since I wouldn't compromise on kids, I started compromising on everything else. It's what I do: make deals.

And then he just *left*.

"You can keep it," he'd said about the loft. And it felt like a stab to the heart. Because he loved the place as much as I did. We lived there together for *five years*.

"You don't want it?" I'd said. Because how could he just walk away?

"Makes more sense this way."

He didn't say it, but I knew what he meant. *Makes sense for you to stay here. Because I'll eventually move to the suburbs, or somewhere for the schools at least. Someplace where it's safer to raise kids. Where they'll have a yard and a swing set—*

I set my bag down on the table in the center of the room. The one that doubles as kitchen table and home office workspace. The one where Miles and I used to eat meals and play board games. Where we laid out all our wedding-planning materials—

I pour myself a bourbon at the bar in the corner. Take a sip. Let the warmth run through me.

I didn't even want the damn wedding. Wanted to elope. Why the hell am I feeling nostalgic about the wedding?

I sit down at the table and open my laptop. Power it up. Navigate to ClandestineTips, start the program. Scan the inbox: nothing from the same username. But there are a couple of new messages.

I click on the first.

To: Alex Charles
From: xxxwxyzxxx
Message: UFOs are real. Look into what happened in Albuquerque, New Mexico, in 1972. The extraterrestrials are here. They're waiting. And they're hostile. I can't say more, or they'll come for me.

I roll my eyes and close the window. Not a day goes by without a tip about UFOs.

Next one.

To: Alex Charles
From: Timothy Mittens
Message: Hello, Alex Charles! I live in the Shenandoah Valley. A home in my neighborhood was recently purchased by the CIA's Director of Operations, Langston West. Why??? Check it out!! 1457 Mountain Bluff Road!! All my best, Timothy Mittens.

Attached is a selfie of a lanky, smiling man—late thirties, I'd guess—with thinning blond hair. Standing in front of a cabin, pointing to it.

Clearly the idea of an anonymous tip is lost on this man. And poor Langston West probably just wants a place to relax. To escape. Guy's been a household name since he famously announced an end to the days of spy swaps, vowed to let spies rot in U.S. jails. Well, good luck with your hopes for privacy, Mr. West, staying next to this fool—

A ding. A new message. I close this window, scan the inbox—

There it is, from Afriend123.

Doesn't matter how I know. What matters is the information. Have you corroborated it?

I write back immediately: *Yes.* And then: *Could we meet?*

The response comes immediately: *No.*

I take a sip of bourbon and consider what to type next.

Do you have any other pertinent information?

What the tipster gave me, it's interesting, but it's not enough for a story.

I stare at the screen, waiting.

Yes.

Another sip. Then I type: *I'd appreciate anything you could share.*

A moment later: *The source. His crypt is Falcon.*

Crypt. Falcon. This *is* an insider. Only an insider would have this info—

Another message appears:

And he doesn't exist.

CHAPTER EIGHT

Alex

Doesn't *exist*?

I just had a CIA case officer more or less confirm that the U.S. gets most of its human reporting on Syrian biological weapons from one source.

A source that might not exist?

Now, *that's* a story.

Adrenaline runs through me like electricity. I love this feeling. The one I get when I know I've got something, and it's something big. "No feeling like it," my mom used to say. And she would know. She broke her fair share of stories. Before she adopted me, anyway.

But how the hell do I confirm it's true? I don't know who Falcon is. Beau didn't seem to have any indication the source wasn't real.

Oh my God—the implications of that. The CIA is relying on a source that doesn't exist. That's a front-page story for sure. A truth that needs to be told.

That's a Pulitzer.

Black women don't win journalism Pulitzers.

I can hear my mom's voice in my ear, at her retirement party. Recounting those words to me. Uttered by a jealous co-worker when she was a young reporter. Long before I came into her life. "I decided then and there I'd prove him wrong," she said to me. She took my hand and smiled at me. "I never did. But *you*. You're another story, Alexandra. *You* can. You have the same passion I did when I was your age. More, even. You have such a strong sense of right and wrong. And you're fearless. You're *determined*."

I stare at the chat on the screen. Force myself to focus.

I need something to work with. A lead I can look into. Something else to corroborate. My fingers find the keyboard.

I need to know more.

I wait. Stare at the screen. Who are *you*, this person I'm communicating with? You know something. How?

How do you know Falcon doesn't exist?

No response.

I type again:

Give me a lead. Please.

Finally, a response:

Find Jill Bailey.

I start with Google. My gut feeling is that she's CIA. She must be, if this source is telling me to find her. If she knows something about Falcon. If she's somehow connected to a CIA source.

But the name, it's too common. Google turns up nothing about a Jill Bailey who works for the CIA. I'm not surprised. But I need to see if this tip is legit.

So I top off my drink and head down into the dark web.

I learned how to do this years ago. Back when I was investigating drug trafficking. Not as hard as you'd think, actually. And there's a treasure trove of information out there. Just harder to access.

It takes me a good hour to find anything useful. But when I do, it's gold. A leak from a whistleblower. A contractor who worked at the CIA. It's a database of names and positions, from five years ago. I've seen these before. Used them to corroborate information about people, case officers and such.

There's a Jill Bailey listed as a reports officer, Syria.

The tip was good, again. This source, whoever it is, knows a hell of a lot.

And I'd be willing to bet this Jill Bailey does, too.

I stand up from the table and stretch. It's getting late and I haven't eaten. My stomach's growling. I pad into the kitchen. Look in the pantry. Sparse contents.

I grab a container of noodles. Peel off the paper lid, fill it with water. Stick it in the microwave. Watch the digits changing. Time ticking down—

A ring. My cellphone, on the table. The screen's lit up, vibrating. I walk over to check it—

Miles.

I stare at the name. I don't have to pick up.

I shouldn't. I should let it go to voicemail. Let him wonder what I'm doing. Let him think I don't want to talk to him.

But I can't. And I hate that I can't.

"Hi," I say.

"Hi."

That *voice.* So familiar. So many damn memories.

"How are you?"

"Fine. You?"

"Doing well."

The microwave beeps. I walk back over. Hold the phone with my shoulder, reach for the noodles.

"What are you up to?"

"Working."

"Of course." He says it lightly. But I hear the judgment.

"What do you want, Miles?"

"I just . . . wanted to say hi. And . . . you know . . . just wanted to make sure you're doing okay."

"I'm great." The words sound flat. "Busy."

"Maybe you should take a break. Everyone needs a vacation, Alex."

He can't resist, can he? Being so damn judgmental. Questioning my decisions. Acting like he knows better.

The mention of a vacation irks me. Because it's another area where I compromised. I always wanted to explore new places; he wanted to return to familiar favorites. Our last few vacations? We ended up renting the same cottage in Ocean City each time.

I grab a fork and start fluffing the noodles. Steam escapes in little puffs. I bring the bowl over to the couch. Sit down, curl up. Phone's still pinned to my ear with my shoulder.

"There's one more thing," Miles says. "One more reason I called." I can hear the hesitation in his voice.

"Yeah?"

"I thought you should hear it from me first. You know, before you see anything on social media, or any of our friends say anything . . ."

I go utterly still. No. Not possible—

"I'm seeing someone, Alex."

My heart drops. I've been so focused on the fact that he's no longer with me. But the thought of him with someone else . . .

"We're still *married*," I say.

"Legally separated—"

"You didn't waste any time, did you?"

"Alex—"

"I gotta get back to work."

"Alex, please—"

"Bye, Miles."

I press end and sit staring at the phone. He's seeing someone. He's moved on.

Who is she? That means they've been out on dates, doesn't it? Had those awkward-as-hell first conversations, maybe talked about the future—

The thought makes me sick to my stomach.

In my mind I'm back on our own first date. At that trendy Mexican place in Dupont Circle. Sitting at that table outside. Laughing. Talking.

"Do you want kids?" he'd asked.

I hesitated. I'd told the truth on other dates. Said no. Seen the recoil. Heard the empty promise to call. And truth be told, I was enjoying this date. This guy's company. I didn't want the date to end. "I'm not sure. You?"

"I'm not sure, either." There was a beat of silence, then he added, "But I'm leaning toward no."

The topic didn't come up again until a couple of months later. We had dinner at his college buddy's house in the suburbs, with the buddy's wife and two kids. The kids were terrors. Throwing tantrums. Refusing to eat. The husband and wife were fighting with the kids. Fighting with each other. It was awkward and uncomfortable and we couldn't get out of there soon enough.

"I don't think I want kids," I said on the car ride home, because it seemed as good a time as any to break the truth.

He laughed. "Thank God. Me neither."

And that was the end of it, then. We talked about it more later, of course. I told him I'd just never felt any sort of maternal pull. I wasn't like my mom in that respect. She always told me that being a mother was one of her life's goals. And thank God it was. I bounced around the foster care system until I was five, until she adopted me. I don't know what would have happened to me if she hadn't.

Miles and I fell in love quickly. He was as ambitious as I was, a consultant with an MBA. Worked just as long hours. We bonded over a shared love of jazz music and sushi, modern art and historical fiction. He wasn't perfect—no one was—but I found his quirks to be endearing. The fact that he took such pride in his appearance, even if he did hog the bathroom for far too long most mornings. His penchant for documenting his life on social media, which would give us a fun trip down memory lane in the future.

We got married, we bought the loft, we focused on our careers. We ate at nice restaurants, took nice vacations. We had the perfect life.

Or so I thought.

And then last year, we brought over dinner to his co-worker, a few weeks after the co-worker and his wife had welcomed a new baby.

"Would you like to hold her?" the wife had asked. To my surprise, Miles agreed. He took the baby into his arms gingerly. And then, it was like he melted. He just stared at the baby in his arms. Mesmerized.

I got nervous.

"Maybe we should have one," he said on the way home.

"A kid?"

"A baby."

"Babies become kids."

He didn't say anything else the rest of the ride home. And then, two days later, when we were getting ready for bed, he said the words I was dreading.

"Alex, I want to have a baby."

I was in the middle of brushing my teeth. I kept brushing, then spit. Looked at him in the mirror. "I don't."

"Where does that leave us?"

I rinsed the brush. Rinsed my mouth with water. Then looked at him in the mirror. "You're just saying this because you held that baby. But you're not thinking about—"

"I've been thinking about this for years."

I turned and faced him. "You've never said a word to me about it."

"That doesn't mean I haven't been thinking it."

"I've told you. I just don't have that maternal instinct. I don't *want* a child."

"Or are you just focused only on yourself?"

I stared at him. This person I thought I knew. "That's a *terrible* thing to say."

I couldn't believe he said that. *Thought* that. I loved him. Deeply. I loved my mom. Missed her every day. My friends. My *country*. For God's sake, I was passionate about my career because finding the truth *helped* people. I wouldn't be able to do my job the same way with children. Just look at my mom.

"What if you change your mind later?" he asked.

I wasn't going to change my mind. I felt confident about that. But I considered the possibility anyway. "Then we'll cross that bridge when we come to it."

"But by then, it might be too late. It's not like you're getting any younger."

The words cut, even if he didn't mean them to. "Then there are plenty of kids sitting in foster care."

"I don't *want* a kid from foster care. I want my *own* kid."

He couldn't have chosen more hurtful words to say. Couldn't have touched on my worst fears in a worse way. "It would *be* your own child. That's what happens when you adopt."

"I know, I know," he said dismissively. "It's just . . . Don't you want to have it all?"

"I thought I *did*." It's true; I never felt like anything was missing.

"Alex—"

"I'm not changing my mind," I said quietly.

He looked me right in the eye. "Neither am I."

I blink and focus on my surroundings. The fireplace in front of me. The built-in shelves on either side. Filled with classics, hardcover favorites. A framed picture of my mom. And one of Miles and me. My favorite one from our wedding day. Our arms around each other, our cheeks pressed together. The biggest smiles—

I look away. Stare down at the cup of noodles in my lap. The liquid's been absorbed. The noodles are thick and soft. My appetite's gone.

It's the last one left of us, that picture. The last one in a frame, at least. There's still the giant corkboard in the kitchen, with loads of pictures tacked to it. But the framed pictures—I'm almost there. Just one to go. The wedding picture. The one that's hard as hell to put away. Almost like an admission that the marriage is over.

I don't know why this is so damn hard.

I look at the picture of my mom. God, I wish she were here. Not a day goes by I don't wish I could talk to her again.

In my mind I can see her here, in the loft. On the couch, where she was the last time I saw her.

"If you and Miles have kids—" she said, mid-conversation.

"Mom, I told you we're not having kids."

"I know. But you might change your mind." She gave me a loving smile. "I did."

"And we might not."

"And you might not," she conceded. She reached for my hand. "I just want you to be happy, Alexandra. And there are many different paths to happiness."

"I have Miles. And *you*. And I have my career."

"And you're kicking ass at it," she said, drawing a laugh from me. "Really. I saw your latest on the wiretapping."

"There are bigger stories out there. And I'm going to find them."

She gave me a quizzical look. "Doesn't have to be the biggest story, Alexandra. Just has to be a truth that people need to hear."

I shake off the memory. Stand up, head to the kitchen. Throw the noodles in the trash. Sit back down at the table, at my laptop.

I have Miles. And you. *And I have my career.*

I don't have Miles anymore. He's moved on. He's going to get what he wants. A wife and kids. The kids that he wants more than the life we had.

And I don't have Mom, either. She's gone. That damn heart attack stole her from me.

I force those thoughts from my mind. I need to focus. Now that I know the tip is good, I just need to find the right Jill Bailey.

Five years ago she was at the CIA. Is she still? I focus on that time frame, because that's the last confirmation I have. I look up every Jill Bailey who's lived in DC, or Northern Virginia, or Maryland. I narrow them down to a few. Cross-reference. Check other databases, court records—

Here's something. A Jill Bailey who changed her name, four

years ago. And not right after a marriage, either. An out-of-the-blue name change. She became Jill Smith.

I dig into the address associated with the name. The house sold just weeks after the name change.

I get that feeling again. That tingly rush of adrenaline. I've found something.

This is someone who wanted to disappear. Who *tried* to disappear. But no one can truly disappear.

It doesn't take long to find the new address, in Florida.

I throw it into Google Maps. Look at the house on satellite view. Then street view. Nice little house, nothing too flashy. Palm trees. A golf course nearby. Looks almost like the kind of place you'd take a vacation.

Miles's words run through my head. *Everyone needs a vacation, Alex.*

He's wrong, though. I don't need a vacation.

I need a Pulitzer.

I fly down to Fort Lauderdale the next day. The flight costs too damn much, but it means getting to work right away. This isn't the kind of story you sit on. This is the kind of story you run down. Whatever it takes.

I rent a compact sedan at the airport. Head to a Hampton Inn. Close to Jill's house, and cheap. I drop off my suitcase, then drive to her house. It's evening by the time I arrive. I sit across the street and wait. There's a RAV4 in the driveway. Sidewalk chalk scribbles on the pavement. A trike outside, and a stray ball in the grass.

Typical suburban house, typical suburban family.

The kind of thing Miles wants.

There are lights on inside. I can see figures moving behind the curtains. They're probably eating dinner. Probably settled in for the night.

I drive back to the hotel, stop in the McDonald's drive-through on the way. I eat the burger and fries in bed, watching mindless TV.

Early the next morning, I drive back to the house. I sit on the street and I wait.

The husband pulls out of the garage at seven. I don't get much of a look at him.

She leaves an hour later. Comes out the front door, two kids in tow. She looks average. Boring. Yoga pants, baggy shirt. Hair tied back, minimal makeup.

One of the kids is a boy. Serious-looking. The other's a girl. Younger, like a toddler. With a full head of dark curls.

I watch Jill load the kids into the SUV, strap them into car seats. It takes forever.

She backs out of the driveway slowly, then drives off down the street. I wait a moment and follow. I try to keep my distance, at least a little.

She heads to preschool first. Joins a line of cars, mostly SUVs. The occasional minivan. I pull off into the parking lot of a nearby bank and watch.

When her car reaches the front of the line, a teacher opens the back door. She leans in—unstrapping the car seat, maybe? Helps the boy out. Adjusts his little backpack, takes his hand. Walks him inside.

Jill's car drives off.

I leave the lot and follow, leaving two cars between us.

She heads directly home. Parks in the driveway, walks inside. Never looks around. She has no idea I'm following her. No idea I'm watching.

Three hours later she leaves the house again. Hurries out, drives off. I follow.

Back to preschool, back into the line of cars. A different teacher walks out with the boy, holding his hand. He's clutching something in his other hand. Some sort of paper. An art project maybe.

When she drives off, I follow.

She doesn't go straight home this time. Stops at the grocery store. I park in the next row over and watch as she gets the kids out of the car seats. God, it's a time-consuming process, isn't it? She lifts them into a cart shaped like a race car, belts them in. The girl grabs the plastic steering wheel, jiggling it.

I head inside after them. Grab a basket, never taking my eyes off her. I pretend I'm examining produce, and a couple of times I get close enough to hear her speak. She's refereeing an argument between the kids. Speaking calmly. A peacemaker.

I stand behind the table of tomatoes and watch her.

She's a normal suburban mom. What does she have to do with Falcon?

Maybe nothing. Maybe I have the wrong person—

She looks up, notices me. Her face transforms. Tightens.

She knows I'm watching her.

She forces a smile. But it's too late. Her face has already given her away. This is someone who's been watched before.

Someone who knows there's a *reason* she's being watched.

This is the right Jill Bailey.

I drift away, out of sight. I have the answer to my first question.

I drop the basket by the door, head back to my car. Sit there and wait.

She takes forever to come out. Her cart's loaded down. The little girl looks asleep. Jill loads the kids into the SUV, one by one. Then the groceries—

She sees me. Goes still, stares right at me. I stare back, from behind my shades.

She finally gets in her car and drives off. Slowly, past my car. I watch her the whole time. She doesn't intimidate me.

I don't bother following her. I don't need to. I got what I came for.

I pick up a six-pack and a sub sandwich on the way home. Eat and drink sitting cross-legged on the bed, watching bad television.

The next morning I'm back on her street, farther away this time. I follow her at more of a distance. She heads to the park. I watch her watch her kids. She looks like a good mom. Attentive. Cautious. *You can never be too cautious, can you, Jill?*

The little girl bumps her chin on the seesaw. Gives me my opening. I make my way over to the little boy. "What's your name?" I ask him.

"Owen."

"And how old are you, Owen?"

"Four and a half. But I'm not supposed to talk to strangers."

"I'm not a stranger. I know your mom."

"Oh."

It's too damn easy. "Is that your sister over there?"

"Yes. Mia."

"How old is Mia?"

"Three."

"Owen!"

I look up, and Jill's hustling toward me, Mia on her hip. Her face is unnaturally pale. Her eyes look wide and panicked.

I watch her calmly. *Why so scared, Jill?*

What are you scared of?

She reaches for Owen. Pulls him toward her. Steps in front of him, like she's shielding him.

"Who are you?" she says. "And what do you want?"

"I'm Alex Charles. And I want to talk about Falcon."

The color drains even further from her face. Leaves it a ghastly shade of white. She reminds me of a deer caught in headlights.

Yes, Jill Bailey—Jill *Smith*—knows about Falcon. There's not a doubt in my mind.

"We're leaving," she says. She grabs the boy's hand, practically drags him away.

I watch her go. That's her instinct, isn't it? To flee. The same instinct that brought her to Florida, I'd bet. That led her to change her name from Jill Bailey to Jill Smith.

What are you running from, Jill?

"I'll be at the Starbucks on Shore Drive tomorrow at ten," I call. She doesn't turn around, but she must hear me. "If you don't show, I'm going to press with the story I have."

I say the words with as much confidence as I can muster. I don't know if I'm overplaying my hand. If she knows I'm bluffing.

I don't have a story, not yet.

But I'm sure as hell going to find one.

CHAPTER NINE

Jill

I get to Starbucks at nine-thirty and sit in the parking lot, watching, waiting. It's habit, from my Agency days: arrive early, scope the place. I need to make sure that no one's watching us. That no one sees me talking to a journalist—and a *Washington Post* reporter, at that.

I didn't sleep last night. How could I? This reporter, this Alex Charles, she knows about Falcon. She knows about *me*. Does she know I approved the source? That Owen was kidnapped? Whatever she knows, it's too much, that's for sure.

And she threatened to go public with it, whatever it is.

It's dangerous, being here. But I'm terrified it's more dangerous *not* to be. That voice from the past has been echoing in my head, on an endless loop: *If this* ever *comes out, we'll be back. We'll take your son. And we'll kill him.*

I called work this morning, said I'd be in late. I hate lying, but it's what I've been doing for the last four years. Maybe not directly, maybe not in actual words, but the very fact that I'm in Florida, that's because I'm living a lie, isn't it?

I need to figure out what story this journalist thinks she has. And if it's the one I think, the one I fear, I need to find a way to stall. Stall, and convince her she doesn't have a story, make sure she doesn't publish anything. I don't know how I'm going to do it, but I have to.

She pulls up at nine forty-five in the same white sedan I remember from the grocery store, parks in the first row, near the door. She sits for a few minutes with the engine off, looking at her phone. Then she heads inside. I watch as she orders something, then hovers near the pick-up area, tapping on her phone. When her drink is ready, she carries it to a table in the back, out of my sight. At least she's got enough sense to pick the back, away from the windows.

I look around one last time, then leave my car, walk inside, head down. I bypass the counter and walk straight to the back. She's at a two-seater, her coffee cup in front of her. I sit down across from her.

"Hi, Jill."

"Hi."

"Coffee?"

"I'm fine." I don't want to be here longer than I need to be.

She takes a sip of her coffee, watching me the whole time. This woman, she's not afraid to stare at people, that's for sure. There's something unnerving about the way she's looking at me, like she's trying to read me, or *can* read me.

"You mentioned going to press," I say. "What's the story?"

"You tell me."

"I have no idea."

"We both know that's not true."

I fold my hands on the table and stare directly at her. I'm not going to blink first. If she wants something from me—and she wouldn't have asked me to come here otherwise—she's going to have to give me something.

There's a clang in the kitchen, something falling to the floor. Then quiet again, just the distant din of activity at the counter, the soft strains of background music from the speakers.

"I know the U.S. is entirely too reliant on Falcon," she finally says.

I fight to keep my face impassive. "Why do you think that?"

"A source."

"Who?"

"Doesn't matter. The information's correct, isn't it?"

I say nothing. If that's all she has, fine. It's not the real story, the one they want me to keep secret. And it couldn't possibly be *attributed* to me, wouldn't look like I broke their rules and talked. I've been out of the game for four years. I have no idea how much the U.S. relies on Falcon, or what he's providing—

"And I know Falcon's not a real source."

Dammit.

That voice rings in my head again. *If this ever comes out, we'll be back—*

"*And* I know you're involved in this."

"I don't know what you're talking about." I say it automatically, like a reflex, one born out of fear.

She takes another sip of her coffee, her eyes never leaving mine. "When did you find out he wasn't a real source?"

"I'm telling you, I don't know what you're talking about."

"Did you know from the beginning?" she presses. "Because you were a reports officer. You worked Syria. You worked *Falcon.*"

How does she know that? *Does* she know that, or is she guessing?

"I worked a ton of different sources," I say. "That name doesn't ring a bell."

"Didn't look that way yesterday. At the playground. Looked like that name most certainly *did* ring a bell."

My pulse is racing. I don't know what to say, how to get myself out of this, how to shut this down.

"It would have been up to you to vet the source. So how'd you miss it? That he's not real."

If she publishes this, they'll come for Owen. Mia, too?

I need to find a way out of this. Stall. Convince her this isn't a story—

"If I missed something, it was an accident."

She nods. "You were just back from maternity leave, weren't you? Probably tired?"

It's an out, isn't it? A way to convince her there's no story here, or at least that *I'm* not part of it. Distance myself as much as possible from whatever she's going to write—

I nod.

"I thought the name didn't ring a bell."

Shit.

"Truth is, you remember that name very well. You approved the source, and then you changed your name and fled to Florida. Why?"

Oh my God. How is this coming out *now,* after all this time?

"Did they pay you?"

"No!"

She shrugs. "I didn't really think so. Blackmail? Did you have some kind of secret affair?"

"Of course not."

"Well, here's the thing. If you don't tell me *why,* the story's just going to be full of speculation."

I stare at her. She can't publish this. *Can* she?

"If anything happened on my end, it was a *mistake*." If I can convince her of that, maybe it'll force her to keep digging. Maybe it'll delay her going to press, or at least keep my name out of it. "I'm not your story."

"So what *is* the story?"

"I don't know."

"Give me *something*."

"I have nothing to give."

"Then you're the story, Jill." She leans back, folds her arms across her chest.

That voice is back again, in my head. *If this* ever *comes out—*

"Why'd you run?"

"What?"

"You *ran*. Changed your name. Moved. *Why?*"

I don't know what to say, so I just stare at her.

"Let's say it *was* a mistake. *Why did you run?*"

A young guy in all black ambles toward the back of the shop. He sits down three tables over, opens up a laptop.

Alex leans forward and speaks more quietly. "Let's put it this way. Hypothetically, if *someone* made a mistake, why would she run?"

"Maybe she didn't want to be in a position to ever make a mistake like that again."

That part, at least, is the truth.

Alex leans back, eyes me. "She thought she was doing the right thing."

I shrug. "Maybe."

She watches me a moment longer. Then she reaches down into her bag, pulls out a folded piece of paper. Opens it, lays it on the table between us, facing me.

It's a list of names, a half dozen. Most are familiar to me, case officers who worked Syria over the years. A. J. Graham is second from last.

"Where'd you get these names?"

"They're online. Dark web. They were part of one of those big leaks, years ago."

I look up at her and say nothing.

"Now, I'll be honest," she says. "I think there's a bigger story here. I think you screwed up, and you know it. But I think there are others who did much worse." She taps one manicured fingernail against the paper. "Give me a name."

"No."

"I'm going to track down each of these guys, and I'm going to talk to them."

Good. That'll take time. "Knock yourself out."

"But first I'm going to press with what I have. *You.* And your source."

"You can't do that—"

"I'll hold the story. For three days. *If* you tell me who recruited him."

I look down at the list again. She'll find A.J. eventually. She has his name. All this would do is buy me time. Time to disappear, to keep my family safe.

"Whoever it was, he put you in this position."

She's right. He *did* put me in this position. Because if Falcon is a fake source, A.J.'s to blame. A.J. didn't do his due diligence and properly vet his source. Or worse, A.J. was in on it, *knew* Falcon wasn't real. The idea's been in the back of my mind for years, but I've tried not to dwell on it, mostly because it inevitably led me to question who Falcon was, and why, and I didn't want to think about either. Didn't want to think about what I'd done.

"A week," I say.

"Four days. That's it."

My eyes settle on the name, and I feel like I'm betraying him, but then, he betrayed me, didn't he? How else did they know I was the one with the cable in my queue?

And she already has his name. I'm just buying myself enough time to protect my kids.

I point to A.J.'s name.

She nods, and I stand to leave.

"Here's the one thing I don't understand," she says evenly, folding the paper carefully in half, and then half again.

I wait, and finally she shifts her gaze to me, gives me a steely look. "If you made a mistake, and that's all it was—a *mistake*—why didn't you just *admit* it?"

The way she's watching me sends a chill through me. I turn and head for the door without saying a word, because I don't have an answer for her, not in the least.

The rest of the morning passes in a blur. I go through the motions at work, by rote. It's hard to focus on my students, on *anything* besides Alex.

Four days. Four days until she goes to press, until this comes out. I tried to convince her that I'm not the story, that at most it was a mistake, but she saw through me. When she writes this story, I'll be part of it.

We need to run, don't we? Pick up and leave, again.

All these years, I did what they said. Never breathed a word. Even now, even meeting with Alex, I never said a word about Owen's kidnapping. Isn't *that* what they wanted me to keep quiet about, more than anything?

But it doesn't matter. All that matters now is this article that's going to come out, and what those people will do when they see it.

When I get home at five, everything seems normal. I stand in the kitchen and look out the window into the backyard. The kids are playing on the swing set, and I can just barely hear the faint sound of their happy shrieks. The sun's sinking lower in the sky; the lake is calm.

I open the sliding glass door and step outside.

"Mommy!" Mia yells, bounding over, pigtails bouncing. She wraps her arms around my leg in a hug. Owen's on the swing, trying hard to pump his legs. He raises one hand in the quickest of waves, grips the chain again, a proud smile on his face.

Drew walks over, gives me a peck on the lips. "How was your day?"

"Fine." There's a pit in my stomach when I say it.

I'm going to have to tell him what's happening. There's no way around it. What's he going to say? What's he going to *think*?

If I were in his shoes, if he'd kept a secret like this from me, I'd be furious.

"Daddy! Let's play pirates!" Owen says, slowing himself to a stop with his toe in the dirt, then hopping off the swing.

"Arrgh, matey," Drew says, giving me a wink.

He jogs off after Owen, who's waving an invisible sword, heading toward the swing set.

We're going to have to leave all this. And we're going to have to do it on our own.

A shiver runs through me. I fold my arms across my chest and watch my family.

How is this even going to work? We can't leave a trail this time, like we did last time. No credit cards, no ATMs. We'll have to pull out all our money before we leave town, live off cash. But we don't *have* much cash. Most of it's tied up in the house. And it's not like we can sell the house before we go.

Where will we live? *How* will we live? We'll have to take whatever jobs are available, the kind that don't require any sort of experience, that don't check references, or even IDs. Will they pay enough for us to afford housing, and food?

I watch Mia spin in the grass, her head tipped back toward the sun, her arms outstretched, and my heart hurts.

I thought I was doing the right thing for my family all those years ago. But I wasn't, was I? I should have come clean when the government could have helped us. Settled us, given us stipends, helped us find jobs, made sure we had a safe place to live.

Now we're on our own. No one to protect us. No one to give us guidance.

Drew picks up Owen, holds him sideways over his head, and Owen dissolves in a fit of giggles, the sweetest sound. So happy, so carefree.

What will this do to the kids? Where will they go to school? What will they think? What about their toys, their books, everything that's important to them? We'll only be able to bring what we can fit in the car. How do I fit our whole lives into a car?

And our families. Will we tell them we're leaving? We can't just disappear. They'll be convinced something terrible happened to us. But what in the world would we say?

"Jill? Everything okay?" Drew's looking over at me, squinting into the sun.

Four days. I can let them have these last hours of normalcy, can't I? I'll tell him tonight, after the kids go to bed. And then we can put plans into motion. Find a way to disappear before the four days are up, before the article hits the press, and our lives change forever.

"Yeah," I call back, but it's a delayed response, and he's already back to his swordfight, laughing with Owen.

Once I tell him the truth, nothing will ever be the same again.

I head back inside, close the sliding door behind myself, look around. I don't even know where to begin. Packing, maybe? Gathering what little we can take, the most precious things that can't be left behind?

I walk out into the garage, to the recycling pile, pull out an old Amazon box, one with some packing paper still inside. I bring it into the study, set it down.

I unlock the fireproof safe, take out the folder of important documents: passports, birth certificates, Social Security cards. A diamond pendant that belonged to my grandmother. An external hard drive where I've backed up all our pictures. I drop everything into the box.

The back door slides open, and I hear footsteps, then Mia's high-pitched chatter, Drew's voice, Owen's. The door closes behind them. I stop what I'm doing, slide the box to the corner of the room, go out to greet them, a big smile plastered on my face, like everything's normal. Like I'm not in the midst of packing up our lives.

We make homemade pizza for dinner, with toddler radio playing in the background, the kids on stools at the counter. Drew rolls out the dough, even tosses it clumsily, much to the kids' delight. Owen spreads the sauce, Mia sprinkles on cheese. I just watch, nostalgic about something that isn't yet gone, because I know it's about to be. Because everything's about to change. We can't stay here, can't keep living this life, not when Alex has this story.

After dinner we give the kids baths, get them into PJs. I help Owen with his, but he wants to do it himself, and as he's struggling into his pajama top, I look around his room. He has a twin-size bed now, with Spider-Man sheets. But I remember when it was a crib, when we first moved in. When I found that note. *You can run, but you can't hide.*

How right they were.

And now? Now we're about to run again.

What if they're right? What if we can run, but we *can't* hide?

We're only safe if we can hide.

We watch *Finding Nemo* in the family room, all four of us cuddled up on the couch. Mia falls asleep in my lap. I bring her upstairs, place her in her bed, and watch her sleep, one arm stretched over her head.

I turn on her nightlight and walk back down the stairs, footsteps heavy—

The doorbell rings. I go still, frozen with fear.

Is it them? Are they here?

I rush down the remaining stairs, make a beeline for the front door. I want to make sure Owen's nowhere near it—

I look out the peephole, and it's Alex.

I swing open the door, fear replaced by anger. She can't be here. Her presence puts us in more danger.

"What are you doing here?" I practically hiss. "You should be talking to A. J. Graham."

"I can't," she says matter-of-factly, looking me straight in the eye. "He's dead."

CHAPTER TEN

Jill

"What do you mean he's dead?" I ask. A.J.'s *dead*?

She's giving me one of those intense stares again, like she's trying to read me. Is she trying to figure out if I knew that? Of course I didn't know that.

"Honey?" comes Drew's voice, from the family room. "Who's there?"

I ignore him. "When?" I ask Alex. "*How?*"

It was *them,* wasn't it? And here I am talking to a journalist, in full view of the street—

Reflexively I look around. Nothing that I can see—

"Come in," I say, ushering her inside, quickly closing the door behind her.

I hear footsteps, and Drew rounds the corner.

"Oh!" he says, catching sight of Alex. He extends a hand. "I'm Drew."

"Alex," she says, shaking it.

Awkward silence follows. He looks flustered, like he thinks he's supposed to know her, like he's trying to place her. Probably thinks she's another preschool mom, that I mentioned she was coming over, that he wasn't paying enough attention.

"Daddy, can I have more popcorn?" comes Owen's voice.

"Duty calls," he says with a smile, looking relieved. He quickly disappears.

"Come on," I say, ducking into the study. She follows me, and I close the door behind us.

She unlocks her phone, holds it up. There's an article on the screen. "Four years ago. Right before you moved to Florida."

Right before I moved. I take the phone from her and start reading.

The date is the first thing that registers. I remember clearly the last day I was in the office, the day I left my career, turned in my badge. *A.J. died the very next day.*

If I'd been at the Agency a day longer, I'd have known about this, for sure. He'd have been memorialized internally, even if his death didn't make a splash publicly. Once I turned in my badge, though, I was cut off from this kind of information. A.J. was undercover; technically there's no reason a CIA employee like myself would have been working with him. And if any old colleague had broken protocol to let me know, they'd have to call on an open line or in an open setting, risking their clearance to do so. But *why*—

"Overdose," she says, even though I'm reading the same thing myself. The article calls him a State Department employee. Says he was found at his home, deceased. Lethal amount of fentanyl in his system, along with a significant amount of alcohol.

That's why I didn't hear about it on the news. He wasn't killed in the line of duty, in an operation. It was opioids, in the middle of an opioid epidemic. He was nothing more than a statistic.

"Accidental?" I ask.

"You think it wasn't?"

I look down at the phone again, stare at the article, like it has the answers I'm looking for. My brain is spinning—

"What's that?" she asks. She nods toward the cardboard box in the corner of the room. Our passports are lying atop framed pictures, an external hard drive. "Where are you going, Jill?"

I say nothing.

"Running, again? Why?"

I glare at her, this woman who's in my home, who brought this fear back into my life. "I gave you what you asked for. A lead."

"It's not a lead when he's dead."

"You don't think a dead case officer is a story?"

"Tell me *why* it's a story, Jill."

I hand her phone back to her. "You need to leave."

She takes it from me without breaking eye contact. "You're covering something up, and that makes you part of the story. It's all going to come out eventually."

I believe her. But what can I say? What can I possibly tell her?

"You're afraid of something, Jill. Why are you afraid? Who are you afraid of?"

"I'm not the story."

"Tell me what you're afraid of."

"I can't."

"Why?"

"I just can't."

She stares at the cardboard box. "I think you tried to do the right thing before. Leaving the Agency, running. Because you were compromised, and you didn't want to do anything else wrong."

I watch her.

"And I think you're about to run again because you're afraid someone's going to come after you."

Her words make me angry. I *am* afraid they're going to come after us. If she'd just go away, this would all go away. If she'd never appeared, the past would still be the past, and I wouldn't be in this situation.

"I'm not saying anything. You need to leave." I point to the door.

"I believe you when you say you're not the story. So help me find the story. Give me something."

I open the door of the study, give her a hard look. "I did. I gave you A.J.'s name."

"And he's dead. I can't talk to a dead man."

I say nothing, and she watches me for another moment, then finally walks out of the study, toward the front door. She opens it, then pauses, turns back around. "It wasn't an accident, was it?"

Not with that timing. Right after Falcon became a source.

"I don't know," I say.

"It was them, wasn't it? The same people you're running from?"

Them.

Was it them?

Did they get what they needed from A.J., and then eliminate him? Falcon was a source. A.J. had given him COVCOM—

A.J. had *just* given him COVCOM.

The overdose was right after my last day of work, and *that* was the day he gave Falcon the COVCOM.

They killed him, didn't they?

"If they got to A.J.," she says, "what makes you so sure they won't get to you?"

———

I stand alone in the hall and stare at the closed door, trembling. Strains of the Disney movie in the family room reach my ears; her voice echoes in my brain. *If they got to A.J., what makes you so sure they won't get to you?*

I'm not sure at all. And that terrifies me.

A.J.'s *dead*. How did I not know that?

Because I stayed away from the news. Because this, it probably didn't even *make* the news, not really. A State Department employee in another country. An overdose. Not exactly breaking news.

I walk into the family room, numb. Sit down beside Owen, put my arms around him, pull him close. He doesn't take his eyes off the screen.

"Who was that?" Drew asks.

"Alex."

I leave it at that. And he doesn't press it, probably thinks he should know who that is.

I watch the screen but don't see a thing that's happening. My mind is racing.

I've followed the rules. I still haven't breathed a word, haven't told Alex anything. Haven't told *anyone* anything.

Did A.J. do the same thing?

For years now, it's been in the back of my mind that he was in on it. That he knew Falcon was a fake. But now, hearing that he's *dead* . . . it makes me wonder if he was in the same position as me. If they got to him. Warned him to be quiet, like they did to me.

Maybe they got to all of us, everyone in the approval chain.

It wouldn't have been hard to do. There weren't very many of us, thanks to those new streamlined procedures. After me it was just COPS and the Director of Operations. Who knows if they'd have even *needed* to get to those two. They were rubber stamps, for the most part.

And there was only one person between A.J. and me. Vaughn Craig, the Chief of Station in Damascus when Falcon was recruited. A.J.'s boss, the person who approved the cable before it got to me.

"Come on, Nemo," Owen whispers intently, beside me. I glance over, and his eyes are wide, focused on the screen.

I pull my phone from my back pocket, unlock it with one hand, pull up the browser. Type the letters of the name into Google: *Vaughn Craig*.

I can't help myself. What happened to him? Something terrible, like what happened to A.J.? Did he resign, like me? Or is he still employed, doing someone's bidding?

I scan the results, then click on the first.

A bio appears, with a picture. That's him. I recognize him, encountered him a few times while I was at the Agency.

Looks like he retired a few months ago, started his own security consulting agency, Security Solutions. In Miami.

Miami. That's less than an hour's drive from here.

I watch the fish swimming on the screen, pull Owen closer.

A.J.'s dead. Vaughn Craig isn't. He might know how to navigate this.

And he's *close* to here. It's like a sign.

I think it's time that Vaughn Craig and I have a little chat.

I leave the next afternoon, as soon as Drew gets home from work. I called my boss at the Language Academy, said I'd come down with something, that I needed the evening off. Drew still thinks I headed into work; there's no way I can tell him what I'm really doing.

What *am* I doing?

I'm not going to breathe a word about my own situation. If he reports back to *them,* at least I'm still following their rules. But I need to understand what's going on. And I feel like Vaughn Craig might have answers.

His website was flashy. Touted his experience as a twenty-year veteran CIA operative, in charge of numerous posts around the world. His "unparalleled experience and expertise." It promised "security solutions for your business, designed by an expert." I plugged the address from the contact page—minus the suite number—into Google Maps, and I've followed the directions here.

I was expecting a high-rise, something equally flashy. But the map directs me to a strip mall, a dingy one. The "suite" is wedged between a dry cleaner and a liquor store, a generic sign above the door. SECURITY SOLUTIONS.

This isn't what I would have expected, at all.

I pull into a parking space out front. The lights are off inside, and there's a sign in the window that says Closed. It's not quite five o'clock. I knew this was a possibility, but I'm disappointed nonetheless. This was a complete waste of—

Another car pulls up beside me, two spots over. A Jeep, open on all sides, music blaring. A man steps out of the driver's seat, a takeout bag in one hand, soft drink in the other. Vaughn Craig. He's in a Hawaiian shirt and loafers. Aviator sunglasses, a dark tan. He looks like a walking cliché.

He unlocks the door, steps inside. Turns on the lights, flips the sign to Open. I watch through the windows as he settles himself into the single desk, pulls a sandwich from the paper bag, opens it up, smoothing the paper flat.

I get out of my car and walk to the door. A chime rings when it opens. "Afternoon," he says, getting to his feet. "Something I can help you with?"

"Vaughn, right?"

"That's me." He walks closer. "And you are?"

"Jill Smith. We used to work together. I was a reports officer. Syria. I was Jill Bailey back then."

"Jill. Of course." He extends a hand and smiles broadly, exposing a row of bright white teeth. "I forget names, but I never forget a face. What can I do for you?"

"Do you have a minute to chat?"

"I have all the time in the world. Have a seat." He gestures toward the two chairs opposite the desk and lowers himself back into his own chair.

I sit down and realize I'm not sure how to begin. "So you're in the business world now."

He laughs. "This probably wasn't what you expected, if you looked me up online."

I smile. "You have a nice website."

"It's all most of my clients see. They never see this." He shrugs. "Rent's cheap."

"You left the Agency recently?" I need to dig without making it obvious I'm digging.

"Six months ago. Thought about going green." He uses Agency terminology for becoming a contractor, trading in a blue badge for a green one. "But I'm making the same doing this, for half the hours. And I'm *here,* outside the hellhole that is Washington."

He leans back in his chair, clasps his hands behind his head. "Are you in need of some *security solutions?*" He gives me a wry smile.

"Actually, I'm here about an old friend of mine," I say carefully. "A. J. Graham."

At this, his demeanor changes. He drops his arms and leans forward. "A.J., huh?" He shakes his head. "Such a shame. He was one in a million, that guy. Top-notch case officer."

I search his face, but I don't see what I'm looking for. Don't see fear, or reticence, or anything I might expect if he's wrapped up with *them*.

I press ahead. "I left the Agency right before he passed. Last case I worked was Falcon. That was the last cable I approved."

He gives me a quizzical look. "Hold that thought."

He stands up, walks over to a closet. Opens it, pulls out some sort of electronic device, a long black wand. Turns it on, starts sweeping the room, waving it toward each wall, the ceiling, the furniture. The device emits a slow, quiet beep the entire time.

Finally he turns it off and puts it back in the closet. "You can never be too careful."

He looks almost disappointed not to have found anything.

"Now," he says, settling back into his chair. "Falcon. What an incredible source. A.J.'s legacy." He looks wistful.

He has no idea, does he?

I don't know what to do with that information, what to think. This wasn't what I was expecting. I thought for sure they'd have gotten to him, too.

The fact that they didn't leaves me bewildered.

Get some answers, Jill.

"I'm trying to learn more about his final days. The overdose . . . it was fentanyl?"

"It was."

"That doesn't sound like A.J."

Truth be told, I don't know if it does or not. I never knew him all that well. But how else am I going to dig for more information, ask if it wasn't an accident, if he was *killed*?

"That was my reaction, too." Vaughn shakes his head.

"And the fact that he overdosed—that makes it even more surprising, doesn't it?"

He gives me an even stare. "You're asking if it was a hit, aren't you?"

"Yes." No sense denying it. I want to hear what he has to say. "I mean, it was a dead case officer."

"*And* a lethal drug. Naturally that was an immediate concern. But we didn't find a shred of evidence to suggest that was the case."

I process those words. Not a shred of evidence. Couldn't that just mean it was someone sophisticated, someone who covered their tracks?

"On the contrary, we found something that most certainly indicated it *wasn't* a hit."

"What did you find?"

"Can't get into that."

"I'm really just trying to understand—"

"I can't get into it."

I can tell from the look on his face he means it, that he isn't going to say a word, whatever it is he knows.

I try a different path. "What about the timing?" I'm heading into dangerous waters here.

"What timing?"

"It was the day after Falcon got COVCOM."

"Where are you going with this?" He gives me an even stare.

"I'm just trying to find out about A.J.'s last days," I say, but it sounds like a lie, even to me.

"This isn't about A.J. This is about Falcon. *Why?*"

What am I supposed to say?

I could insist it's just about A.J. Find a way to end the conversation, make my way home. I came because I thought Vaughn and I were in the same boat. I was wrong.

But then what? Alex is publishing in three days. I have three days to find a way out of this. And right now I don't have a clue how to do that.

"Was Falcon a dangle?" I ask. It's impulsive, and it's probably a step too far. But I'm sitting across from the person who knows more about this case than just about anyone.

He raises his eyebrows. "You know our processes are rigorous. Why do you ask?"

I notice he doesn't immediately say no. "Don't you think the timing's suspicious, with what happened to A.J.?"

He leans back in his chair. Steeples his fingers, watches me closely. "And what would be the goal?"

"COVCOM."

"Using it to penetrate our network?"

"Exactly."

He taps his fingertips together, looks thoughtful. "Well. If it *was* about COVCOM, I doubt they'd still be wasting their time on Falcon."

"Why's that?"

"The COVCOM system Falcon has—it's pretty useless at this point. We've got a better system now. *That's* what we're deploying in the most aggressive countries. And only for the most trusted sources. There's only so much damage one could do with that legacy system."

"Any sign that Falcon's been angling to upgrade systems?" It feels strange to be asking such specific questions, but we're already having a conversation that shouldn't take place outside

Agency walls, aren't we? He swept the room. And he doesn't seem
to have the same qualms I do; I've always found that field-based
operatives are far looser when it comes to talking shop outside
secure spaces.

"Nope. On the contrary, actually. He wants to avoid face-to-
face meetings as much as we do."

"When was the last face-to-face?"

"When A.J. handed off the COVCOM."

"I mean with his new handler."

"No one else has met with him."

I stare at him, speechless. "How's that possible?" It's been *four
years*.

"We didn't want to spook him. Besides, there was no need,
once he was on COVCOM. We were intentionally trying to limit
face-to-face contact. The Syrians were trying too hard to root out
spies."

It's got to be about COVCOM. A.J. died *the day after* giving
the source COVCOM, and no one else has met with him. Some
fake source has access to our COVCOM—

"Getting access to the system—could that have been the goal,
four years ago?"

"Could have been." He cocks his head to the side. "But I don't
know. Falcon provided reporting that checked out. Things about
the Syrian regime that the regime wouldn't have planted. Wouldn't
have wanted us to know."

"Maybe he wasn't run by Syria. Maybe he was run by another
country."

"It's possible," he says. Then his brow furrows deeply. He goes
quiet, looks deep in thought, troubled.

"What is it?" I ask, because it's obviously *something*.

He hesitates, then speaks. "Falcon's reporting changed, right
before I left. His access improved significantly. There was more

detail to his reporting. *Much* more detail. It began to attract a lot of attention."

"Someone took over the COVCOM?"

He shakes his head firmly. "No. Same person from beginning to end. I'm sure of it. Phrasing, expressions, tone—all of that was entirely consistent."

"What was the new reporting?"

"That Syria had developed a super strain of anthrax. One so lethal it would kill ninety percent of those exposed. And—even more disturbingly—that the government was making preparations to deploy it."

I process the information. That's incredibly explosive reporting.

"When I left," he says quietly, "we were considering military action to put an end to it."

Maybe it's not about using COVCOM to try to infiltrate our networks. Maybe it's about planting false information.

"Does someone want us to go to war with Syria?" I ask.

"Sure. Every country that wants us weak."

"So someone else could be behind this. Planting this info. China or Russia or—"

"Maybe." He holds up a palm in a stopping motion. "*If* it's a fake source. I'm still not convinced. A.J. was my best case officer. And there's a whole approval process—"

"You were the next person in the chain."

I can tell from his expression he dropped the ball, and he knows it. "And you were after me."

He thinks *I* dropped the ball, too.

"That's why you're here, isn't it?" he says. "You know something—"

"I don't know anything." I'm going to stick to the story I told Alex, the one I've been telling myself for years. "But I don't know if I was careful enough. I don't know if I sent the cable through too quickly."

"Someone would have caught it."

"Who? COPS? The Director of Operations?"

His face falls, like he's realizing that *no one* would have caught it if we didn't. "COPS was a lazy piece of shit. And the DO didn't care about anything after he got those Russian operatives locked away, except talking tough in the press, gunning for the director's job. Ambitious prick, that guy." He shakes his head. "You think A.J. was in on it?"

"I don't know."

His brow has furrowed even deeper. "A.J. was a good guy. One of the best case officers I ever had."

"I know," I say quietly. That was his reputation, at least. And until Falcon came along, I never would have questioned it.

"He didn't have a price, Jill. No amount of money, no blackmail, *nothing* would have made him turn on his country."

I believed the same thing about myself, once. No amount of money would have made me do what I did. No one could have talked me into it, under any circumstances.

The Agency spends so much time digging into employees' finances, and their foreign contacts, looking for vulnerabilities. But with me, there was one thing the Agency security team missed. The one thing that was truly a vulnerability. My family. That was how they got to me.

"Everyone has their price," I say.

I drive back home completely unsettled. I was so sure, heading out here, that Vaughn Craig was somehow involved. That they got to him, just like they got to me.

But they didn't. He didn't know anything. He had taken A.J. at his word, approved Falcon, and then the cable went on to me. He wasn't part of this.

And what he shared with me, the reporting that's been coming from Falcon—

It gives me chills, just thinking about it.

I drive in silence, the stereo off, the only sound the hum of the engine. Cars pass me on either side, nothing more than blurs.

Someone's fabricating intelligence that could lead to military action. People could get *killed* because of this intelligence.

Someone already *did* get killed.

These people got to A.J. They kidnapped Owen. And they'll be back as soon as Alex publishes her story.

What *now*?

What am I supposed to do?

A police car approaching on the opposite side of the road draws my attention. I listen to the wail of the sirens, keep my eyes on the flashing lights until it passes.

I could go to the police.

It might be time to consider it.

Going to the authorities means jail time. Jail would be worth it if it would protect the kids. But *would* it?

They would still be out there. And if I talk, they'll come after Owen. They vowed they would.

Until I know who *they* are, until I'm sure the authorities can keep them away from my kids, how can I risk coming clean?

There's a red light up ahead. I slow to a stop and sit in the silence, staring at the light.

Abruptly I reach for my phone. Scroll through the contacts until I find the name I'm looking for. *Jeremy.* I place the call.

The light turns green and I press down on the gas.

One ring. Then two—

"Jill!" comes Jeremy's voice. So familiar, like a blast from the past. "My God, it's been years."

"I know. How have you been?"

We're still friends on Facebook. I've been able to keep up with his life, and he has with mine, though neither of us posts much. We haven't talked in person since I left the Agency.

"Really good." His dog barks in the background, a deep booming bark.

"Still working in reports?"

"Still."

"Same portfolio?"

"Same one."

Perfect. He has access to information on Falcon.

"How are you, Jill?"

"Oh, fine. Hey, I have a question for you."

There's the briefest hesitation, the realization that I'm not calling to chat. "Shoot."

"I know this is unusual. And it's not a discussion we should be having on the phone. But I need help. It's important."

He doesn't say anything for a moment. "We're friends. Of course I'll try to help."

"Falcon." I say it softly, even though it doesn't matter, even though if someone's listening in, they'll hear me say it either way. "If he were a double, who would be running him?"

"Yikes. Jill, what in the world?"

"I know, it's out of left field. It's just . . ." What am I supposed to say? "If you could just give me your opinion."

"*Is* he a double? Because that—"

"I'm just saying *if*."

He says nothing. I can hear Max chewing on a squeaky toy in the background.

"Please, Jeremy?"

"I don't know, Jill. It's not something I've ever thought about. I'd have to look back through his reporting—"

"Could you do that?"

Another long pause. Then he speaks. "I'll see what I can do."

CHAPTER ELEVEN

Alex

Tuesday morning, and I'm back in my own car. Away from that ridiculously oppressive Florida heat. Back to the mildly oppressive mid-Atlantic kind.

Chasing a lead.

I had left Jill's house on Sunday night completely unsettled. Couldn't sleep at all, tossed and turned all night. Every time I closed my eyes, I saw *her* eyes. That haunted look when I asked if it was *them,* the people she's running from. The fear when I suggested she might be next.

She didn't know A.J. was dead. That much was clear. And even before she learned the truth, she was planning to run. I saw that box. The passports. The pictures. She wants to disappear. Again.

I kept working from my hotel room and tried to focus. Tried to work on other stories. But it was useless. This is the only story that matters.

I checked ClandestineTips religiously. Nothing from my source. I wrote my own message: *Thanks for the tip on Jill Bailey. Is there anything else you can share?*

Nothing. No response.

I dug more into A. J. Graham. Found his obituary. It was short, to the point. He left behind his mother, and a fiancée, Blaire Delaney.

More digging. I found a Blaire Delaney who worked for an NGO in Damascus at the same time A.J. was there. Bingo.

She's still working part-time for the same NGO, remotely. Her profile said she lives in Bethesda, just outside DC. In her headshot she looks young. Younger than I'd have thought. Blond and tan and pretty.

Property records next. I found a Blaire Delaney listed as an owner of a home in Bethesda. I wrote down the address.

Then I booked a flight back to Washington. I had a lead.

I'm driving through Bethesda now, getting close to Blaire's address. The streets in her neighborhood are winding. Mature trees everywhere. Sprawling houses with big front lawns.

I'm not sure exactly what I hope to get out of this. Confirmation he was killed, maybe. That an overdose would have been completely out of character. But mostly, I'm here because she's a lead. I don't have enough to publish right now. I might be bluffing and telling Jill I do, but I don't. I need more. I need to get to the bottom of this story.

I knock on the front door. It's one of those ornate ones flanked by long opaque windows. I can see a figure approaching from deeper in the house. A moment later the door opens.

It's Blaire Delaney. She looks just like her picture. Blond and perfect—and taller than I'd have thought. She's dressed in white linen pants and a soft pink top. Her left hand is resting on the edge of the door. There's a gigantic diamond on her ring finger. She looks at me expectantly.

"Hi, Blaire. I'm Alex Charles, from *The Washington Post.* I'm wondering if we could chat."

Her face registers surprise. And interest. I always find it telling how someone responds to an intro like that. Fear, if they're guilty of something. Curiosity, otherwise. "About?"

"A. J. Graham."

A shadow crosses her face. "What about him?" She makes no move to open the door wider, to invite me in.

"I'm hoping you can answer some questions."

Still she doesn't move. Eyes me suspiciously. It's almost a hostile look. "About?"

"The night he died."

Surely there was a more tactful approach. Oh well.

"Blaire, honey?" calls a male voice from deeper inside the house.

"I've got it," she calls back.

I look behind her into the house. Everything's stylish and perfect and *white*—so much white. Reminds me of all those damn neutrals Miles insisted we have.

She turns back toward me. "It's been a long time since anyone's asked me about A.J."

"I'm sorry for your loss," I say, because I feel like I need to say something. The words sound emotionless. But really. How sorry should I be for her? Clearly she's moved on.

"Thank you." She looks just as discomfited by the statement as I feel.

I don't know why the hell I'm begrudging the fact that she moved on. It's been four years, and her fiancé *died.* It's not like she's still married to him.

"The night A.J. died," I say. "Can you tell me about it?"

"What do you want to know?"

"I read that it was an overdose. Fentanyl."

She nods.

"Is there any more to the story?"

Hurt flashes across her features, just for a moment. "Meaning what?"

I consider what to say. "Was he a frequent drug user?" I almost cringe at how that sounded.

"No," she says tightly.

"There's more to the story, isn't there, Blaire?"

Her eyes search mine. The hurt's still there, but something else, too. Anger. "Why are you dredging up the past?"

"To find the truth."

"Does it matter? Whether it was an accident or it was intentional . . . so what? He's dead."

Intentional? She's talking like she thinks it was suicide. *Was* it suicide? "Can we just talk?"

"I've talked. To the *authorities*, years ago. I told them everything I know. They have the message. I have nothing else to add. *Especially* not to a journalist."

The message? A *suicide* message? "Please, Blaire—"

"No." She shakes her head. "I have nothing else to say."

A man approaches from behind her. Blond and tanned and built like a quarterback. Barbie and Ken—

And there's a toddler trailing behind him. In a white onesie, unsteady on his feet. Blond, naturally.

I can't help but stare at the kid.

Four years since A.J. died, and she has a completely new life. *Miles will, too.*

"Is there something we can help you with?" Ken asks, putting his arm protectively around Blaire.

"She's just leaving," Blaire says, her eyes on me.

"Blaire, I—"

"Listen, that chapter of my life is over." She says it so definitively there's no doubt in my mind she means it. That she decided it ages ago.

She reaches down and picks up the toddler, rests him on her hip. He gives me the same even stare as his parents.

"Okay," I say. I might not be a people person, but I can tell when a door has closed. And this door is most definitely shut. "Thanks for your time."

I walk back to my car, strangely energized. She might have turned the page on that chapter. Done her best to forget about A.J. Moved on.

But you can be damn sure I'm not going to. I'm going to get to the bottom of this.

I hit dead end number two when I call CIA Public Affairs and ask about A.J. No surprise there. State Department is strike three. Luckily, this isn't baseball.

Next I track down A.J.'s mother. She lives in Rockville, Maryland. Just outside the Beltway. That's where I'm headed now.

She lives in an older neighborhood. Hilly and treed. Hers is a split-level halfway down a cul-de-sac. Overgrown landscaping, a missing shutter. A house that's seen better days.

I knock on the door—the doorbell's missing—and a few moments later, it opens. A stooped older woman stands there. She has tight gray curls and a deeply lined face. One that looks set in a permanent frown.

"Hi. Mrs. Graham?"

"Yes?"

"My name's Alex Charles. I'm a reporter with *The Washington Post*."

Her face doesn't change. "And?"

"I'm wondering if I can ask you some questions. About your son. A.J."

She stares at me without blinking. "A.J." She repeats it back, almost like an exhale. And then she just stands there.

"Do you have a few minutes to chat?" Strike four's coming any second. Wonder what lead to go after next—

"Yes."

I sure as hell didn't expect to hear that.

She opens the door wider. "Come in."

I step into a narrow foyer, follow her up a short flight of stairs. Then into a living room. Furnishings look old, like she's lived here for decades. Probably has.

She sits down in a flowered recliner. I perch on the edge of a slip-covered sofa.

"You're here about A.J.," she says. I catch a hint of wonder in her tone.

"I'm looking into his final days. The overdose . . ."

She clasps her hands in her lap. Goes very still.

"Was it accidental, Mrs. Graham?"

"Ruth." She corrects me quietly. And then, "You mean was it suicide?"

I nod. *Was* it suicide?

Or was it *murder*?

"Why are you asking? I don't want his name besmirched."

"I have no intention of doing that, Ruth. I just want to find the truth."

She turns to look out the window. I follow her gaze. The branches of large oaks sway in the breeze.

"If you're asking, you must not have seen the video," she says.

"No, I haven't."

I wait for her to say more about the video, but she doesn't. It's silent, except for the methodical tick of a clock somewhere in the room.

"What video?" I finally say. Can't help myself.

The hint of a smile crosses her face. Seems like a reaction to my bluntness. Not a permanent frown after all. "There was a message. A video. He sent it to his fiancée right before he died. Blaire was her name."

The message. The one Blaire mentioned. "What did it say?"

"Did you know she's married? Has a child, too." It's like she didn't even hear my question. Or ignored it completely. "Got engaged not six months after A.J. passed," she adds bitterly.

"Too damn soon." The words slip out before I can filter them.

There's that shadow of a smile again. "I certainly thought so."

Silence descends again. Filled with that relentless tick of the clock. I wait for what seems like an appropriate interval before switching topics.

"The message—what did it say?"

The frown returns. Deepens. "That he was sorry for what he was about to do. That he made a mistake."

Sounds like a suicide message.

"That's what I've been told, anyway."

Been told? "You haven't seen it?"

"No."

"Why?"

She lifts her shoulders in a shrug. "He sent it to Blaire. She says she turned her phone over to the government, never got it back. And no one ever shared it with me."

"Did you ask?"

"Of course." She says it harshly. "CIA. State Department. I exhausted every avenue. One roadblock after another. Never got it."

"He's your son."

"That didn't make a difference. If I had been mentioned in the video"—her voice breaks, and she turns again toward the window—"I was told it might be a different story."

Well, this is awkward as hell. I have no idea how to respond.

"He was raised Catholic," she says quietly. "I just . . . it's hard to believe he'd have done that. Taken his own life."

I nod.

"But it's hard to imagine him doing drugs like that, too."

"I'm sure. You know, the stories I read—they only mentioned an overdose . . ."

"You mean they didn't say it was suicide."

"Yes." I leave the *why?* unspoken.

"It didn't come out. The government has a way of putting a lid on things."

An orange tabby cat saunters into the room, rubs up against Ruth's legs. She doesn't seem to notice. The cat eyes me suspiciously.

"Do you have kids?" she asks.

God, I hate that question. "No."

She gives a brusque nod. "Good."

Well, that's a new one. Especially from a mother.

"Don't look so surprised. Kids become everything too easily. Next thing you know, you don't know who you are anymore without them."

The tabby cat sits down by Ruth's feet, its eyes still locked on me, and begins purring.

"That saying—''Tis better to have loved and lost than never to have loved at all'—whoever came up with that never lost everything." She fixes me with a stare and adds quietly, "Losing everything changes you."

I feel a pang of sympathy. Almost makes it hard to think about anything else.

"The CIA shipped me a box of his belongings, months after he passed," she says, back to business. "His phone was in there."

"And you weren't able to see the video?"

"Couldn't get into the phone. Don't know the password, and Blaire didn't either. I tried the cellphone company, the manufacturer. No one would help me."

She reaches down and pets the cat. "I found some people on the Internet who said they could unlock phones. But apparently not that one. It had some extra encryption or something." She leans back in her chair and shrugs helplessly. "I just wanted to understand, you know?"

I do, too. "Do you still have the phone?"

"Of course. I still have everything of his." Her eyebrows rise. "Can you get in?"

"I can try."

I can see the wariness on her face. "If you do, what will you do with it? I don't want—"

"Mrs. Graham—"

"Ruth."

"Ruth, I want to understand, too. I'm not going to smear your son. I just think there's more to the story."

"I do, too."

She turns toward the window again. This time, I watch only her. She looks deep in thought. The sound of the cat's purr fills the room.

Finally she turns back to face me. "Come on." She rises to her feet. "Let's get you that box."

CHAPTER TWELVE

Alex

I carry the cardboard box into my loft late that afternoon. It's one of those small white ones, meant for files. A.J.'s name is written on the side in black marker. There's a shipping label attached to the top, addressed to Ruth. Remnants of the original packing tape on the sides. New packing tape wrapped around, to keep it closed.

I set the box down on the table in the center of the room and walk over to adjust the thermostat. It's hot as hell in here, and stuffy. I'd turned down the AC before I left for Florida. Hadn't expected the temperature to rise as much as it did. Must have been too damn preoccupied to check the forecast.

I lower the dial, and it kicks on a moment later. The hum is the only sound in the room.

I make my way over to the junk drawer in the kitchen. Dig around, pull out a box cutter. I slice through the tape on the box. Lift the lid, look inside.

There's a gallon-size Ziploc on top. I pull it out. A bunch of old receipts, some spare change, a phone charger, a tube of Chap-

Stick. The contents of his nightstand, maybe. Or his glove box, something like that.

Books, underneath. Thick nonfiction tomes about Syrian history. Conflict in the Middle East. A couple of dog-eared paperbacks, too. Crime fiction. I take them out one by one, flip through them. Just to make sure nothing's inside.

Next, the cellphone. A bit battered, a long crack in the screen protector. I press the power button. The screen stays black. No surprise there. It's been years.

I open the Ziploc and pull out the charger. Plug it into the bottom of the phone—it's a fit—and then into the wall.

The last thing in the box is a framed picture of A.J. and Blaire. I set it on the table, standing up. They're on a beach with turquoise water and white sand. In swimsuits. They have their arms around each other, and they're both smiling broadly. Not fake smiles, either. Real, honest, natural ones. They look genuinely happy. She's holding out her hand to the camera. Showing off a diamond ring.

This must be when they got engaged.

Now she's got a new ring. New partner, new life.

A.J. was replaced, just like I was.

Does she have a copy of this picture? If so, it's probably in a box somewhere, in storage. Maybe she's thrown it out.

I glance at the phone, charging. Then I walk over to the kitchen, fill a glass with ice water.

When I sit back down at the table, I pull out the receipts from the Ziploc. Start looking through them. Can't decipher most of them, but nothing looks particularly odd or out of the ordinary.

I reach for the phone, try the power button. This time, it works. It powers on. I take a sip of water and wait.

A lock screen appears. A prompt to enter a passcode. Room for six digits.

I try the obvious, 1-2-3-4-5-6. Then the reverse.

Doesn't work.

I reach for my own phone. Scroll through the contacts until I find the name I want. Damian.

I press the green button. As the phone's ringing, I put the call on speaker and set the phone down on the table.

"Hello?" he answers.

"Damian, it's Alex."

"Hey, Alex."

"Listen, I need help getting into a phone."

"Do you have *permission* to get into this phone?"

"Of course." It sounds like I'm snapping, but come on. I don't need that from him.

"Read me the serial number on the back."

I slide the phone out of its case—it's much thinner now—and flip it over. Look closely for the number—there it is. I read the string of digits to Damian.

"Got it," he says, and I can hear the clack of keys on his end, like he's running a search on the number.

I take another sip of water while I wait.

"No dice," he finally says. "Won't be able to get into this one."

Dammit. "For real?"

"Yeah. This series has an added layer of encryption. Only way you're getting in is with the passcode or a fingerprint."

That's not what I want to hear. But it explains why Ruth couldn't find anyone to unlock it. "Absolutely nothing we can do?"

"Nothing. Sorry, Alex. Wish I had better news."

"Thanks, Damian."

I disconnect the call and look down at A.J.'s phone.

Another dead end.

I'm so sick of dead ends.

I push the phone aside and pull out my own laptop. Open it up. Navigate first to ClandestineTips. Nothing from my source.

I'm out of leads.

A. J. Graham—sure looks like it was suicide, but what if it wasn't? If I could see that video message—the *suicide* message—maybe it would help answer some questions.

Blaire's moved on. His mother never will. And I can't get into that damn phone.

Then there's Jill. Clearly she's hiding something, but I don't know what it is.

I scan the rest of my inbox. I catch sight of a name that's familiar and roll my eyes. But I double-click nonetheless.

To: Alex Charles
From: Timothy Mittens
Message: Hello, Alex! I have a critical update for you.
CIA spook Langston West is in his new house AND HE
BROUGHT IN TWO LARGE BLACK SUITCASES.
Why??? Check it out!! 1457 Mountain Bluff Road!!
All my best, Timothy Mittens.

Another picture, unbelievably. The same blond guy with the goofy grin. Standing in front of a house, pointing to it. Inexplicably using a system set up for anonymous tips. I close the message and scan the inbox.

"You've got to be kidding me," I mutter, opening another message.

To: Alex Charles
From: xxxwxyzxxx
Message: They've taken over my brain. They're controlling
my thoughts. Research Albuquerque before it's too late.
I can't say more.

No shortage of messages from the crazies, but nothing from my source.

I look over at the photograph of A.J. and Blaire. I focus in on her. In my mind I see her in the house in Bethesda. The new diamond, the new husband, the new baby.

And then I see Miles. On a beach with a woman—

I turn back to my laptop. Start typing a new message:

To: Afriend123
From: Alex Charles
Message: Your information has been invaluable.
Please, do you have any more tips?

I need something. I'm stuck right now, and I hate being stuck. I need this story. This is *the* story. I rack my brain, try to figure out something I could offer the source. Some quid pro quo.

I look over at the picture again. This time my gaze falls to the bottom. There's a date stamped there in the corner. Almost covered up by the frame, but not quite. 05/22/16.

My gaze drifts to his phone. A tingle of excitement runs through me. Birthdays, anniversaries, someone must have tried those dates already. But an engagement day?

I reach for it, touch the home button. The screen with the numbers appears. *Enter passcode.*

0-5-2-2-1-6

That screen disappears, and rows of colorful icons take its place.

I'm in. Oh my God, it worked.

Finally I caught a break.

I press the text message app. Blaire's name is on top, the most recent conversation. I open up that chain—

A video. The last thing he sent. All I can see is a black screen. I press the play button—

There's movement, but it's still just a black screen—

There's A.J.'s face. A close-up, a selfie. His eyes are bloodshot. The camera wobbles.

I'm filled with an overwhelming sense of anticipation—and fear.

He starts speaking.

"Blaire, babe, I'm so sorry."

His speech is slightly slurred.

"I couldn't reach you, so I'm sending this instead." The picture shakes, like he's moving around. *"I need to talk to you before . . . before anything happens."*

His eyes are glassy.

"I've made mistakes. I just wanted so badly to protect you." His voice breaks, and a tear leaks from each eye, runs down each cheek. He wipes them away with the back of his hand.

"People aren't always who they seem."

He turns his head, toward a window. Then looks back at the camera.

"It's time for me to find a way out. Before I do, I want to tell you I'm sorry, Blaire. I'm sorry I wasn't stronger. Just know . . . know that I'll always love you."

The picture freezes. That's the end. I stare at the screen, the frozen image of his face.

It *could* be a suicide message. Recorded right before he killed himself.

But my gut tells me it wasn't. That it was shot by a man who knew he was being hunted—

A noise, outside my door. A loud clap. Like something falling, hitting the ground with force. My heart leaps in my chest, and I spin toward the door. But it's closed, and nothing's out of the ordinary. Everything is silent once again.

Thoughts of the story suddenly take a backseat to something else. *Fear.* A sense that I'm in too deep.

I look back at the phone, at A.J.'s frozen face.

A chill runs through me.

Why was he being hunted?

And *who* was doing the hunting?

CHAPTER THIRTEEN

Jill

Tuesday passes like any other day, even though it's *not* like any other day. Because I've met with Vaughn Craig; I know what sort of intelligence we're getting from Falcon. And I've talked to Jeremy, suggested Falcon might be a double agent, asked his opinion on who might be behind it. Both of those things—they're the closest I've come to talking, to *breathing a word*.

But Owen still needs to go to preschool. Mia needs attention. And Drew's at work, poring over contracts no doubt, making judgments about what's right and wrong, with all the information he needs right there in front of him, in black and white. So it's up to me to pretend that life is normal.

It's almost dinnertime now. Owen's playing with plastic dinosaurs, one gripped tight in each hand, tilting them toward each other and talking in two exaggerated voices. Mia's absorbed with her electronic dancing unicorn, the one that scoots around the floor, plays the most annoying tinny song on a loop.

When Drew walks in, I'm at the stove, stirring pasta into a pot of boiling water.

"Hi, honey," he says. He walks over and gives me a kiss on the cheek, peeks into the pot. "Spaghetti and meatballs?"

I nod. "I felt like a drama-free meal." It's one of the only meals both kids consistently eat without complaining. And tonight I just need *something* to be easy.

"Rough day?" He rolls up his sleeves, goes to the sink, turns on the faucet.

I turn toward the counter, where my glass of water sits. I take a sip, my back to him.

"Honey, are you okay?"

I turn toward him. "Can you stop asking me that?"

He keeps his eyes on me a moment longer. Then heads to the utensil drawer, starts setting the table.

I shouldn't snap at him. He's just trying to make sure I'm okay. He's done nothing wrong.

I'm the one who has. And I'm about to ruin everything.

"There's something we need to talk about," I say to him.

The words fill me with a strange combination of fear and relief. Fear because I don't know how he'll react, because I've kept this secret from him for so many years, and he might not forgive me, and I couldn't blame him for that. Relief because I have to do this, and I just committed myself to it.

He looks over expectantly.

"Tonight," I say. "After the kids go to bed."

"You're not leaving me, are you?" He says it with a devilish grin.

"No," I say, forcing a smile.

I'm not leaving *him*. But we're all going to need to leave here, one way or another.

———

I give the kids baths while he cleans up the kitchen. Then it's on to story time—Mia picks *The Very Hungry Caterpillar* for the umpteenth time, insists I read it three times, and Owen chooses *The Book with No Pictures,* laughs uproariously. I tuck them both in, give them good-night kisses, and head back downstairs, dread settling over me.

The kitchen's clean. Drew's picking up toys in the family room, tossing them into baskets. I walk into the room.

"Time to talk?" he asks.

I wish it weren't. I wish I could avoid having this conversation.

But I need to do this. These people will *kill*. They'll come back for Owen. For Mia, too. Our kids aren't safe.

It's been two days since I made that deal with Alex. Two more until she publishes. I need to do something to protect the kids. Disappearing, or coming clean, accepting my punishment, getting my family into some sort of protection program. I'll be in jail, won't be able to see them, but as long as they're safe—

My phone rings. The sound startles me.

I turn toward the kitchen. It's on the counter, screen lit, vibrating. I pick it up, check the screen—

Unknown.

Panic washes over me.

"Who is it?" Drew asks from the other room.

"Not sure."

But I am sure, aren't I? It's *them*.

I answer the call, expecting to hear that robotic voice, the one that still haunts my dreams. "Hello?"

"Jill? It's Alex."

Alex. I let out a breath. "Thank God."

"I talked to A.J.'s fiancée. Blaire."

Blaire Delaney. The name comes to me now. I met her on a trip to Damascus once, but I'd completely forgotten about her.

"And his mother, too."

"The overdose—was it suicide?" I ask. I want to say *Or was it murder?* but Drew's within earshot.

"I don't think so."

I don't, either.

"I found a video. A message. He recorded it before he died."

"Yeah?" Apprehension is swirling inside me.

"Family thinks it's a suicide note."

The authorities do, too, I'd be willing to bet. That's probably the evidence Vaughn mentioned. "But you don't?"

"Could have been. It's clear he was feeling extremely guilty about something. Any idea what that could be?"

Requesting encryption for a dangle? Giving him COVCOM? A.J. died the day after giving Falcon the COVCOM. And *that* was four days after Owen was kidnapped—

Did he *know* they were going to come for Owen?

"Jill?"

"No. I don't know."

She's quiet. She doesn't believe me.

"It may not have been a suicide message," she finally says. "But either way, it was a *goodbye* message. He knew he might not see Blaire again."

I glance into the family room. Drew's watching me, concerned.

"He knew they were coming for him."

"I need to go," I say. I need to get off this call. Get away from this conversation.

"A.J.'s secret, whatever it was—it got him killed. If he'd have just come clean, told someone the truth . . ."

She trails off. And I know what she wants me to think. That all would be well. That he'd be alive right now, that he'd be safe.

Would he?

When the call disconnects, I place the phone down on the counter and stare at it. Drew walks into the kitchen.

"An overdose?" he asks quietly. "Who?"

"An old co-worker."

"Dead?"

"Yes."

He pulls me into a hug. "How terrible."

I rest my head against his chest and listen to his heartbeat. I need to tell him the truth, but my mind is spinning right now, trying to make sense of it all.

"I can see why you didn't want to talk about this in front of the kids," he says.

There's my out. He thinks this is what I wanted to tell him. That I found out an old co-worker died. I can keep my secret a little bit longer.

Alex's voice rings in my head. *A.J.'s secret, whatever it was—it got him killed.*

I pad downstairs into the darkened kitchen before dawn. Flip the switch on the wall, flood the house with light, squint as my eyes adjust. I turn on the coffee maker, listen to the gurgle as it brews, the only sound in the silent house.

I think about last night's conversation. Alex, the revelation about A.J.'s video message. He felt guilty about something. Was it sending the cable? Did he know the truth about Falcon?

When the coffee's done brewing, I take the steaming mug and wander through the house.

I stop first in the doorway of Mia's room. She's sprawled practically sideways on her bed, unicorn sheets twisted awkwardly around her, wild curls splayed everywhere. Her stuffed bear has fallen to the floor. I walk over quietly, pick it up, place it back in her bed, beside her. She never stirs, her chest rising and falling slowly, methodically.

Then on to Owen's room. I lean against the doorway and watch him sleep. He's on his side in the center of his bed, Spider-Man sheets still tucked neatly around him, his stuffed elephant just barely peeking out from where it's nestled in his arms, like it is every night.

He's safe, but he won't be once this story comes out.

I did the unthinkable once to protect him. Made the worst decision of my life, but made it for the best possible reason. I did what I thought was best, at the time.

And that's what I need to do again.

I'm going to tell Drew.

No more of this indecision. It's time to act.

I take the coffee back down into the kitchen. Sit, looking out the sliding glass door, as pink streaks appear in the sky, as the birds begin chirping.

Drew's alarm starts chiming at five-thirty. A few minutes later he walks into the kitchen, squinting into the light. "You're up early."

He grabs a mug from the cabinet above.

"Drew, we need to talk."

He turns, blinking as his eyes adjust.

This is it. This is the moment everything's going to change, forever.

I take a deep breath. "Four years ago, Owen was kidnapped."

I tell him everything. Every last detail. I owe him that, at least.

He listens quietly, just taking it all in. Must be that lawyer training. Listen, don't talk, maintain a blank expression. But I wish he'd react. I wish he'd say something.

I finish telling him about Alex, and then I go quiet. That's it, that's everything.

He just stares at me, says nothing. Silence descends. Outside, I can hear a neighbor rolling a trash can to the street.

I'm desperate for him to say something. To know what he's thinking.

"Why did you keep this from me?" His voice is low. I can hear the anger simmering underneath.

"They told me to keep quiet—"

"I'm your husband. Owen's *father*."

"I know, and maybe I should have—"

"*Maybe?*"

"I should have." I don't know if that's true, but I know it's what he needs to hear.

He shakes his head. "And now it's all going to come out? They're going to come *back*?"

My throat feels tight. I nod.

"Why didn't you go to the police?"

This is why I didn't tell him years ago. Because in his mind, everything's black and white. There's a right and a wrong. He doesn't see the gray, never has.

"I didn't know if that would put him in more danger—"

"So you decided *you'd* protect him?" It's practically a shout. He throws up his arms. "On your own?"

I can hear one of the kids getting out of bed upstairs. Little feet on the floor. "I thought I was doing what's right."

"And what about now? Are you ready to go to the police *now*?"

"Probably. But I don't know. I wanted to talk—"

"What *do* you know?"

"That if we go to the police, I'll go to jail."

"Well, maybe that's exactly where you belong."

The words sting, coming from him. But it doesn't mean I wouldn't do the same thing over again, if given the opportunity. It doesn't mean that I didn't protect Owen.

I'll do it. I'll go to the police, admit everything. Because I have to do *something* before they come back. And running seems impossible. There's just no way we could give the kids a decent life if we run—

My phone rings, and I reach for it. Drew's glaring at me.

I check the screen. *Jeremy.*

"Hello?"

"Hi, Jill." His voice is tense.

I cover the mouthpiece and say to Drew, "I need to get this."

"Seriously?"

I open the sliding glass door and step out onto the back patio, feeling his eyes on me the whole time.

"Did you look into the source?" I say to Jeremy, once I've closed the door behind me. There's no one outside at this hour; I'm completely alone.

"What kind of encryption apps do you have on your phone?"

"I'm sorry?"

"We can't have this conversation on an open line. What do you have? WhatsApp? Signal? Stronghold?"

"I don't have any of those."

"Okay. I'm going to send you a link. Download the app, wait for my call."

The call disconnects. I pull the phone from my ear, stare at the screen. A moment later the text comes through. I click the link, and the Stronghold app begins downloading.

I look out at the lake in the distance, still and quiet. *What's he going to tell me?*

The app finishes downloading, and immediately there's a call. A different ringtone; the icon for the app flashes. I tap it, and Jeremy's number appears. I tap again, and the call connects.

"Hi," Jeremy says.

"Hi."

There's a pause, like each of us is waiting for the other to begin.

"Well," he says, breaking the silence, "first things first. I confirmed a person with the same name as our source works for Syrian defense, with access to biowarfare programs."

I wait, because he said "with the same name," and that makes me think there's more.

"But I can't corroborate it's the same person A.J. was meeting with. Doesn't mean it's not the case, just means I can't confirm it."

I wouldn't have been able to, either, if I'd done the work I was supposed to do, vetted the cable the way I was supposed to. Is that what they didn't want me to find? "So he's a dangle."

"Well, not necessarily. He could be legit. He gave us a lot of good information in the beginning. Real information, the kind that only an insider would know. And the kind the Syrian regime wouldn't want getting into our hands."

That's the same thing I heard from Vaughn Craig. "But?"

"But the reporting's changed. It's much more . . . sensational now. Says the regime has a weaponized strain of anthrax ready to go. And that it's prepared to use it."

"Which makes you think he's not a real source?" I'm not sure where he's going with this, what he's thinking.

"It makes me unsure. We don't have anything else to corroborate this line of reporting. But that's because we don't have access. So it *could* be real."

"Or it could be fake."

"Exactly. But I'll tell you this: Policymakers are eating it up. It's led to an increase in military expenditures, a troop buildup in the region—"

His dog starts barking like crazy in the background.

"Max! Quiet," he yells. Then, to me: "Sorry."

"It's okay." I'm still trying to process everything he's saying, everything I'm learning. "Could it be someone else using the COVCOM?"

"No. Everything checks out. It has, in every message. Verification protocols, biometrics, style and language, everything's been consistent."

I watch a trail of ants on the other side of the patio, heading toward crumbs under the kids' plastic picnic table.

"Fact of the matter is, I can't say whether he's legit or not. But that's not what you asked. You asked who I thought it would be running the source if he *is* a dangle."

"Right. So who do you think it is?"

"Well, I'll say this. The source's reporting has been bringing us ever closer to war."

And inching toward war means expending resources unnecessarily. "So it's an adversary that wants us weak? Russia? China?"

He's quiet. "It's possible."

"But?"

"But you asked my opinion. And my opinion is it isn't either of those countries."

In the distance I can see a fish jump in the lake. It lands back in the water, disappears, and all that's left is ripples.

"If either of those countries were running the source, there's no way they wouldn't be trying to use him to get access to our new COVCOM system. It's all their security services care about right now."

The new system. Vaughn mentioned the same thing. And Falcon has no interest. Won't meet face-to-face with anyone.

I rack my brain, trying to think of another adversary that would have the capabilities and the motivation to run this source.

"I think their goal is for us to dramatically increase our military expenditures," Jeremy says. "And right now it's working. That's exactly what we're doing."

"Okay. So who's running the source?" Why's Jeremy being so cagey?

He hesitates. "I don't think anyone is."

"What do you mean?" That doesn't make any sense.

"The messages *look* like they all originate in Damascus, right? But I found an anomaly in the way the IP addresses are recorded. Did some digging, talked to a friend in Science and Tech. Figured out why it looks that way."

"Why?"

"There's a device attached to the COVCOM. Something called a Z23. State-of-the-art technology. Changes an IP address, makes it very difficult to ascertain the true origination point."

"It's not so unusual we'd install that, is it?"

"No. But what *is* unusual is where these messages are coming from."

"You figured it out?"

"Once I understood how the system works, I was able to back-trace. Got as far as the country of origin, no further."

He's going to say China. Or Russia.

But he also said he doesn't think it's either of those countries.

"You're losing me here, Jeremy. Who's running the source?"

"That's just it, Jill. I don't think there's a source to be run. I think it's all made up."

A breeze blows through, rustling the palm fronds.

"Who's making it up?" There's a pit forming in my stomach. I can hear the hesitancy in Jeremy's voice, the *fear*.

"*Us*, Jill. The United States Falcon's messages came from *inside* our country. I think *we're* fabricating this information."

CHAPTER FOURTEEN

Jill

Of all the things I expected to hear, *imagined* hearing, this wasn't one of them. I feel like the floor has dropped from under me.

"You think *we're* running this source?" I say it quietly. I shouldn't be having this conversation out here. Shouldn't be having it over the phone. Shouldn't be having it at all.

"The messages are being sent domestically. The source, if he's a dangle, is a perfect avenue for stealing our new COVCOM, and *no one's tried*."

My mind is spinning, trying to make sense of this. "Agency?"

"It's Agency hardware. Seems likely."

I feel like pieces are snapping together in my mind. If it's *us*, if it's people on the inside, that explains how they knew about me, about my role. How they knew the cable would end up in my queue.

And when they told me to put the phone in my pocket, it's because they knew I was wearing pants and not a skirt, because they were watching me. They were probably right there in the building.

They weren't bluffing when they said they'd know if I didn't follow their instructions. And they weren't relying solely on my phone, either. If I'd have slipped someone a note in the office, there's a good chance they'd have seen it.

The thought chills me. Thank God I didn't try anything.

That means this is coming from the *inside*. Intelligence about another country possessing a weaponized strain of anthrax, intel that's leading to a troop buildup in the Middle East, that's leading us ever closer to war. It's fabricated, and my *own country* is fabricating it.

My *own country* had my son kidnapped to keep the truth hidden.

The thought makes me sick to my stomach.

"Coordinated, or some rogue operation?"

"No idea. I don't even know for sure it *is* the Agency, or even the U.S. That's just my guess. Because nothing else makes sense."

I watch a seagull drift by slowly overhead, almost like it's lost, like it's strayed too far from home.

He's right. This makes the most sense. Syria couldn't pull this off, and the source provided information Damascus wouldn't want us to have. More sophisticated intelligence services would be making a play for the new COVCOM system—

"Jill, will you tell me what's going on?" he asks.

The sliding door of the next house over opens, and old Mrs. McIntosh steps outside onto her screened-in patio.

"Listen, I need to go," I say quietly. "Let's chat soon."

I end the call and stare out at the lake. It's still and peaceful, just like before. But now it doesn't seem calming, reassuring. Now it seems dangerous. Like the calm before the storm.

What am I supposed to do now? My plan was to go to the authorities, the FBI. But the *authorities* might very well be behind this. Anything I say might be shared with the wrong people.

I can't trust our own law enforcement agencies.

I don't know who I can trust.

No one can protect us from the *entire* CIA. I need to know *exactly* who's behind this, or talking to the authorities is just going to put my family in grave danger.

I pull open the sliding glass door and walk back inside. The kids are on the couch in the family room, bowls of Cheerios in their laps, eyes glued to Elmo on the television screen.

Drew's in the kitchen. He's dressed for the day now, khakis and a collared shirt, and he's pacing. He stops when I approach. "We're going to the police, Jill," he says quietly.

"We can't."

"This isn't up for debate."

"You're right, it's not. We're not going to the police." I can dig my heels in just as much as he can.

He throws up his arms. "Unbelievable."

"The local police wouldn't do a thing here, Drew. It's the FBI we need. The FBI works with the CIA"—I throw a glance toward the family room, but the kids are absorbed in the show, paying no attention to us—"they might be in on this, Drew."

"What the hell are you talking about?" He looks furious. I barely recognize him right now.

"We're not going to the authorities. That's all you need to know."

"I'm so tired of you deciding what I deserve to know. It's infuriating." He stares at me, breathing hard, nostrils flaring.

I swear I'm looking at a stranger.

"My *son* was *kidnapped,* and you didn't think I deserved to *know*?"

The words cut through me. I can't imagine finding out that something so terrible had happened to one of my children and I didn't know. That my *spouse* had hidden it from me. It would feel like the ultimate betrayal.

"I remember that night, Jill. When you came home and said

you resigned. I remember thinking you were hiding something from me. I *asked* you about it. You lied to me. You *promised* me you weren't hiding anything."

I remember it, too. Clear as anything. "I was going to tell you the truth."

"Yeah? *When?*"

"That night. It's just . . ." I trail off. "I didn't know what you'd do."

"You didn't trust me to do what was best for *my son?*"

I don't know what to say. It seemed like the right move at the time. The safest one. But now, from his perspective . . . If I were him, I don't know if I'd be able to forgive this.

"Are you going to tell me more *now,* or not?" he asks.

"I don't know what you want me to say. The CIA might be behind this. And if we go to the authorities, the information could very well get back to them."

"So what now? What the *hell* are we supposed to do now?" His voice is too loud.

Owen walks into the room, a worried look on his face. Mia's trailing behind him. Neither of them says a word; they just stare at us.

I force a smile at them, one intended to be reassuring, but I can feel how twisted, how pained, it must look.

"I'm not just sitting around waiting for someone to come after us," he says, more quietly this time.

There's no way he should be saying that, not in front of the kids. I shoot a glance in their direction. Owen looks flat-out scared now. "I'm not asking you to."

"Yeah, Jill, you are."

He stands there, hands clenched in fists at his sides. I've never seen him so angry, and it's not like I can blame him. It's not like I didn't see this coming.

"If this is how it is, then we"—he points to himself, and to the kids—"are leaving."

Leaving.

The word hangs in the air as he storms out of the kitchen. I watch him go, shoulders hunched, tense with fury. He disappears into our bedroom, and the door slams shut behind him.

I look at the kids. Mia's quiet and still. Owen's eyes are filled with tears, his bottom lip quivering. I walk over, bend down, pull them both close, hug them. I don't know what to say to them, so I don't say anything at all.

We've never fought like this. We have a solid marriage, always have. We've always been on the same team—

But teammates *talk,* don't they? Teammates don't keep secrets, not huge, life-changing ones like this. Maybe we *haven't* been on the same team, not the way I think.

I pull my kids tighter, bury my face in Mia's baby-soft curls, breathe in the scent of no-tears shampoo.

Never in my wildest dreams could I have imagined Drew threatening to leave with them. Or me *agreeing* to it, not fighting it with every fiber of my being.

But what am I supposed to say? I can't put up a fight. They're safer away from me. Away from here.

My *own country* is behind this.

My marriage is unraveling.

My family is falling apart.

I need to find a way to fix this, before it's too late.

An hour later the car is packed and the kids are strapped into car seats. They're going on a surprise vacation, I told them, and Mommy and Daddy were arguing because Mommy needs to stay behind and work. I've done my best to say cheery goodbyes, even though my heart is breaking. Drew will barely look at me. He says nothing as he starts the car, backs down the driveway, into the street. As the car pulls away I can see Owen through the window. He cranes his neck to wave goodbye.

Tears stream down my cheeks. I wave and blow a kiss.

What have I done? All I wanted was to keep him safe. Now I'm on the verge of losing everything.

I watch the car until it's out of sight.

When I walk back inside, the house is incredibly quiet. I head upstairs to Owen's room, stand in the doorway. His Spider-Man bed is neatly made. The stuffed elephant's gone. The room looks empty, sterile.

I walk over to Mia's room next. Everything's in its place, bed made, books on the nightstand neatly organized. The nightlight's still on. I walk over and turn it off. Take one last look at the room before I leave.

I walk back into the kitchen, sit down at the table. The silence is overwhelming. I don't think I've felt this powerless since the day Owen was kidnapped.

The U.S. is doing this. Fabricating a story about Syria possessing a virulent strain of anthrax, making up intelligence that's leading us to *war*. And keeping it a secret, at any cost.

Whoever's responsible, they took my son. And they're coming back. Soon, because Alex is going to publish tomorrow. And really, they're here *already*, because they're Americans. Insiders. And that might be the most terrifying aspect of all. Because it means I can't go to the authorities. How can I depend on the government to protect my family when they might be the very ones *threatening* my family?

I look down at my phone, at the background picture. Owen and Mia in the yard, arms around each other, big smiles on their faces.

If I can't go to the authorities, can't get them to protect my kids, I need to do it myself. I need to find the truth, get to the bottom of exactly who's behind this. And I need to get them locked up, away from my kids. Whatever it takes.

I've been quiet for too long. I've been *scared* for too long.

Owen and Mia are in danger, one way or another. Whether I'm silent, or whether I talk. As much as I hate to admit it, as much as it terrifies me, it's true.

I'm done following their rules.

I unlock the phone, pull up a number, and place the call.

CHAPTER FIFTEEN

Alex

I wasn't expecting the call. The change of heart. This willing-ness to talk, to come clean. And I certainly wasn't expecting her to fly to DC the next morning, show up at my loft. I don't know what she's going to say. But I know that whatever it is, I sure as hell need to hear it. It's a lead. And right now I don't have any-thing else.

I open the door. She steps inside, and I close and lock it behind her.

She looks different to me. I try to pinpoint what it is.

And then it hits me. Every time I've seen her, she's looked afraid. She doesn't look afraid anymore. She looks *determined*.

"Coffee?" I ask. There's a pot ready.

"Sure." She's standing near the table, looking around the loft. "Nice place you've got here."

"Thanks."

I pull two mugs from the cabinet, fill them both. "How do you take it?"

"Black."

I add cream to mine and carry them both over to the table. "Want to sit?"

She nods and pulls out a chair. I sit down across from her.

"What is it you want to talk about?" I ask. I've never been one for small talk. She doesn't look like she wants to chat, either.

"I need you to promise me something first," she says, wrapping her hands around the mug.

"What's that?"

"What I'm about to tell you—you can't publish a word of it until my kids are safe."

I raise my mug to my lips slowly, watching her face the whole time. She looks deadly serious. "They're in danger?"

"Yeah." She doesn't elaborate. And she still doesn't look afraid. Surely they're not in any immediate danger—

"Where are they right now, Jill?"

"With Drew."

"At home?"

"No."

I wait for her to say more, but she doesn't.

"What kind of danger are they in?" I press. Because she can't say something like that without elaborating.

"I need that promise first."

I take another sip of my coffee and eye her. "Have you gone to the police?"

"I can't."

The way she says it makes me want so damn badly to hear what she has to say. "Well, I can't agree to sit on a story."

"You should make an exception."

"Why?"

"Because, trust me, you *want* this story."

Absolutely I do. I can't think of anything I want more right now. But still . . . "I don't make deals like that."

"And I don't talk to journalists."

"Then why are you here?"

She never breaks eye contact. "Because I'll do whatever it takes to keep my kids safe."

A.J.'s tearstained face in that video floats through my mind, unbidden. *I just wanted so badly to protect you.*

This is connected, isn't it? She thinks they're going to hurt her kids. Did they threaten her kids?

This is why she ran in the first place. Why she's planning to run again.

I want to hear what it is. I *need* to hear what it is.

"You came to me looking for a story," she says. "This is the most explosive story you'll ever find."

My gaze drifts to the framed picture on the shelf. My mom, smiling. I can hear her voice in my head. *I never did. But* you. *You're another story, Alexandra.* You *can.*

I turn back to Jill. "And you'll tell me everything you know?"

"*Everything.*"

I believe her. She's telling the truth.

I feel that itch of excitement. Adrenaline running through me. "Deal."

Jill tells me a shocking story. One that will sure as hell make the front page. A child was kidnapped. His mother—a CIA employee—was coerced. A source was planted.

And then she gets to the kicker. The U.S. is behind it. The CIA, most likely. Our own government. Fabricating intelligence. *Explosive* intelligence. Intelligence that's leading us closer to military conflict.

When she's done, she goes quiet. I try to process what to say.

"Who's responsible?" I finally ask.

"That's what we need to figure out."

I stare down at my mug. The coffee's long since gone cold.

My mind is racing. I need names, and I need proof.

"Your turn," Jill says.

"I'm sorry?"

"I came clean. Will you?"

"About?" I ask.

"Your source, for one. How'd you know about Falcon? How'd you know about *me*?"

"I don't reveal my sources."

"I don't expect you to. But was it someone in the Agency? Do they know more?"

She's right; she *did* come clean, and she wants to work together. My best chance of getting to the bottom of this—*our* best chance—is if we work together.

"I got an anonymous tip," I say. "I don't know who the source is."

"Can you find out?"

"I tried."

"What did he—or she—tell you?"

"Falcon's crypt," I say. "That ninety percent of our intelligence on Syria biowarfare comes from him. And that *you* would know more."

"He gave you my name?"

"Yeah."

Her brow furrows. "Do you know where he's getting his info?"

"No."

She doesn't respond. The loft is exceptionally silent.

"I want you to see something," I finally say. And I reach for A.J.'s phone. Pull up the video. Press play.

She watches in silence. When it's over, she looks up at me.

"What do you make of it?" I ask.

She's quiet for several moments. "My guess is he learned the truth. That Falcon was a fake. That's what he meant when he said 'People aren't always who they seem.'"

"He was telling her what was going on, without saying it in so many words."

"Probably thought it would put her in more danger to know the truth," she says. "He sent the encryption cable. Handed over the COVCOM. *That* was the mistake."

"That's why he said he should have been stronger."

"And I bet they threatened to hurt Blaire. '*I just wanted so badly to protect you.*' Just like they threatened to hurt Owen."

"And A.J. caved."

Jill nods. "Can you blame him?"

I sure as hell *can* blame him. He had a responsibility—

"I know what you're thinking," she says, watching me carefully. "But until you're in that position, you don't know how you'd react."

Sounds like a load of crap to me. But there's no sense arguing with her.

"The video makes it seem like he was going to come clean," I say.

"He was probably just trying to figure out how to make sure they wouldn't come after Blaire."

We both go quiet. In the distance, down below on the street, I can hear the wail of a fire engine.

"He never got a chance to tell the truth," she says. "They killed him first, didn't they?" She wraps her arms around herself like she's suddenly cold.

The thought of the truth dying with him makes me sick to my stomach. "He waited too long."

"So what do we do now?" she asks.

"Get to the bottom of it. Figure out who's behind it."

"*How?*"

"I don't know," I answer honestly.

"You're a journalist. Isn't that your job?"

"You're CIA. Isn't it yours?"

"Maybe it's up to both of us," she says, and goes quiet.

Maybe it is. Silence falls over the room.

"What's the endgame?" she finally says. "War?"

"Could be. Wouldn't be the first time fake intelligence led us into a conflict."

In the distance a car horn blares.

"But we've learned our lesson, haven't we?" she asks. "We wouldn't go to war over unverified intel, would we?"

Unease creeps through me, because she's right. Intelligence alone wouldn't be enough.

And whoever's planting this information, *they know that.*

After Jill leaves, I open up my laptop. Tap the touchpad, bring the screen to life. Every fiber of my being wants to start typing this story. To *publish* this damn story. But I need names. I need proof. And I made a promise to sit on it. To wait. Her kids' safety depends on it.

I navigate to ClandestineTips, scan the inbox. Another message from Timothy Mittens, and one from the UFO guy. Neither of which I bother reading.

Nothing from my source.

I start typing a new message:

Who's fabricating the intelligence?

I hesitate, then add:

We have reason to believe it's someone on the inside.

I watch the screen, even though I know the odds of an immediate response are next to nil.

And then a message appears:

I've given you enough. Any more is a danger to me.

A tickle of excitement runs through me. My fingers find the keyboard:

I protect my sources.

I stare at the screen. Wait for a new message to appear. But there's nothing. No response.

I type again:

Who's behind this?

I watch the screen as seconds turn into minutes. Still there's nothing.

Finally I close the program and open an Internet browser. Pull up Google. Type a single word.

Anthrax.

I start reading. Syria and numerous other countries—and non-state actors, like terrorist groups—have reportedly worked on strains. It's not difficult to produce. The U.S. and the Soviet Union used to have stockpiles but destroyed them.

I type in another search term.

Super strain anthrax.

I find an academic article on the characteristics of the most lethal strain of anthrax. Resistant to penicillin and antibiotics. Weaponized spores delivered by aerosol and inhaled. Engineered to quickly kill ninety percent of those exposed.

The symptoms: chest pain, shortness of breath, high fever.

Death within twenty-four hours.

I close the browser, uneasy. Then I open ClandestineTips again, search the inbox in vain.

Nothing from my source.

I look at the last message sent, the one that hasn't been answered.

Who's behind this?

The question echoes in my mind, and is soon followed by another.

And why?

I'm moving the cursor to close out of ClandestineTips when a new message appears. From my source. I double-click, pulse quickening.

Why haven't you published your story?

I hesitate. Why the question? I don't understand.

Because I need more information, I type. It's not just that. But that's part of it.

I wait. There's no response.

I look back at the chat—

A response, from my source:

You need to publish soon.

Unease runs through me like a current. I type:

Why?

The response comes seconds later:

Do it soon, before it's too late.

CHAPTER SIXTEEN

Jill

I leave Alex's loft and check into a Hilton around the corner, one that caters to business travelers. It looks quiet and clean, and I can be anonymous here. Exactly what I need.

The room is small and dark, and pleasantly cool. The hallways are silent. No noise from surrounding rooms. If the kids were here, I'd be shushing them, trying to keep them occupied with activity books and toys so they wouldn't bother other guests.

God, I wish they were here.

How are they? *Where* are they?

I perch on the edge of the king-size bed and unlock my phone. I find Drew's name, the first in my list of favorites. Press call. One ring, then another, and another. Voicemail connects. *Hello, you've reached Drew. . . .*

I listen to his voice, heart hurting, and disconnect just before the beep.

I lower the phone and walk to the enormous window, look out through the sheer curtain. A typical city view, buildings around, streets below packed with cars, dotted with pedestrians. Typical weekday rush hour. The activity makes me feel lonelier than ever.

I did the one thing I've avoided doing for four long years. The one thing they warned me not to do.

But I got what I needed: more time. Alex made the deal, agreed not to publish until the kids are safe.

The kids. I look at my phone again. Nothing from Drew. Just the time, and the picture of Owen and Mia in the backyard.

I unlock the phone with my thumb, search for another contact. Jeremy. I press send and listen to it ring.

Voicemail. I end the call without leaving a message.

I sit back down on the bed and reach for the remote, turn on the TV. Flip through a few channels. A sitcom I don't recognize. A cartoon. News. All of it mindless, irritating.

I turn it off, and an overpowering silence descends.

I need to get out of here.

I grab my purse and key card and leave the room, head down to the parking lot. Slide into my rented Ford Focus, start driving.

I don't have a destination, don't have anywhere to go, anywhere to be. It's just aimless driving, on roads that were once familiar. Four years ago, I knew these roads like the back of my hand. Seems like yesterday, and a lifetime ago.

I drive past the Tidal Basin, where Drew and I had one of our first dates, walking through the cherry blossoms. Take I-395 over the Potomac into Virginia. The Pentagon's just up ahead, on the right. On the left is that hotel with the revolving restaurant on top. Drew and I went to a wedding there once.

I exit off to the right and wind my way past Arlington National Cemetery, onto the densely treed George Washington Memorial Parkway. I took this road countless times over the years. Quickest route between Langley and DC.

I exit onto Route 123, follow it west into Vienna. I used to fight traffic on this road every morning, every evening. I've hit the sweet spot right now, midday, between rush hours. Cars are few and far between.

I pass All Children's on my right, and my throat tightens. Looks just the same as it did years ago. I remember the panic I felt the last time I pulled into that parking lot. The sheer terror of not knowing whether Owen was safe.

I'm near the turnoff to our old neighborhood now. There's a row of new fast casual restaurants on the corner. The corner grocery's been taken over by one of the chains, and it's twice the size. They must have knocked down the hardware store.

I pull onto our old street. It's quiet at this hour; everyone's at work. I'm the only car on the road.

There's our old house. Still standing. The ones on either side have been knocked down, huge new houses erected in their places. The little ranch looks the same, but somehow older and smaller, overshadowed as it is by the giant houses on either side.

I park on the street and just look at it. So many memories here. It's the place where Drew and I started out our married life, where we brought home our first baby. I try to focus on *those* memories, but what keeps pushing its way to the front of my mind are those final weeks. The ever-present fear, the desperation.

It's someone on the inside. Someone on the inside is responsible for Owen being kidnapped. For threatening us. For taking away all semblance of safety, of security. The thought infuriates me. It's not fair, what they've done. It's just not fair.

I take one last look at the house—I'm sure it won't be here much longer—and pull away from the curb. I wind my way back out of the neighborhood. Past the new restaurants, back toward the city.

I'm on I-66 when I first notice the car. A black sedan, traveling in the same lane, same speed, about five car lengths behind me. Probably nothing, so I switch lanes, just to be sure.

The black sedan switches, too.

I maintain my pace, watching it in the rearview mirror. Gradually I ease off the gas, lower my speed. The sedan stays in the same lane, same distance back, lowers its speed to match.

My pulse quickens.

I'm being followed.

It's *them,* isn't it?

Do they know I met with Alex?

I thought her loft would be safer than a public place, but maybe I was wrong. Probably doesn't matter, either way. If they were watching her loft, they'd have followed her anywhere we'd have met.

If they know I met with her, they know I talked.

And that means the kids are in danger.

My hands tighten on the steering wheel. I'm crossing the bridge into the District now. The Potomac shimmers below, postcard-perfect.

That car is still behind me. Too far away for me to see the driver or read the plates. But as soon as we hit Constitution Avenue, there will be traffic. Stop and go. I'll be able to see something, won't I?

Onto Constitution now, coming up on a red light. Small clusters of tourists mill about, strolling down the sidewalks, headed to the Lincoln Memorial. I slow to a stop, but the black sedan slows sooner, lets two cars in between us. I can't see a thing.

The light turns green, and I inch forward, watching the rearview mirror. Slow enough for those cars to pull around me, I hope.

One veers into the next lane, speeds around me.

Then the other follows suit.

Another red light—

I stop, and the black sedan does, too, but at a distance, leaves too many car lengths between us. An SUV pulls in behind me from the other lane, blocks my view of the sedan.

I slam a hand against the wheel. This isn't working. They're *here,* right behind me, and I don't know who they are.

They're back—and this time, I don't want them to disappear. I want to confront them. I want to know *exactly* who's behind this.

When the light turns green, I press down on the gas. Past the White House on my left, the Washington Monument on my right, eyes flitting to the rearview mirror the whole time. The car's still behind me.

A quick right on Fourteenth—the car follows—and then a left on Jefferson. A one-way, flanking the National Mall. The black sedan's right behind me, at a distance.

The Mall's crowded. With pedestrians, and with cars, parallel parked on either side of the street. I inch along, but the sedan keeps its distance—

Bingo. Ahead of me, just across from the Hirshhorn Museum, a minivan pulls out from a parallel spot along the left side of the street, adjacent to the Mall. I press down on my brakes. The sedan slows to a distant stop behind me.

The minivan speeds off and I parallel park in the vacant space, quick turns of the wheel, watching the rearview mirror the whole time. The sedan keeps its distance.

I'm parked. That car's still behind me, stopped at a distance—

Another driver lays on his horn, and the sedan inches forward. Nowhere to go but forward. Past me.

My heart's beating fast. I watch the rearview mirror as it approaches. Nissan Sentra, DC plates, letters and numbers I memorize. And the person—a man, someone wearing a hat pulled low—

I spin my head to the side as the car accelerates past. The driver turns his head as he passes. I can't get a look at his face.

I slam my hand against the wheel, again. Watch as the car speeds down the street. It takes the first left to cut across the Mall—

Then a left down the other side of the Mall. The car slides parallel into a space near the National Gallery of Art, directly across from me.

He's not going away.

He's still watching me.

And I still want to know who he is.

Abruptly I open the car door. Get out, start walking, cut through the Mall. I catch sight of his car—

The driver's-side door is open. There's a man stepping out. Dark baseball cap, pulled low. Gray hooded sweatshirt.

Let's see if he'll follow me on foot.

I take a right on the dirt path, head in the direction of the Capitol. I force myself to keep my eyes forward, to avoid making it obvious that I saw him, that I know he's getting out of his car and following me.

But I intentionally keep a slow pace. I want to give him time to catch up.

I focus on each of my footsteps. Long enough now that he's probably crossed the Mall, caught on to my trail—

I turn and cast a furtive look back. There he is, following at a distance, hands jammed in the pocket of his sweatshirt, head down; all I can see is that black baseball cap.

My pulse is racing. This is dangerous.

But I need to know who he is. He's got to be one of the people behind this.

I walk another block, forcing myself to keep looking straight ahead. My skin is crawling, knowing he's behind me, but not having eyes on him, not knowing exactly *how* close. I need him to get comfortable, need to catch him by surprise—

I turn abruptly, heart pounding, and start walking toward him.

It catches him off guard. He stops, lifts his head just enough for me to catch a glimpse of the lower half of his face. Facial hair, a thick beard. He's too far away to see more, especially with that hat pulled low—

He does a 180 and starts walking away from me.

I start jogging toward him. I'm gaining on him—

He glances back, face still shielded by the hat, then starts running—

I break into a full run after him, chasing him.

This is crazy. I have no weapon; I'm not prepared for any sort of confrontation. But these people are a threat to my kids. I don't know who they are, and I *need* to know. I need to find the truth. The only way I can keep my kids safe is by figuring out who's behind this.

I have tunnel vision. I'm dimly aware of tourists around us, stopping and staring, but all I can see is him. His back, his sweatshirt, jeans. He's a big guy, solid. And *fast*. He's lengthening the distance between us.

The Metro station, straight ahead. The Smithsonian one, the one that's right on the Mall, a bank of long escalators heading down into the station, underground. He veers slightly off course, and I know he's heading for it. I push myself to run harder, faster.

He ducks into it, and I lose sight of him. I'm almost there—

I run for the escalator on the right, start running down—

There he is. Near the bottom of the escalator, pushing his way past a couple of tourists. I continue running down, hand grazing the rail, my eyes never leaving his back.

He's on the landing now. Runs past the ticket machines on the right, toward the turnstiles on the left—

He leaps over the turnstile. His hat flies off, and I can see thick, dark hair.

I don't have time to stop. Straight for the turnstiles now. There's a large woman in a flowered dress touching her card to the reader. I run straight forward, crashing into her, pushing my way through the turnstile behind her. She turns, shocked, scared, then gives me an angry look, but I'm already past her.

Down to the next bank of escalators now. I catch sight of that gray sweatshirt again. He's near the bottom already, and there's a train there, doors open—

I push past two men in suits, running down the steps as fast as I can.

He leaps on board. I can hear the chime, the warning that the doors are closing.

No, no, no.

I'm at the bottom now, and the doors are closing. I'm almost there—

The doors slide fully closed with an audible click. I didn't make it.

He's on, and I'm not.

I slam a hand against the side of the train in frustration. Then I stand back, breathing hard, and desperately scan the windows—

There he is. Standing, facing me. Gray sweatshirt, jeans. He has a thick beard, bushy eyebrows, and he's looking directly at me.

The sight makes a shiver run up my spine. I recognize this man from the headshot in the Agency cable, years ago.

He's *Falcon*.

CHAPTER SEVENTEEN

Jill

I watch the train until it disappears, swallowed into the black tunnel. When I turn, there are clusters of people standing a safe distance away from me, some outright staring, some casting furtive glances in my direction. The woman in the wide flowered dress from the turnstiles is watching me with her hot pink lips pursed, her handbag clutched tight to her body.

I catch sight of a guard in uniform ambling this way. Metro security. I turn, start walking away from him.

Up the escalator now, taking the stairs two at a time, and back out into the blinding sunlight, onto the green grass of the Mall. I blink to adjust my eyes.

Falcon.

Did that just happen?

Or was my mind playing tricks on me?

No. That was him. I'm absolutely convinced of it. That face has been imprinted on my brain for years. The round face, the wide-set hazel eyes. The thick beard, the bushy eyebrows. I'll never forget what he looks like.

But why is he *here*? And why is he following me?

There's a tour group approaching, everyone in bright yellow shirts, the guide holding a matching yellow flag above her head. I angle past them, head down, back toward my car.

He's here because he's not the person who works in the Syrian lab, with access to biological weapons programs. That person was never our source. We don't *have* a source. What we have is people—people within our own government—planting fake intelligence through our COVCOM system. And this guy's in on it.

But one thing's for sure: he isn't acting alone. Someone—or more likely, some *group* of people—deep within the CIA must be involved. That's the only way to explain the proprietary Z23 device. And this guy can't be CIA, because *his picture* is in CIA cable traffic.

Jeremy's right, isn't he? If there was any doubt in my mind that the U.S. is behind this, it's gone now. This man is *here,* in Washington.

And he's watching me. Following me.

I need to warn Drew.

I pull out my phone, dial Drew again. One ring, then another. No answer. *Again.*

I reach my car, unlock it. Slide into the driver's seat, shut and lock the door behind me. Then I sit in the silence, the air around me heavy and hot.

I can't reach Drew, don't know where the kids are, *how* they are.

I slam a hand against the steering wheel. Nothing's going the way I want it to.

I breathe hard, trying to marshal my thoughts, trying to figure out my next move.

Then abruptly I start the ignition, pull away from the curb. I know exactly where I'm going.

I should have done this years ago. I considered it then, decided against it. At first I didn't want them to see, was afraid of what they might think. And then I told myself I didn't need it. That they were gone, that we were safe.

Turns out I was wrong.

Twenty minutes later, I'm there. I pull into the gravel parking lot, the car bumping almost violently. A place I used to pass, back when I lived in Virginia. Dilapidated building, plain sign hung from the rafters. FIREARMS AND RANGE.

"Buying or shooting?" asks the woman behind the counter when I step inside, a dull chime announcing my arrival. She's leaning on the counter, a bored expression on her face, a web of tattoos covering her thick arms.

"Both."

Her expression doesn't change. "Do you know how?"

"*Knew* how. It's been a long time."

"What do you want to use?"

"A Glock." I scan the display on the wall behind her, then point to the smallest model, small enough to slide into a purse or a pocket. "That one."

The woman nods, then slides a sheet of paper in front of me. "Waiver," she says. "Sign this, get your eye and ear protection from the bins by the door. I'll meet you out in the first stall." She walks away without bothering to make eye contact.

I sign the paper, don clear goggles and ear protection that looks like oversize headphones, and head through two sets of doors to the range. It's empty, and quiet.

The woman walks out a moment later, Glock and a box of ammo in hand. She sets them down on the table between us. "Want me to explain?"

I pick up the Glock and turn it over in my hands, examining it.

"I think I've got it." It's been years since I've held one of these, but it's all coming back to me.

I open the box of bullets, load them into the magazine. Slide in the magazine, lock it into place. It's heavier now, more substantial.

The woman hangs a paper target, uses the pulley system to send it back. She stops it a short distance away. "This good?"

"All the way to the end, please."

She smirks and sends it all the way back. "Ready?"

"Ready."

I step into position. Adopt the stance I remember, my legs shoulder width apart. I grip the gun with both hands.

I raise my arms, straighten them. Focus on the target, through the sights. Press down on the trigger, slowly, just like I was taught . . .

Pop. The gun recoils in my hand, the smallest bit. I'd forgotten how loud this is, even through the ear protection. *Pop pop pop pop pop.* Six shots. I look over the sights at the target. There's a tight cluster of holes on the bull's-eye, dead center.

"Damn," the woman says. She looks at me approvingly. "Where'd you learn to do that? CIA or something?"

I smile. "Something like that."

Paperwork and payment complete, I walk out the door with the pistol in my purse. Once I'm in the car, I reach over and place it into the glove box, slam the door shut. Then I start the engine—

The phone rings. It's in my bag, on the passenger seat.

I reach for it, dig through the bag until I find it. Pull it out, hoping to see Drew's name, to be able to talk to the kids—

Unknown.

Dammit. It's not Drew, it's Alex.

I press the button to answer. "Hello?"

The instant I hear that deep, robotic voice, I know I'm wrong. It's not Alex. It's *them*.

"*We know where your kids are.*"

CHAPTER EIGHTEEN

Jill

The line goes dead before I can respond.

I lower the phone from my ear and stare at the screen, at the picture of Owen and Mia. My heart is racing.

I unlock the phone, my hand trembling. Find the list of recent calls, touch Drew's name. One ring, then another.

Not again. He needs to answer.

Why isn't he answering?

He doesn't know surveillance detection like I do. Doesn't know how to shake a tail. Hasn't been trained in it, the way I have.

I thought they'd be safer, away from here, away from me. Did I make another terrible mistake?

Another ring—

The click of a connection, and then his voice, tight and short. "Hi, Jill."

Thank God.

"Drew. Is anyone following you?"

There's a beat of silence. "What?"

"You need to leave. Wherever you are, find a new place. But watch for anyone following you—"

"Jill, what's going on?"

"Please, Drew, just leave. Pack up the kids and go somewhere else."

Another pause on his end of the line. I can hear the kids in the background, very faint, talking. "They followed us?"

"I think so."

He curses softly.

I wish I knew where he was. But I can't ask, not on an open line like this. Not when they might be listening. Maybe they *don't* know where he is. Maybe it's a bluff. And the last thing I want to do is lead them to him.

"Drew, I need you to leave behind your phone."

"What?"

"You need to stop somewhere and pick up a new one. A *few* new ones."

"Burner phones? Are you kidding me, Jill?"

"No, I'm not." God, I wish I was. "We're going to start talking through an encrypted app, too. Stronghold."

"Jill, this is—"

"Get all the cash you can—you can't use a credit card. And google 'surveillance detection route.' Learn how to make sure no one's following you."

There's no response. In the background I hear Owen's little voice. Mia's giggle.

My heart feels like it's being squeezed.

"It's up to you to protect them, Drew."

"Yeah," he says bitterly. "I guess it is."

I lay the phone down on the passenger seat. I'm still idling in the parking lot of the range. Through the windshield I see the front door. The woman with the tattoos is sitting on the stoop, smoking. Eyeing me suspiciously. I've been sitting here a while now, haven't I? I took some shots, bought a gun, and then I just sat here.

I shift into reverse and back out of the spot, then forward out of the lot, tires grinding noisily over the gravel.

I pull out onto the street, my stomach in a knot. They know where my kids are, and I'm not there to keep them safe. It's up to Drew, and he's an *attorney,* not a spy. He doesn't know how to do this.

I feel a gnawing sense of panic.

I need to figure out who's threatening my kids. That's how I can protect them.

I take a right and start heading back into the city. The engine hums as I pick up speed.

I reach for the phone, on the passenger seat. Find Alex's number, eyes flitting between screen and road and mirrors. I'm headed back to the hotel on autopilot, watching for a tail, mind spinning.

"Hi," I say when she picks up. "Can we talk on an encrypted app?" I don't know if they're listening. I have to assume they are.

"What do you have?"

"Stronghold."

"Got it. I'll call you back."

I set the phone down on the center console, focus on the road, and the mirrors. Traffic's light. No one's following me.

A moment later the phone buzzes, and the Stronghold icon flashes on the screen. I tap it, then tap her number, and the call connects.

"What's going on?" she asks. Her voice sounds taut.

"They know where my kids are. They called."

There's a pause on her end of the line. "They could be bluffing."

"Or not."

More silence. The hum of the engine fills the void. "What are you going to do?"

"What *can* I do? I told Drew to leave, to stop using his phone, to watch for a tail . . ."

I trail off, and she says nothing.

"We need to know who's behind this. Did you get anything from your source?"

"No." The disappointment in her voice comes through, crystal clear.

A motorcycle speeds by on my left, far too fast, the driver hunched low. I watch him weave around another car, switching lanes recklessly.

"Someone followed me today," I say. "When I was driving."

"Did you get plates?"

"I got more than that. I saw who it was."

"And?"

"It was Falcon."

"*What?*"

"The guy . . . I recognized his picture from the cable at work. I remember his face, Alex. I'll never forget it. The guy who followed me was the guy we thought was Falcon."

A tractor-trailer barrels past me on the left, draws my attention. I watch it speed ahead, lengthening the distance between us.

"What does that mean?" she asks.

"That Jeremy's right? That it *is* the U.S.?" I glance in the rearview mirror, almost reflexively. Turn on my right blinker. Time to switch lanes, just to check.

"Jeremy—did he find out more?"

I veer into the right lane, slow my pace, watch the mirror. No one follows, no one slows. "I haven't been able to reach him."

Out the passenger-side window, a big green sign catches my eye. The next exit is Alexandria.

Alexandria. Jeremy's still in the same place, I think, judging from Facebook. His townhouse is a few blocks from King Street. I bet I could find it—

There's the exit. I veer to the right, pull off. "Listen, I'll call you later," I tell Alex.

I set down the phone on the center console, check the rearview mirror. No one's pulled off behind me.

I follow the signs for King Street, head toward the commercial district, still keep an eye on the mirrors. Still clean.

I see a street that looks familiar. The one I've turned down in the past to reach his house. I take a left, then wind my way through the neighborhood until I see another turnoff that looks familiar. I take a right this time, continue on—

There it is, with the yellow shutters, and the American flag. Jeremy's townhouse.

I parallel park along the street, grab my bag, head toward his place, climb the three concrete steps to the landing. The door's painted black, with oval-shaped decorative glass in the center. Just to the right of it there's a small ceramic figurine of a Great Dane holding a Welcome sign.

I ring the doorbell and take a step back, hear it chime inside. A moment later, a figure appears through the glass. Jeremy. It's almost like looking at him through a kaleidoscope; he's fragmented, but it's definitely him, and he's stopped in the foyer and looking right at me.

He turns and walks away.

Weird. But I've done that before when someone's come to the door. Walked away to pick up a crying child before I answered—

Jeremy doesn't have a child. But he has Max—

Where's Max? The silence inside suddenly hits me. No booming barks, no giant Great Dane bounding toward the door, pummeling into it—

And still no Jeremy.

I knock twice, hard. There's a knot forming in the pit of my stomach.

"Go away, Jill," comes his voice, shouted through the door.

"Jeremy, what's wrong?" I call back.

"Leave."

I look through the window in the door. No sign of Jeremy. No sign of the dog, either—the knot in my stomach is twisting harder.

"Where's Max?"

No answer. Then Jeremy appears again on the other side of the door, fragmented in the glass. Growing larger, coming closer—

The door swings open. Jeremy gives me a look, fearful and angry and suspicious all at the same time. He's not wearing his glasses, and his eyes are puffy and red; he's been crying. "What do you know about Max?" he demands.

"Nothing." My pulse is racing. "What happened, Jeremy?"

He blinks quickly.

"What'd they do? Where's Max?"

He reaches for a piece of paper laying on the table in the entryway. Holds it up for me to see. Black marker, block letters, the same handwriting I saw on that note in Owen's crib.

STOP DIGGING. STOP TALKING. OR MAX IS DEAD.
AND YOUR PARENTS ARE NEXT.

"Who's behind this, Jeremy?" I ask, because he's been trying to find that answer. He might have *already* found that answer.

He shakes his head, quick and firm.

"You can't let them get away with this," I say.

"They'll stop at nothing." His chin quivers.

"What have you learned?" I ask. I can hear the desperation in my voice.

"Nothing."

He closes the door, and the last thing I hear is the turn of the deadbolt.

CHAPTER NINETEEN

Alex

The office is starting to empty for the evening. There's that late afternoon buzz, those final conversations of the day. The see-you-tomorrows and the have-a-good-nights. I'm dimly aware of the chatter, focused on my computer screen. Monitoring the latest developments out of Syria. Or trying to, anyway. It's damn near impossible to concentrate.

Jill said she saw Falcon. Following her. What the hell does that mean? I don't know if she's safe. Or if her family is. And they *need* to be. I protect my sources, and right now Jill's one of them.

And then there's those last messages from my tipster. They've been replaying in my mind. The request to publish. The vaguely threatening follow-up: *Do it soon, before it's too late.* I never got an answer to my question: *Too late for what?*

Better not be too late for a scoop. This is *my* story. I can't lose it.

Marco, the college-intern-slash-social-coordinator, stops at my cubicle. "Brewster's?" he asks.

"I'm going to pass tonight."

"Next time," he says with a grin. Heads off to the next occupied cubicle, off to round up more participants.

The mention of Brewster's brings Beau Barnett to the forefront of my mind. I wait until Marco's moved on to the next row of cubicles, then I reach for my phone.

I try his cell first; it's late enough he might have left work. He picks up. "Hello?"

"It's Alex."

"Alex. Twice in two weeks."

"Friends chat, don't they?"

"What do you need?"

A smile pulls at the corners of my mouth. "I have a hypothetical for you."

"I love hypotheticals." His voice drips with sarcasm.

"We need to go encrypted. Do you have Stronghold?"

There's a beat of silence. "Yes."

"I'll call you back."

I hang up, touch the Stronghold app on my phone, place the call through the app. He answers before the first ring.

"What's the hypothetical?" he asks.

I glance around to make sure no one's listening. Then I speak more quietly. "Say someone in our government wanted to plant intel through a fake source. How plausible would that be?"

He whistles. "Come on, Alex. Even with encryption we shouldn't be having this conversation. Are you trying to get me fired?"

"Where are you right now?"

"Home."

"Text me the address."

"Alex—"

"You owe me. Those sources in Baghdad, those tips I gave you—"

"Pretty sure I've paid down that debt."

I say nothing.

"Why are you asking me this? Is it another anonymous tip?"

"I thought you didn't want to talk on an open line."

"I'll take that as a yes."

Again, I say nothing.

"Fine. I'll text you the address. But, Alex?"

"Yeah?"

"Same deal we had in Baghdad. I talk, so do you. I want some details on these sources of yours."

I show up at his apartment in Georgetown an hour later, a six-pack of Sam Adams in hand.

"Come on in," he says, opening the door wider, ushering me forward.

I step inside. It's a small one-bedroom, decked out like a bachelor pad: shabby threadbare couch, old coffee table with water rings, giant television, video game systems. No décor, nothing on the walls.

I hold up the six-pack and he takes it from me, heads to the kitchen. "Want one?"

"Sure."

He pops the caps off two of them. Walks back into the room, extends one toward me. I take it, and he plops down on one end of the couch. I sit on the other.

"So, this latest source of yours," he begins.

"This *scenario* I described." I'm getting the answers *I* need first. "The U.S., using a fake source. Planting intel. How plausible would it be?"

He takes a swig. "Not very. It's the kind of thing you see in movies, but not real life."

That's not what I want to hear. "Why?"

"There'd be too many people involved. Sources aren't run by just one person, you know? It wouldn't *just* be a case officer making something up. There are a bunch of people who vet the source—"

"Say the source made it through the vetting process."

He raises an eyebrow. "How?"

"It's a hypothetical." I lift the bottle to my lips, take a sip. Avoid his stare.

"Okay. Let's say that's true. But every meeting with the source—it's an operation, you know? Multiple people involved, beyond just the case officer."

"What if there were no in-person meetings?"

"COVCOM?"

"Exactly."

He leans back, looks thoughtful. "Well, that makes it more plausible. Just leave whatever message you want, and it's in the system as reliable intelligence." He seems to be thinking aloud. "But *getting* that COVCOM is not an easy process."

I nod. So he's saying it's possible.

"You still haven't explained how—in your *hypothetical* scenario—the source made it through the vetting process." He uses air quotes.

I answer the question in my head. *Threats. Kidnapping.* But I sure as hell can't say any of that. So I settle for "It's possible, isn't it?"

"Depends on the source, I guess." He looks thoughtful again. "If it's someone reporting on a hard target like China or Russia, it's pretty unlikely. There are way too many sets of eyes on a source like that. Going through everything with a fine-tooth comb. You have to, with those counterintelligence concerns."

"But another country?" *Like Syria?*

He shrugs. "More of a possibility. Fewer sets of eyes. Quicker encryptions. Especially for a high-priority reporter. Someone with access we desperately need."

Like someone reporting on biowarfare. I don't say the words, and he doesn't either. But I can tell from the expression on his face that he's connected the dots. Last time we chatted, I asked him about Syrian biological weapons programs. And now I'm asking him about this—

"Did you get both tips from the same source?" he asks.

I grip the bottle in my hand tighter. "Yes."

"Someone who claimed to know the percentage of reporting we're getting from a specific source. Someone who now claims to know that we have a *fake source*?"

"Yes."

"Alex, that's . . ." He shakes his head slowly. "I don't even know what to say."

"I know." I don't know what to say either. I pick at a loose thread on the cushion beside me. "So, *hypothetically*, who would be doing something like that?"

He examines his bottle, looks deep in thought. "The hurdle would be getting the source encrypted, getting him COVCOM. Once the COVCOM's in hand . . ." He shrugs. "Anyone could be using it."

"But to get to that point . . ."

"Well, it would *have* to be CIA. The whole recruitment process—it would all be documented in operational channels. No one outside the Agency would have access to the level of detail needed to pull something like that off." He nods, looking more confident. "But, Alex, we're not doing anything like that. I'm positive."

"CIA as a whole, sure. Could there be some sort of rogue faction?"

His expression is haunted. "I can't believe we're having this conversation."

"I know. I can't, either."

I wait for him to say something, but he's quiet.

"What if I said there was a Z23 involved?"

"A Z23? How the hell do you know about that, Alex?"

"I have my ways." My ways are Jill. And her contact. I'd never heard of it before. Proprietary CIA scrambling technology. But according to Jill's friend, it was attached to the COVCOM.

He looks uncomfortable. "If there's a Z23 involved, then it's someone senior."

"Yeah?"

"Yeah. No one junior can access those."

"How senior? Like *your* level of seniority?" Beau's been a Deputy Chief of Station out in the field. Number two in charge. Now he's a Deputy Group Chief at headquarters, overseeing operations in the Middle East. Pretty damn senior.

"Oh hell no. I can't get anywhere near a Z23. Higher. I'm talking about someone who's read into everything. Every compartment."

Apprehension is swirling inside me.

"Someone at the highest level of the CIA."

It's dark by the time I get back to my loft. I step inside, drop my bag onto the table in the center of the room. Hover there in the silence, considering what to do next. I'm too disconcerted to sleep right now. Too damn tense to have any appetite.

Someone high up in the CIA. That's Beau's guess. Before I left his apartment, he pressed for information about my source, but I didn't have much to give. Told him it was an anonymous tipster. Someone who knew Falcon's crypt. Knew how much intel he's providing, knew he was fake. That that's all I've got. And he didn't press it. I think he's as unsettled by the information as I am.

I carry my laptop over to the couch. Sit down cross-legged with it in my lap. Open it up, check ClandestineTips. Nothing. The last thing I got was the request to publish. *Do it soon, before it's too late.*

And my response, still unanswered: *Too late for what?*

I set the laptop beside me on the couch and reach for the remote. Turn on the TV. Flip through a couple of channels. A sitcom. A crap reality show. I could pull up Netflix, but I know I won't be able to concentrate right now. I turn the television back off.

Silence, again.

My gaze falls onto the framed picture on the built-ins. The wedding picture.

I pull the computer back onto my lap and open Facebook. I haven't checked the site in days. Weeks, even. I log in, and the news feed appears—

Miles. It's the first update in my feed. A picture of him with a woman, their arms around each other—

I feel like I've been punched in the gut.

They're outside, somewhere sunny and green. He's smiling, and it's a genuine one. I know his smiles. The pose-for-the-camera ones, the I'll-smile-if-I-have-to ones. But this one's real. He's *happy.*

She's smiling, too. She's pretty and young and she looks *nice.* That's the toughest damn part. It'd be easier if she looked unpleasant.

I close Facebook. Stare at the background picture on my screen. The stock photo.

Then I look over at our wedding picture.

Don't you want to have it all?

Impulsively I open up Word. Start typing. Writing down every-thing I have.

It's enough now, with Jill's info. Sure, it'd be better with names. More convincing with proof. But she's not an anonymous source. I know exactly who she is. I know her access. I can tell this story.

The words flow easily. Far more easily than I would have expected. I reach the end and stare at the draft. It's a damn good piece. Ex-plosive. Front-page worthy. It's not everything, not the whole story. But enough to make a splash.

Enough to make sure *I'm* the one who gets the scoop.

Jill enters my mind and I try to push her out. But I can hear our conversation replaying in my mind. I made a deal with her. I got that information because I made a deal. I promised to stay quiet until we got to the bottom of this. If I break that promise, if I publish something attributed to her, her kids could be in jeopardy.

More of my mom's words run through my head.

You have such a strong sense of right and wrong.

I hit save and close Word, frustrated as hell. Nothing's working out the way I want it to. My marriage is over. A failure. I can't get to the bottom of this story. It's my job to figure it out, and I just can't.

I pull up the browser again, still open to Facebook. Look at the picture of Miles with that new woman.

My gaze shifts to my phone. I shouldn't do this. Shouldn't even be considering it.

But he's the one I always turned to when things weren't going my way.

Maybe this was all a mistake. Maybe I made the biggest damn mistake of my life.

I reach for the phone. Unlock it, find the text chain with him. It's not at the top anymore, like it always used to be—

My thumbs tap out a message and I hit send before I can change my mind.

Can we meet?

I watch the space below my message and wait for those dots, the ones that show he's writing back—

There they are. He's writing something—

The dots disappear.

I watch the screen.

They're back. He's typing again. He must have written something, erased it, reconsidered—

A reply.

Sure.

I stare at the word. He just agreed to meet.

Want to come by? I tap out.

I wait for the dots—

There they are.

Still there.

Still, like he's typing something long—

The message appears:

No, Alex. I don't think that's a good idea. How about that new place, Bar Ten? Halfway between my place and yours . . .

My place and yours. The phrasing hurts, even if it's true. My place isn't *ours* anymore. He has his own.

I can be there in fifteen, I type.

See you then.

I stare at the screen. What the hell did I just do? *Why* did I do it?

My gaze shifts to the wedding picture on the shelf. How did we get to this point? How did everything fall so spectacularly apart?

I glance at the clock, then reach for the laptop. Time to close it up, time to go. I pull up ClandestineTips for one last check—

A new message, from my source.

I double-click—

They know you're digging around, and they're not pleased. Be careful.

CHAPTER TWENTY

Alex

It's a warning. That much is clear. They're threatening me because I'm digging around. They want me to stop. To stay the hell away from this story.

But what strikes me even more powerfully is the fact that my source knows *exactly* who's behind this—and is close enough to those people to know what they're thinking.

Who? I type. *Who's not pleased?*

I stare at the screen and wait, but there's no answer.

I glance at the clock again. Fifteen minutes. I'll check ClandestineTips when I get back. Right now I need to see Miles. I close the laptop and head for the door.

Bar Ten is one of those trendy bars. Couldn't be more different than Brewster's. The lighting is dim but strategic, the kind designed for flattering Instagram shots. Everything's modern, streamlined, minimalist. The music makes me imagine people meditating on a beach. The bartenders look straight out of the pages of *GQ*.

Miles is at the bar. In a suit, his tie loosened. He looks good, even better than the last time I saw him. He catches sight of me and stands. I walk over, and we exchange an awkward hug.

This feels all wrong.

"This place is great, isn't it?" he asks, sitting back on his stool. There's a martini glass in front of him, filled with liquid that looks fluorescent green. I sit down slowly beside him.

This place isn't great at all. This is the kind of place I hate, and he should know that.

"How've you been?" I ask in return.

"Really good," he says with a smile. "How about you, Alex? I worry about you."

The words feel condescending as hell. "Also really good."

An awkward silence follows. He reaches for his drink and takes a sip.

A bartender dressed in all black walks over. "Have you had a chance to look over our martini list?" He lays down a long, skinny drink menu in front of me.

"No." I skim it, then look behind him, try to catch sight of a bourbon, or beer taps, but it's a lost cause. Maybe all they *have* is martinis? "You know what, just a water would be great."

"Sparkling or still?"

Tap would be fine, but that doesn't seem like an option here. "Still. Thanks."

He purses his lips and turns around.

"You should get a martini," Miles says.

"I don't like martinis."

Another awkward silence ensues. I watch the bartender pour Evian into a stemless martini glass.

"Alex, why are we here?" Miles asks. "What do you want?" He says it gently, but the words sound harsh.

What *do* I want?

Him.

The life we used to have.

"I want things to go back to the way they were," I say. And the moment the words are out of my mouth, I wish I hadn't said them.

"Have you changed your mind? About, you know. *Kids.*"

"No. Have you?"

"No." He shoots me a wry smile, and in it I see the old Miles. The one I used to banter with. The one I used to be *happy* with.

"Aren't you worried your life will be empty without kids?" he asks. He says it lightly, but it doesn't blunt the blow of the words.

"That's a terribly offensive thing to say."

"Even your mom wanted you to have kids. You told me about that conversation—"

"The one where she said there are many different paths to happiness?" He's not going to use my mom's words against me.

"Like what? Like winning some award? *That's* going to give your life meaning?"

"Are *kids*? Why do you think my life can't have meaning without kids? And no, I don't mean some award. I mean love, like the love I feel for you, and for her—"

"You don't owe her anything," he says. "Certainly not some award."

"I owe her *everything*. She never accomplished her goal because of me."

"That's ridiculous, Alex."

"It's the truth."

"But she had *you*. Didn't she always tell you that was better?"

"Well, of course she's going to say that to me."

"You don't believe her?"

The bartender sets down the martini glass full of water. I'm pretty sure he heard that.

"I don't want kids, Miles. I never have. You didn't, either, re-member?"

"I changed my mind."

"Well, I'm not going to."

"Then this is where it ends, Alex."

The bartender pretends to examine the row of mixers just to the right of us, clearly listening to our conversation.

"And besides," he says. "I'm seeing someone. I told you that."

"You do remember we're still *married*?" I'm not sure if I say it more for the bartender's sake or his. Or maybe *mine*.

"Our marriage has been over for a long time."

"It might have been useful to share that information with *me*."

"I filed for divorce."

"Was that before or after you got a girlfriend?"

"Does it matter?"

"Yeah, I'd say it does."

"You had this damn *quest*. I could never compete."

"What the hell are you talking about?"

"Finding the biggest story. It mattered to you more than any-thing. Even me."

He swirls his drink around in its glass like it's wine, watching the martini instead of me.

"So you were *jealous* of my *career*?"

"I wanted to matter more."

I stare at him, this man I once knew. "No, you wanted my ca-reer to matter *less*."

The bartender slinks away. This conversation is too much even for him.

"My career makes me happy," I say. "I shouldn't have to apolo-gize for that."

Miles says nothing.

"*You* made me happy, too." I realize I've just used the past tense. And it doesn't sound wrong.

"You didn't," he says.

"What?"

"You *didn't* make me happy. Not toward the end. Not the way she does."

The words cut like a knife. And looking into his eyes, I'm pretty damn sure that's how he intended them.

I've forgiven a lot of what he's said. Given him the benefit of the doubt. Tried to get past it.

But I'm done now. And frankly, I should have been done a long time ago.

"I'm going to go," I say, sliding off the stool.

"Alex—"

"I'm leaving."

He glances over at the bartender. "Alex, stay and talk. Don't run out on me."

I shake my head and continue toward the door.

It's all about him, isn't it? He doesn't feel guilty about what he just said. He's not worried that I'm leaving, upset. He just doesn't want to be left alone at the bar.

It was *always* all about him, wasn't it?

Maybe not always. Maybe not right in the beginning. Or maybe I just didn't see it. But in any case, our problems ran deeper than just whether or not to have kids.

Why the hell didn't I want to admit that?

I push open the door, and I answer my own question. Because I didn't want my marriage to fail. Because he's the only family I've got left. Because he's been trying to paint *me* as the selfish one in this relationship—and maybe, just maybe, I was starting to believe him.

"You can't hide from the truth, Alex," he calls after me.

"I know," I say, without ever looking back. Because for the first time I feel like I'm actually *facing* the truth.

It just doesn't look the way I wanted it to.

Tears blur my vision, turning streetlights and headlights into giant puddles of brightness. I blink them away, focus on my surroundings. The street outside the bar, cars whizzing past. A group of women in their early twenties, scantily clad, heading for another bar, one that's sending a low pulse of bass out onto the sidewalk. One of them says something funny, and the others laugh uproariously.

I turn away and start walking toward home.

My marriage is over. But it's been over for a long time now, hasn't it?

Miles is right. I can't hide from the truth.

Being true to myself doesn't make me selfish, no matter what he wants me to think.

Choosing not to have children doesn't mean I don't care about other people.

I gave that relationship my all. I gave my mom my all. And my sources, and my stories.

In my mind I see Jill. Her kids. If all I cared about was breaking a big story, I'd have published one by now.

I care about doing the right thing. How dare he say otherwise?

I cross the street and veer right into the park. Quickest route home, a cut-through. It's lush and green, a fountain in the center, shut off for the night. There's a statue beside it, some war hero I can't remember.

I pass a row of empty benches. The whole park's empty at this hour. Completely deserted. The streetlight just up ahead is flickering, casting an eerie glow on the park. I pick up my pace—

Footsteps, behind me. Loud, and heavy. A quick pace. Close, like someone approached without me hearing. Too close, since there's no one else around—

A wave of apprehension washes over me.

I turn my head and catch a glimpse of the man. Large, with a thick beard. Wide-set eyes staring directly at me—

The apprehension morphs into full-blown fear.

He lifts something over his head—

And then everything goes black.

CHAPTER TWENTY-ONE

Alex

Muffled sounds break through the quiet darkness in my mind. Voices. Garbled, unintelligible.

I force open my eyelids. I blink, and my surroundings gradually settle into focus, my brain making sense of what I'm seeing.

I'm on the ground, looking up. Figures are leaning over me. Two people, a man and a woman. College kids by the looks of them. A streetlight flickers overhead.

My head feels like it's splitting. I reach up, touch the back of it. There's a bump there, a huge goose egg. But nothing wet, nothing sticky. No blood at least.

"Are you okay?" the man asks, a worried look on his face.

"Do you think we should call the police?" the woman asks him, quietly, urgently.

"No," I say, answering for him. It comes out like a croak.

"She's probably drunk," the woman says, in an exaggerated whisper.

"Probably," the man says.

I struggle into a sitting position. Everything around me is spinning. My head throbs and I feel like I'm going to vomit.

"Whoa, are you sure you're okay?" the man asks.

"I'm fine."

I sit, wait for the dizziness to subside—it doesn't, but it lessens slightly—and then force myself to my feet. I sure as hell don't want the police getting involved. I need to show these people I'm fine.

"Hey, is that yours?" the woman asks. She's pointing at something down by my feet, something that must have been under me—

I look down. It's a piece of paper, folded in quarters. I reach for it. It's not mine, or *wasn't* mine, but I have the strangest sensation it *is* mine. That it's meant for me.

I hold on to it and give them an even look. Focus on standing still, not swaying. Looking normal.

"Come on," the woman murmurs to the man, reaching for his hand. "She's fine."

The man gives me one last look, like he's unsure if he should leave, but he lets her pull him away.

I watch them leave, and then I slowly unfold the piece of paper under the light of the flickering streetlight.

A message. Block letters, black marker.

BREATHE A WORD, AND NEXT TIME YOU DIE.

When I'm back inside my loft, dead bolt firmly engaged, I pull open the freezer, dig around for a bag of peas. Then I sink down on the couch, hold it to the back of my head.

I could have been killed. I was knocked out cold, and another blow could have finished me off.

The only reason I'm still alive is that whoever did this didn't *want* to kill me. This was just a message. A warning.

In my mind I can see the man's face. Those eyes, focused directly on me—

I shudder and reach for the beige blanket draped on the couch. Wrap it around myself.

They want my silence. They want this story quashed.

They're terrified that I'll find the truth.

My mind turns to Jill. I'm not the only one searching for the truth. Far from it. If that man came for me, is she in danger, too?

I put down the bag of peas and pick up my phone. I hesitate, the message flashing in my mind.

Breathe a word, and next time you die.

That means publishing, right?

Or does it mean talking, too?

I tap the Stronghold app, then tap Jill's number. She answers after the first ring. "Hello?"

"Hey. Listen, someone came after me tonight."

"What?"

"A guy, in the park. Hit me over the back of the head—"

"Are you okay?"

"Yeah." I reach up with my other hand, touch the goose egg on the back of my head. It's still cold from the bag of peas.

"Who was he?"

"I don't know."

"What'd he look like?"

"Big guy. Beard. Wide-set eyes." I can picture his face in my mind, and shudder.

"Falcon."

"Huh?"

"That's Falcon. Really thick beard, right?"

"Yeah." My mind is churning. That was *Falcon*? "He left a note. 'Breathe a word, and next time you die.'"

There's silence on the other end of the line. Then, "Are you out?"

Just three words, but they're loaded. I can hear the emotion in her voice. The fear, the anticipation. Almost like she's standing on a precipice. Like she knows in a moment she'll be elated or face crushing disappointment. No middle ground.

Am I out? I sure as hell should be. I should let this go. Stay quiet. It's the safest thing to do.

But this story's too important. I have an obligation to keep going. To find the truth.

"No," I say. "I'm all in."

After I end the call with Jill, I sit down at the table and open my laptop. I need to find out what's going on. What kind of secrets justify these threats, this violence.

I open ClandestineTips. There's a new message from my source.

Why haven't you published yet?

I read the words and almost want to laugh. While I was being attacked, warned to stay quiet, my source was urging me to do the exact opposite. What are the odds?

Why *haven't* I published yet? Because I promised Jill I wouldn't. Because her family's safety depends on it. And now . . . now there's another reason, too. *Because I want to stay alive.*

I give my head a quick shake, which sends it throbbing. I can't think like that. I can't let them get to me. Can't let them win.

Because I need more, I type.

"And you sure as hell know more," I murmur.

I watch the screen and wait for another message.

Nothing. I focus on the last one the source sent. *Why haven't you published yet?*

There's something about it that doesn't sit well with me.

I lift my fingers to the keyboard again: *Why do you want me to publish?*

I wait, but there's no response. He's not going to answer that, is he? He didn't last time, either. Just said, *Do it soon, before it's too late.*

What *do* I know? Beau felt like there was someone high up in the CIA involved. Jill's old co-worker thought the goal was to increase military expenditures. Could I find an intersection there? A CIA official with ties to the military-industrial complex?

It's worth a shot.

I find a CIA org chart online. Jot down all the top positions. Director, and the list of deputies below that. The heads of the various directorates: Analysis, Operations, Science and Technology, Digital Innovation, Support. The leaders of the Mission Centers.

It takes some digging, but I'm able to find most of the names of the people who fill the roles. At the more senior levels, most officers are no longer undercover. Mavis Sawyer's in charge. The Gang of Three: Rosemarie Harris, Langston West, Gladys Chen. Rounding out the directorate leadership: Sean O'Leary, Nate Percy. Then on to the Mission Centers. I find names for each one except two: Counterintelligence, Counterterrorism.

I write each name and position on a Post-it. Spread them out on the table.

Next, I write down the biggest names in military industry. Boeing, Lockheed Martin, Northrop Grumman, dozens more. Spread those on the table, too, and look over everything. Who's connected? Who stands to gain the most if we march toward war?

Before long, the connections are appearing, and the table's disorganized as hell. I stand up, stretch. Touch the lump on the back of my head. My whole head's aching.

Then I catch sight of the giant corkboard in the kitchen. Full of memories of Miles and me: tickets from concerts, sporting events, Broadway shows. Photo booth shots from friends' weddings, selfies from our Polaroid, favorite snapshots we had printed. I haven't been able to touch it. Haven't wanted to erase those memories, or admit that we're not making any more.

I walk over and take everything in, my gaze settling on one item after another. The fortune from the Chinese takeout that made us collapse with laughter. A save-the-date card from our wedding. A picture of the two of us holding the keys to the loft, the day we closed on it.

Then I reach up and start taking everything down, piece by piece.

Within minutes the board is empty. I feel strangely lighter myself, like a weight's been lifted. The empty board looks like a fresh start.

I reach for the notes on the table, and I start pinning them up.

Hours later, the board's full. String connects the various people to various companies. Financial interests, advisory roles, any sort of ties between entities.

Everyone has links, some more than others.

My head hurts like hell, and not just from the blow.

I stand back and look at it. The idea that it *could* be these people doesn't seem so far-fetched. That the goal of the fake intelligence could be to feed the military-industrial complex. Looking at the tangled web of connections in front of me, it actually seems pretty damn possible.

But who specifically is behind it? That's the question I need to answer. Any of these people could benefit in some way from a military buildup. And I just don't know.

But my source does.

I sit down at the table and open my laptop. I start a new message to my source, but I hesitate before typing. I don't know if I should tip my hand. But maybe I need to give something to get something.

We think it's coming from within the CIA. Can you confirm or deny?

I walk to the counter to pour myself a glass of water, pop a couple of Advil. When I get back, a message is waiting. *Do you need the information to publish the story?*

Yes, I type. It's not *all* I need, but it's something.

A new message appears:

Confirm.

That prickle of adrenaline runs through me. It *is* from inside the CIA. Who is this source, and how does he know?

And why hasn't he done something about it?

I take a sip of water and type a reply:

If people in our government are dirty, you have an obligation to do something about it.

That was a step too far, wasn't it? Too critical.

The message comes back a minute later.

YOUR government. If I tell you this information, I'm betraying MY government.

CHAPTER TWENTY-TWO

Jill

I pace my hotel room like a caged animal. Alex was attacked. By *Falcon*.

They're getting more aggressive. And I'm terrified they'll go after my family.

I've thought about just getting in my car and driving down to wherever Drew and the kids are. But I don't *know* where they are, and it's a risk to ask. If he tells *me* on the phone, I can't say with absolute certainty that *they* won't hear it, too. Besides, what if they track me down there? It's still safer if I stay away, and if I do everything I can here to figure out who's behind this.

Trouble is, I'm at a loss for what to do. Jeremy seemed like a promising route, but he's not talking. He's not talking because of *them,* because they took Max, the thing that was most important to him in all the world. Because they threatened to hurt his parents, proving they'd stop at nothing to silence him.

It's late when the phone finally rings. I pounce on it. It's a number I don't recognize. "Hello?"

"It's me." Drew's voice.

"Thank God."

"I'm going to send you a link. Stronghold. I'll call you back through that."

"Fine." He sounds tense.

I hang up, place the call through the app, and a moment later we're reconnected.

"How are you?" I ask. "Are you in a new hotel?"

"Yeah."

"How are the kids?"

"Worried. Frustrated. Bored." His tone is clipped. "But they're asleep now."

I picture them, tucked side by side under a white duvet in a big hotel bed, fast asleep. God, I wish I was there with them. "Did you get cash, like we talked about? You haven't used a credit card, have you?"

"Paid cash for the room." I can hear the bitterness in his voice. "Do you know what kind of place takes cash?"

I close my eyes and breathe deeply. The thoughts of them in that big plush bed vanish. They're in some dingy motel, aren't they? I'm sick at the thought of them being in a place like that. But it's the only way, until the people threatening us are behind bars.

"You need to go somewhere else tomorrow. Keep moving. Just in case."

"Really, Jill? How long?"

"I don't know. Until we get to the bottom of this. Until we know who's responsible."

"And when will that be?"

"I don't know."

There's silence on the other end of the line.

"I'm doing my best." The words sound almost pleading, like I'm pleading with him to understand, to be on my side.

"I'll talk to you later, Jill."

The line disconnects. I pull the phone from my ear and stare at it. The picture of Owen and Mia, those carefree smiles on their faces. They're worried now, Drew said so himself. And they're going to be even *more* worried when they have to pick up and move again tomorrow. But there's no other choice.

Those people, whoever they are, they knew where my kids were.

They hurt Alex, and threatened her.

They took Max to get to Jeremy.

They're getting close.

Sleep that night comes in fits and starts, and I keep being jolted awake by nightmares: visions of my kids being snatched in front of me, of screaming silent screams. When dawn breaks, I pack up what few belongings I have left, and I check out of the hotel.

It's time to move on. I need to take the same advice I gave Drew, keep moving, because if they get to me, I can't get to the bottom of this.

I run a surveillance detection route, a long one, and then instead of driving directly to the next hotel I've picked out, I detour and stop at Alex's loft. Park two blocks away, approach the building from the rear, walk into the residents-only below-ground parking lot, then piggyback off someone else entering the building. I need to talk to Alex, and it might as well be in person.

"How are you?" I ask after she shuts the door behind me.

"Sore." She reaches up and lightly touches the back of her head. "Have you heard from Drew?"

"They're at a new hotel. I told him to keep moving."

She nods, then motions toward the table. "Want to sit?"

"Sure."

Her laptop's open, and there are Post-its strewn about—

I catch sight of the corkboard in her kitchen. She's created some sort of link chart up there, with pinned-up Post-its and string. "What's that?"

"Research."

"Into?"

"Top CIA officials. And their links to military contractors."

I sink down slowly into one of the chairs at the table, my eyes on her the whole time, waiting for her to say more.

"Beau's guess was CIA brass," she says. "With the goal of feeding the military-industrial complex."

"Who's Beau?"

"A friend of mine. CIA case officer."

If she's telling me this, revealing a source, she must really trust me. "And he knows about this?" I ask.

"Parts of it."

I process those words, looking at the web of connections she's created. "Looks like you think he might be onto something."

"Trouble is, could be any number of people. *If* that's even the real story. Did you ever reach Jeremy? Did he have any thoughts?"

In my mind I can see his face, those red-rimmed eyes. The jarring silence in his home, where Max should have been. "They got to him. He's not talking."

She curses under her breath.

"What about your source? Anything?"

"Actually, yeah." She nods toward her computer. "My source knows *exactly* who's behind this. Said the people know I'm digging around and they're not pleased."

"I think your run-in in the park proves that," I say.

"Also confirmed it's coming from within CIA. But referred to it as *our* government. Said to give us more would be treasonous."

"So he's not an American."

"Apparently not," she says.

"Did you get more?"

"That was it. I asked a follow-up, but there was no response."

Wheels in my brain are turning, trying to make sense of this. "A foreign intelligence service," I say, musing aloud.

"I had the same thought."

"It makes sense," I say, a current of excitement running through me. It feels like a break, at long last. "A foreign intel service is spying on CIA officials. *That's* how they have the information. And someone who works for that service is sharing it with us."

"But *why*? I mean, it's not about money, or they'd be approaching the CIA, right? Offering to sell these secrets?"

"Could be a moral obligation. You know, trying to do the right thing. Could be revenge, someone who was passed over for promotions, something like that."

Alex nods.

"Hard to know without talking to the source," I add. "Knowing his background."

"Right. But he won't agree to meet. Won't tell me who he is."

"Can we track him down? Is there anyone who could access the back end of the tips system, find an IP address?"

"It's designed so that that's not possible."

I hate having so little information, being completely dependent on this source to *provide* information.

"If it *is* a foreign intelligence service," Alex says, "which country's most likely?"

I consider the question. "China and Russia are the most capable, the most aggressive. Just behind there's Iran, Israel, Ukraine. Could be any number of countries. Anything in the messages to indicate what country it might be? Unusual phrasing, word choice?"

"Nothing. I wouldn't have even guessed—"

The shrill ring of my phone cuts short her thought. I pull it from my bag, check the screen. *Drew.*

He's not calling from a burner phone. He's calling from *his* phone—

"Hello?"

"Jill?" Instantly I hear the panic in his voice.

"Drew? What's wrong?" I grip the phone tighter.

"The kids . . . They're *gone.*"

CHAPTER TWENTY-THREE

Jill

*N*o. This isn't possible.

"What do you mean they're gone?" I can hear the panic in my voice. "How are they *gone*?"

"I took a shower, Jill. Honest to God, all I did was take a shower. Two minutes max, and they were watching *PAW Patrol*, and I came out, and they were gone."

I glance at Alex and she's watching me, sympathy on her face, an expression that somehow makes this all more real, more terrifying.

It's not possible that I'm living this same nightmare again. Even worse this time, really, because they told me if they took Owen again, they'd kill him. And they have *both* of my kids this time, and they haven't told me what I need to do to get them back.

Is there anything I can do to get them back?

I talked. To a *journalist*. I did exactly what they warned me not to do.

They know. And they took my children because of it.

My heart feels like there's a weight pressing down on it, crushing it.

I imagine the scene he's describing, the kids in their footed pajamas, sitting on a double bed, absorbed in the TV, Drew darting in for a quick shower—

What happened, when he was in there? Did someone break in?

Or did someone come to the door, and the kids answered it? I've told them never to answer the door, not without a parent there, but did I stress it enough? Would they have known what to do if they were in an unfamiliar setting, if the only parent there was in the shower?

They're gone. My kids are gone. Someone has them. I don't know who, or where—

"Where are you?" I ask Drew.

"Atlanta. A budget motel off the interstate. It's all that would accept cash."

It's my fault. It's my fault they were in a cheap motel, that they had to leave home in the first place, that anyone was after them, *took* them—

"Call the police," I say, and I see the surprise on Alex's face. But really, how can we not? They know how to track down missing people, and *my children are missing*.

"Already done."

"What did you tell them?"

"Just that I came out of the shower and the kids were gone. I didn't tell them any of . . . you know. The other stuff."

"Good. So what now?"

"They're on their way." He pauses, then adds, "I hear the sirens now."

My stomach is in a knot. The police are on their way. Drew's talking to the police. But it's *him,* not me, and he's not saying anything he shouldn't.

Would it matter if he did?

My reason for staying silent all these years was so they wouldn't come back, wouldn't come for Owen. *They came.*

"They're *gone*," he says. His voice breaks. In the distance, behind him, I can hear the wail of sirens approaching. "Jill, what are we going to do?"

"We'll find them." Even as the words come out of my mouth, they sound like a lie. My vision blurs, but the tears stay put, almost like they're frozen in place.

CHAPTER TWENTY-FOUR

Alex

Jill lowers the phone. She's pale. Looks stunned, almost like she's in shock.

This is what I've always worked so hard to avoid. Something terrible happening to a source of mine. I can't help but feel responsible. And *scared*. For her. For her kids.

I don't know what the hell to say. I finally settle on the last words I heard *her* say. "We'll find them." But the words ring hollow, and she hears it.

Silence descends. She stares down at the black screen of her phone, unblinking.

There's got to be *something* I can say. But everything that comes to mind sounds like a damn lie.

"We need to figure out who has them," she finally says. She looks up at me. "Your source knows."

"My source won't say a thing."

"These people have my children!"

Now she looks wild. Unstable.

I turn toward my laptop. "I'll try again."

I open up ClandestineTips and type a new message:

Please tell me who's behind this.

The response comes a moment later:

Publish what I gave you.

"What?" Jill asks, looking at the screen.

"He wants me to publish the story."

"You promised me." She looks terrified.

"I know. That's why I haven't. But I'm afraid he's not going to give me more until I do."

"If you *do*, they'll hurt the kids."

If they haven't already, I think. But I say nothing. I'm pretty sure by the look on her face she hears my unspoken thought. I turn back to the keyboard, type again:

I can't publish without knowing who you are. I need to confirm your access.

It's not entirely the truth. I could publish a story with what Jill told me. But my source doesn't know that. I can't publish anything *he's* given me until I know who he is.

I don't have any proof right now it's the U.S. I have Beau's speculation, and Jeremy's speculation. And I have some anonymous tipster confirming it. But without knowing who this source is, or his access, I can't publish something that sensational. A new message appears:

I'm an anonymous source. You use them all the time.

I type back:

They're anonymous in print, but I know who they are. Our standards require it.

"Why does he want you to publish?" Jill asks.

"I don't know."

I stare at the screen and wait for a reply. There's nothing.

"See if he'll just give you the name," Jill says. I can hear the desperation in her voice. "I don't care if you publish, as long as I know who has my kids."

I lift my fingers to the keyboard:

Or just tell me who's behind this. I'll confirm it and then I'll publish.

Jill's pacing the length of the loft now. Wringing her hands.

A new message appears:

I can't do that.

I type back:

I protect my sources.

I watch the screen. Out of the corner of my eye I see Jill. Pacing faster now. "What's he saying?" she asks.

"Nothing yet."

I continue to watch the screen.

Finally, a reply:

I'm a Russian intelligence operative.

"He's Russian intel," I say to Jill.

Jill was right. A foreign intelligence officer.

If I can confirm he is who he says he is, I have my story.

She comes over, stands behind me. Reads my screen.

I type a response:

Can you prove it?

"No wonder he's skittish," Jill says.

That's an understatement. If Russia finds out what he's doing, he's toast. And if our government thinks a Russian spy is skulking around, jail it is. Jail, and no swaps.

A message appears. A *picture*. It's a snapshot of the front of an employee badge. Bright blue background, a yellow emblem at the top—three crowns, two feathered wings, crossed swords. Cyrillic writing. And a passport-size photograph in the middle—completely covered with several overlapping strips of masking tape.

"SVR," Jill says.

"Is it real?"

"Looks to be. But for all I know, it's available on Google."

That's true. There's nothing to indicate my source actually took this picture. I lift my fingers to the keyboard.

I need proof it's you.

I wait for a response. Nothing. Maybe I pushed too hard—

Another picture. Same badge, slightly different angle. And it's lying on top of yesterday's *Washington Post*.

"It's legit," I say. My *source* is legit. Adrenaline is coursing through me.

"It doesn't *matter*," Jill says, moving away from the screen, sitting back down. "He needs to tell us who's behind this." There's desperation in her voice.

Another message arrives.

Now do you believe me?

Yes, I type back. *But we need to know who's behind this. Publish.*

"Dammit," Jill says.

I try to figure out what to say next. Lift my fingers to the keys—

Another message appears.

You waited too long as it is. You're too late.

I stare at the screen and try hard not to react. It's damn near impossible. I can feel Jill's eyes on me, from across the table.

"What it is?" Jill asks.

Too late because the kids were already nabbed? It couldn't be that they're dead, could it? The thought fills me with fear.

I don't reply. Instead, I type:

What do you mean?

Jill pushes back from the table, her chair scraping the floor.

She comes up behind me again. My instinct is to close the screen, because I don't want her to see what I'm terrified the source is about to write—

A message appears:

Something happened. And I'm afraid it's just the beginning.

CHAPTER TWENTY-FIVE

Alex

"Wat happened?" Jill says, her voice panicked. "Is he talking about my kids?"

"I don't know." My fingers find the keyboard:

What happened?

My gut feeling is that the source isn't talking about Jill's kids. But who the hell knows. I stare at the screen and wait for a reply.

Seconds pass in utter silence.

Finally, a message appears:

An accident.

"Oh my God," Jill says. "What happened to them?"

My stomach is starting to turn. *Is* the source talking about her kids?

What kind of accident? I type. *Who was involved?*

The loft is utterly quiet. We both stare at the screen.

"Why isn't he responding?" Jill says. It's gut-wrenching to hear her voice.

At the Farm.

"What's he talking about?" I say. "What happened?"

"No idea." Jill looks relieved.

I'm *confused.*

What happened at the Farm? I type.

That message has left me completely unsettled.

Something happened. And I'm afraid it's just the beginning. Look into it. Logging off now.

"No, no, no," Jill pleads. She leans forward toward the screen like she can physically restrain the source. "We have to know who has them."

I feel for her. I do. We didn't get anything to lead us to her kids. But we *did* get a lead.

I open a browser window. Google "the Farm." Then "the Farm CIA." Looking for any recent news. Anything about an accident.

Skim the articles. Just the basics: covert training facility, shrouded in secrecy. No news, though. Nothing noteworthy that's happened recently—

Or at least nothing that's made it into the public domain.

"Can you check the chat again?" Jill pleads. I pull up ClandestineTips. No answer. I leave the window up. Reach for my phone and dial CIA Public Affairs. Kassie answers.

"It's Alex Charles at the *Post,*" I say.

"Hello, Alex."

"I'm wondering if you can comment on an accident at the Farm."

A beat of silence. Then, "We cannot comment on any location popularly referred to as 'the Farm,' nor the existence or lack thereof of any specific training facilities."

Of course she can't. She actually can't ever seem to say a damn thing—

"As for an *accident,* a statement will be forthcoming."

So there *was* an accident.

"Come on, Kassie. Can you give me just a little right now?"

"An official statement will be released soon." She sounds resolute. "Is that all, Alex?"

I'm not going to get the information I want. But I did get something.

Something happened.

"That's all," I say. I disconnect, and then look back at the laptop screen. Jill is pacing the length of the loft, her phone tight in one fist. She looks half crazed.

I scroll up through the chat with the source. Reread the conversation. Skim it, anyway.

Something happened.

You're too late.

"What are we going to do?" Jill says.

I don't know what we're going to do. Feels like we've hit another dead end. At least until Public Affairs releases that statement. And who the hell knows when that will be.

I keep scrolling. All the way back up to the pictures of the ID badges—

And then I have an idea.

CHAPTER TWENTY-SIX

Jill

Fourteen minutes later, Alex has a location for her source.

I know it's fourteen because I've been checking my phone constantly, desperate for any news from Drew. There's nothing new on the kids. Nothing I can do, because I'm *here,* but in order to get *there* I'd have to be in the car for nine hours, or unreachable in the air for two.

But at least this—the location—is something.

A co-worker of Alex's, a man named Damian, used the attachments the source sent to trace the IP address. Apparently it was a loophole in the anonymous system: it was only anonymous until there was an attachment.

The messages originated at the Fenwick-Coats Inn, a small, historic hotel just a few blocks from the White House. Alex and I made a beeline for my car, and then for the hotel.

I park two blocks away, on the street, just in front of a restaurant advertising fish and chips. There was a swarm of valets out front when we drove past, jackets and white gloves, ready to assist with check-in and luggage. Our best bet is to avoid them entirely.

The hotel is stately, a white-columned exterior, large circular drive. There's a small park across the street, neat green grass and perfectly manicured landscaping. Alex and I stop there. We sit on a bench facing the hotel entrance and watch the valets.

"Should I just go in?" Alex asks.

I don't answer. I go through the motions in my mind, the ones I know from my days as a case officer. Formulate a plan. Extract information—

"I'm going in." I say it decisively. I can see the surprise on her face. But there's no question in my mind. This needs to be me. I was trained for this, I've *done* this, albeit a long time ago.

And most important, it's my kids on the line. I'm not going to rely on anyone else right now. I need to do this myself.

"How are you going to do this?" Alex asks.

"I don't know." An honest answer. I *don't* know. And I wish I did, because for an operation like this, I should have a plan. But there's no time to come up with a plan. I need to figure it out on the fly. And that's exactly what I'm going to do. I get to my feet.

"Stay here," I say. "Watch your phone."

"Got it."

When there's a break in traffic, I walk across the street. Across the circular drive, straight to the automatic doors. I nod to the valets as I pass, never breaking stride, like I belong here, like I've walked in and out of this front entrance dozens of times.

"Welcome back, ma'am," one of them says.

First rule of blending in: pretend like you belong.

I'm through the automatic sliding doors now, met with a blast of cool air. The lobby is ornate and dimly lit—lots of reds and golds and rich mahoganies, a huge crystal chandelier above.

There's an elevator and stairwell off to the left, a check-in desk ahead, up three marble steps. One man is behind the desk, in a suit, assisting a guest with a small rolling suitcase by his side. The clerk looks stern, no nonsense, and as exclusive as this hotel is, there's no way he's going to give me names, not with what little I'd be able to tell him.

There's a small lobby bar up the same steps, off to the right. I walk up the steps, angle as close to the desk as I can, commit everything to memory. Behind the desk there's an old-fashioned-looking cubby system, slots for each room, two dozen in total, newspapers sitting in about two-thirds of them, a few with sheets of paper on top. Final bills, maybe. A filing system, filled with items destined for each occupied room.

The bar's just in front of me now. It's cozy, and dark. There's a single bartender behind the counter, in a crisp white button-down, drying a glass with a towel. No patrons at the bar. I keep scanning, all the while walking like I know exactly where I'm going, what I'm doing—

Restrooms. Bingo. I head for those, without pausing, like I was headed there all along. Ladies' room. I push the door open, step inside. It's empty, and I can finally exhale. I feel almost shaky. It's been ages since I've done anything like this. I step into a stall, close and lock the door, take a deep breath.

Twenty-four rooms. How am I supposed to find out which one holds our source?

Think, Jill.

I open my bag, look at what I have. The gun. My wallet. My phone. A tube of lip gloss. A pen, a few stray crayons, a small plastic dinosaur, a notebook. That now-familiar feeling of terror and helplessness bubbles up inside me at the sight of the kids' things.

My gaze settles on the notebook. I pull it out. It's small and spiral-bound, light blue. Owen likes to doodle in it. I open it, tear out the pages with crayon scribbles, stuff them back into my bag. Now it's an *empty* notebook. I reach for my pen, open the notebook to the first page, and write.

Cyrillic letters. I know a handful of words in Russian. *Da* and *dasvidaniya* and things like that. The alphabet, too. I took an introductory Russian course at the Agency, years ago. We started with the alphabet, had it drilled into us. Our instructor, Oleg, insisted we know it like the back of our hands before moving on to anything else. I still remember most of it.

I write random letters in random groupings, but to anyone unfamiliar with the language, it should look like coherent sentences. I write a few sentences on the first page, a few on the second, same with the next few pages. Then I drop the pen into my bag, clutch the notebook, make my way out of the bathroom, back to the front desk.

"Can I help you?" the unpleasant-looking man in the suit asks. His nametag reads THOMAS WORTHINGTON.

I lay the notebook down on the counter. "I found this in the ladies' room. I think it must belong to a guest. A *Russian* guest, by the looks of it." I flip it open to the first page.

He glances down at the page, then back at me. "I know just the guest."

Perfect.

"Thank you, madam." He takes the notebook, flips it closed, lays it down in front of him, behind the counter, out of my reach.

That's not what's supposed to happen. He's supposed to place it in one of those cubbies, at the least.

"Anything else I can help you with?"

I can't just stand here. "No. That's all."

"Have a nice day, madam."

I need to leave. I force myself to turn away from the desk.

Panic begins creeping through me. This was supposed to work. If this didn't work, what else am I supposed to do? Any other attempt to identify the Russian guest and it'll be obvious what I'm trying to do.

I glance back at the desk. Thomas hasn't moved. He's still looking at his computer screen.

I need to figure out something else to do.

I stop in front of a large painting on the wall—a man on a horse, Revolutionary War–type dress. There's a placard on the wall beside it, with a long description. I pretend to read, my mind churning.

Out of the corner of my eye I see Thomas reach for the corded phone, lift the receiver to his ear. He presses a single button. Must be dialing a room—

"Mrs. Ivanova?" he says. "I believe we have an item of yours at the front desk. Would you like to retrieve it? Or shall I send up a valet?"

A pause. I hold my breath.

"Very well, then," he says. "It will be right here when you arrive."

My heart's pounding. I don't turn around, force myself to walk to the next painting on the wall. This one's of a woman in a hoop skirt dress, holding a parasol. I stand back and pretend to admire it for what seems like an appropriate length of time. Then I turn.

There's an antique upholstered bench against a nearby wall. Angled toward the center of the room, but if I sit on one side, I should be able to see the front desk beyond the columns in the center of the room. I walk over, take a seat, pull out my phone. Hold it between myself and the front desk, pull up my texts, the chain with Alex.

Mrs. Ivanova, I type.

MRS? comes the reply.

Stand by.

The elevator dings. The doors open, and a woman steps out. She's in her sixties, probably, fair hair, dressed like she's just come from the office—slacks, a blouse, a scarf, all understated. She walks confidently through the lobby, toward the desk—

I open the camera app on my phone, lift the screen just slightly, tap the button. A series of pictures, silent. She never looks over.

Her back is to me now. She's talking to Thomas. He lays the notebook down in front of her. She shakes her head, and they have a quick conversation. Thank God she doesn't open it, doesn't see the nonsense words, or surely she'd grow suspicious—

She turns away from the desk, toward the lobby, toward me, and I look down at my phone. Pretend to be texting. I can feel her coming closer. I watch her in my peripheral vision—

She walks past me, toward the front door. I pull up the text chain again, tap out a quick message, attach one of the pictures I just snapped.

She's coming your way. Don't let her out of your sight.

CHAPTER TWENTY-SEVEN

Alex

The picture Jill sends shows an older woman with fair hair, dressed smartly. That's my source. She isn't what I expected. Not at all.

She's coming your way.

I lower the phone and watch the front door of the hotel. The sliding doors open—there she is. Nondescript, really. Blends in. A perfect spy.

She steps outside, takes a right. Walks at a moderate pace. There's nothing about her that would attract attention.

I stand up from the bench, start walking in the same direction. Opposite side of the street, a handful of paces behind. She doesn't turn. Doesn't seem particularly aware of her surroundings.

I reach for my phone, tap out a text to Jill. *She headed right. I'm following.*

The response comes an instant later. *I see her. I'm on it.*

Of course she is. She's a spy, too. Or she *was.* She knows how to do this. Hell, she ID'd my source in no time at all. Even got a name. I have no idea how she did it.

I slow my pace a bit as Jill comes into view on the opposite side of the street. Better to let her get close anyway. My source might know what I look like. She reached out to me, after all. Last thing I want to do is spook her.

Past the fish and chips restaurant now. Past Jill's car. My source is still walking at an even pace. Still hasn't looked back. And Jill's still behind her.

I reach for my phone. Scroll as I walk, until I find the name I need.

"Hana," I say when she answers. "It's Alex."

"Alex. What's up?"

"I need your help." It's true. If anyone can help me get to the bottom of this, it's her. A senior counterintelligence analyst.

"And I've told you what you need to do to *get* my help."

I slow my pace. Jill's still clearly in my view. As long as I keep her in sight, I'm good.

"One of the CIA's best sources is a fake," I say.

In the distance I hear a car horn. There's silence on Hana's end of the line. "Who?" she finally says.

"You help me, I tell you."

"How do you know this?"

"A source."

"Who's your source?"

"A Russian intelligence officer."

"Your source is a Russian intelligence officer?" She sounds like she's salivating.

"This is going to be a big story, Hana," I say, stating the obvious. "Biggest damn story of your career."

There's a pause, and then: "What do you need from me?"

"I need you to verify my source's access. Tell me everything you know about this person."

She doesn't answer right away. "And then you'll give me the name of the CIA source?"

"I'll give it to you before it becomes public."

I wait for her to object. She doesn't.

"And one more thing. You can't breathe a word of this to any-one. Especially at the CIA."

"It's an inside job?"

"Looks that way."

She exhales audibly.

"I told you, it's a big story."

I focus on Jill's back, my eyes shifting every so often to the source, farther ahead.

"You've got yourself a deal," Hana says.

I give her the information I have—SVR, female, surname Iva-nova, in the U.S. right now, staying at the Fenwick-Coats—and she promises to call when she has something.

No sooner have I ended the call than I realize I should have asked about the accident at the Farm. I almost call back, but stop myself. Better she focuses on my source. I'll try Beau.

I glance down at the phone as I walk, find his name. Touch the number labeled "Work" and press send.

"Beau, I need a favor," I say when he picks up.

He sighs.

"There was an accident at the Farm. I need to know more about it."

I've lost sight of my source, but Jill is still firmly in my sights.

"Did you get this from your source?" he asks.

I don't answer right away, and I know he takes my lack of re-sponse as confirmation.

"Who is this source, Alex?"

"She's a Russian intelligence officer."

"*What?*"

"She knows what she's talking about."

"She?"

"She."

"I want to talk to her," he says.

I cringe. I had a feeling that was coming. When has he ever *not* gone after my sources? "I'll see if she's willing to talk to you. *After* this is all over and done with."

"Alex, I—"

But I don't hear the rest of the sentence. I abruptly end the call. Because Jill's just broken into a run.

CHAPTER TWENTY-EIGHT

Jill

She knows I'm on her tail.

That's the only explanation for why she just darted right down a side street. I'm running to catch up, to reach the street, my feet pounding the pavement, my hand gripping tight to the purse slung on my shoulder as I swerve around a couple of teenagers, a woman in a suit.

I round the corner—

I don't see her. I scan the length of the street, one filled with boutique stores, coffee shops, and cafés, offices above. There's a relatively small number of people milling about, both sides of the street, heading to and fro, but there's no sign of her, none whatsoever.

It's like she just disappeared.

I start walking down the street, peering into store windows, but I know it's useless. She could be anywhere. She probably ducked into one, has already slipped out a rear door. I don't know which side of the street she picked.

How did she know I was behind her? She never turned around, not once. Did she catch my reflection in a window somewhere?

However she did it, she's good. She knows what she's doing.

Footsteps, behind me. I turn, and it's Alex, running to catch up, breathing hard. "Where'd she go?" she asks.

"I don't know." The words fill me with desperation. This is the only lead I have to my kids. And I've just lost her.

A door opens behind us, a bell sweetly dinging inside. An ice cream store. A man walks out, holding tight to two kids' hands, a boy and a girl, each clutching an ice cream cone, big grins on their faces.

The sight makes me feel even more desperate.

"You want to take one side of the street and I'll take the other?" Alex asks. She crosses the street without waiting for an answer, heads straight for the first shop, a clothing boutique.

I look down the street again. So many stores. There's no point. The source knew she had a tail and she shook it. She's a professional. We're not going to find her—

Vibration, from my purse. Incoming call. I pull out my phone, and there's a single word on the screen.

Unknown.

It's *them*, isn't it?

I press the green button instantly. "Hello?"

"Hello, Jill."

That voice, that deep robotic voice.

"Where are my children?"

"With us."

"Are they okay?"

There's no response, and my heart seizes. They *have* to be okay. I'd know if my kids were dead. I'd feel it. Some piece of me would die, too, wouldn't it?

"For now."

I grip the phone tightly. As terrified as I was when Owen was taken as a baby, this is worse. They're four and three. Old enough to know what's going on. What are they thinking? How are they being treated?

What if they don't listen, and these people hurt them?

"What do you want?"

"*We wanted you to stay quiet, and you didn't.*"

My heart is pounding. They're not saying they're going to hurt the kids, are they?

"*Do you remember what we said would happen if you talked?*"

Oh my God. They *are* saying they'll hurt the kids. "Please," I beg, because I don't know what else to say. "Please don't hurt them."

"*Here's the good news, Jill. The information hasn't spread. Right now your journalist friend is the only one who knows.*"

I take a shallow breath and glance at the clothing boutique, the last place I saw Alex. She's in there now, or she's moved on to the next store.

"*There's still time to fix this.*"

"How?"

"*How do you think, Jill?*"

And then the voice is gone, disconnected, a short string of beeps in its place.

I lower the phone. I feel like I've been punched in the gut.

Alex steps out from the café beside the boutique. Catches sight of me, heads my way. "This is pointless, isn't it?"

I nod. That voice is still ringing in my head.

How do you think, Jill?

"Did she see you?" Alex asks.

"She must have." Must have caught my reflection. She must always be looking over her shoulder, without *actually* looking over her shoulder.

"What now?"

I open up my purse to drop my phone back inside, and my gaze lands on the gun.

There's still time to fix this.

"Jill?"

I'm not actually considering this, am I?

I close the purse tightly. "Come on." I start walking, back in the direction from which we came.

"Where are we going?" Alex asks.

I'd be willing to bet she's headed north, toward the Russian embassy. We could try to intercept her before she arrives, but she's got a jump on us, probably already in a cab, and even if we beat her there, if she sees us at one entrance she'll just make her way to another, won't she?

It would be futile. We'd always be one step behind. And we need to be one step *ahead.*

"Back to the hotel," I say.

"You think she'll head back?"

"No," I say. "That's why we're going."

We walk in silence, because I need to think. Need to come up with a plan. I might know where we're going, but I don't know what we're going to do when we get there.

We're nearly back to the Fenwick-Coats when Alex's phone rings. She pulls it from her back pocket and looks at the screen. "It's Hana. My CIA contact. I've got to get this."

She holds the phone to her ear as we walk. "Hello?"

She listens to something, but I can't hear what it is.

"Great," she says, and then after another pause, "I need more. Everything you have on her. Background, cases, family, *everything.*"

I lead the way back to the park across from the hotel. There's an older man with a cane sitting on the bench now, so I come to a stop under some big shade trees. No one else is around.

"Thanks," Alex says into the phone, and then lowers it, returns it to her back pocket.

"Source is SVR all right," she says, facing me. "CIA has a file on her. Natalia Ivanova."

"What else?"

"She works counterintelligence. She's in the U.S. for a short trip. Attending a conference on emerging technologies."

Is she picking up information that would be useful to Russian intelligence? Attempting to recruit sources?

Does it matter?

"Hana's going to dig deeper. Get me more."

"Good."

My brain is churning. We have a name now, first and last.

I look across the street at the Fenwick-Coats, the gaggle of valets. An idea is beginning to form.

Twenty-four rooms, two floors . . .

I turn back to Alex. "You're going in this time. Be confident. Act like you belong, and no one will question you."

She glances at the hotel. "I can try."

"You saw me do it. It's easy."

"For *you* it was easy."

"Just be confident."

I picture the interior of the hotel in my mind. It's a small place, which will work in our favor. "When you enter, you'll see the check-in desk straight ahead, up three steps. You're going to veer off to the left before you get there. There's a hallway that leads to the rooms."

"Okay."

"What I need you to do is map the first floor. Look for every room with a Do Not Disturb sign. One of those is hers."

I've never met a spy who wants housekeeping. Just doesn't happen. If there's one thing I'm sure about, it's that this woman doesn't want anyone entering her room when she's not there.

"I'll do the same on the second floor," I say. "Text me and tell me what you find."

"Will do."

I look across the street again. There's a red coupe in the circular drive, blocking my view of the front door. "You go first, okay?"

Seems better for us to stay apart.

She crosses the street just as the red coupe pulls out of the drive. She walks to the front door, head held high—

One of the valets steps in front of her, blocking the door.

They're talking. He's not moving out of her way—

When there's a break in traffic, I dart across the street.

"Welcome back, ma'am," says one of the valets, but I don't even see him. My eyes are on Alex and the man in front of her.

"I'll walk you up to the front desk," he's saying, his tone unfriendly, "so you can ask for a replacement key."

"That won't be necessary," I say. "I have mine, and she's with me."

I reach for her arm and walk around the valet, into the cool air of the lobby.

He doesn't follow. Doesn't say a word.

"He was demanding to see my key," Alex says, once the doors have closed behind us.

"Weird. He didn't ask to see mine."

"It's not actually that weird," she says. She looks angry.

"I'm not sure I follow."

"Look at us, Jill. In his mind I don't belong here. All that man saw was my skin color."

That wasn't something I even considered when I asked her to walk in. She had, though. She knew she'd have a more difficult time than I did. I should have known, too.

"Come on," she says. "Let's go."

Thomas Worthington is still at the front desk. His head's down, and he doesn't notice us. We veer left and separate wordlessly. Alex walks down the hall and I head toward the door to the stairwell, just beside the elevator. Push it open, climb the stairs two at a time to the second floor, exit out into a crimson-colored hallway.

Rooms are to the left and right, six in each direction. The doors are painted black, and there are antique-looking plates mounted beside them, each with a room number. There's a housekeeping cart in the middle of the hall to the right.

I head left first. There are Do Not Disturb signs hung on three door handles, fancy little metal plates hung with silver chains. To the right of the stairs, past the housekeeping cart, past a room that's open, in the midst of being cleaned, there's one with a sign. All the way at the far end of the hall.

My phone buzzes in my bag, just as I'm turning around. I pull it out.

Text from Alex. *Two.*

Much better. I wonder if the first floor is largely vacant.

Left or right of elevator? I reply.

Both left.

Even better.

Stand outside. Listen for a ring.

I'm back in the center of the hallway now, near the door to the stairwell, and the elevator. I use the browser on my phone to google the Fenwick-Coats, find the main phone number, and place the call.

It rings once. Twice—

"Good afternoon. You've reached the Fenwick-Coats Inn," comes Thomas's voice in my ear. "How may I assist you today?"

I speak with the hint of a Southern accent, a skill I haven't used in years. "I'm trying to reach a friend of mine. Natalia Ivanova. Could you please connect me to her room?" I'm walking as I'm talking, back down to the left of the elevator, to the cluster of three rooms with Do Not Disturb signs.

"Certainly."

There's a brief pause, a click, and then the sound of ringing. I pull the phone away from my ear and listen to the rooms around me.

Silence.

I start walking quickly back toward the elevator, but the ringing cuts out, and the call disconnects.

Anything? I text Alex.

Nothing.

Keeping listening.

I dial the front desk again, hear the same greeting. "Well, hello again," I say, "I seem to have been disconnected. Would you mind trying Natalia Ivanova's room again?"

"She may have stepped out," Thomas says.

"Maybe. Could you be a dear and connect me once more?" I make my way down the other side of the hall, past the housekeeping cart, loaded with sheets and towels and toiletries. Inside the open room, there's a figure inside, her back to me, making one of the queen-size beds.

"Yes ma'am."

There's that click again, and then a ring—

There's a ring on the other side of that door, the one at the end of the hall, the one with the Do Not Disturb sign. I wait for another ring just to be sure. I hear it through the phone, and through the door, almost in unison.

Bingo. We found the source's room. The plate beside it reads 212.

I end the call, drop the phone back into my purse. Then I look at the door. Solid, tightly closed, outfitted with an electronic key card reader.

Down the hall I hear a noise, like the sound of something being dropped, maybe a bucket against a hard floor—

I head toward the sound, the open door. There's a woman inside, in a housekeeping uniform. She's short with close-cropped dark hair, a spray bottle in hand.

"Excuse me," I say from the hall.

She looks up, meets my eye. Then walks over to me.

"Could I possibly have a couple of fresh towels? I didn't want to trouble you with housekeeping today, but could use some towels if you don't mind."

"Of course." She steps out into the hall, takes a stack of three thick folded white towels from the cart, hands them to me. "Would you like more?"

"This is perfect," I say, taking them from her. "Thank you so much."

"Not a problem. Have a nice day, ma'am."

"You as well," I say. I head back toward Natalia's room. When I reach it, I turn. The hallway's empty. I count to five in my mind, then walk down the hall again, back to the open room.

"Excuse me again," I say, hovering just outside the doorway. "This is embarrassing. I was in such a hurry to catch you, I left the room without my key."

The housekeeper smiles a tired smile. "Happens all the time." She walks out into the hall.

"I feel like such an idiot," I say, yammering away, filling the air with chatter. "I didn't want to trouble you, and now here I am asking you to stop what you're doing to help me."

"It's really not a problem, ma'am. Which room is yours?"

"The one down at the end, 212."

I wait for her to ask my name, to ask for some sort of identification. She reaches for a key card that's clipped on to her uniform, hanging by her side, holds it up to the reader. The lock disengages, and the light flashes green.

"Here you go," she says, pushing open the door, holding it open for me.

"Thank you so much," I say, walking past her into the darkened room. "Promise it won't happen again."

I flip the light switch, let the door close slowly behind me.

That was easier than I thought. I figured I'd have to do more bluffing, more pretending. As soon as I hear the automatic lock engage, I reach for my phone.

Room 212, I type to Alex. *I'm in. Come on up.*

CHAPTER TWENTY-NINE

Jill

It's quiet inside the room. Cold, too; the air-conditioning is set low. The switch by the door illuminated a desk light, but it's dim, and the room still feels dark. The curtains are tightly drawn.

It's a small suite, with a bedroom and bathroom off to the right, a living area to the left. I walk quietly into the room, glance into the darkened bathroom first. Toothbrush and toothpaste on the counter, a makeup bag, a hairbrush.

Bedroom next. A king-size bed, loosely made but clearly slept in. A dresser, empty on top, except for a lamp. A medium-size black rolling suitcase propped up on a luggage rack. Two bedside tables with lamps. A cellphone charger on one of them, and a framed photograph—

I walk closer. It's small, a four-by-six picture I think, in a silver frame. Two boys, around kindergarten age, give or take. One's blond and skinny, the other dark haired and solidly built. Different as can be, just like Owen and Mia.

They're outside in the sun, and their arms are around each other, heads close, big smiles on their faces. The kind of picture I treasure of my own kids, the ones I use as the background on my phone, or put in a frame on the mantel.

It's in color, but it's that sort of muted color that I recognize from pictures of my own childhood. And the way the boys are dressed, the hairstyles, it reminds me of the way my brothers looked in photos from the same era.

These boys are probably my age now. I'd be willing to bet these are Natalia's kids.

Strange that it's here, that she's brought such an old photo with her to a hotel, propped it up next to her bed—

My phone vibrates. I reach for it, pull it out of my bag. Incoming call, through Stronghold. *Drew.*

I answer, "What's the latest?" I'm almost afraid to hear what he's about to say, but desperate to hear it, at the same time.

"We have a lead."

A *lead*. Thank God. "What is it?"

"The hotel's CCTV. A man took the kids from the hotel room. He was carrying Mia, holding Owen's hand—" A sob escapes, a deep guttural sob. "He got into a car with them."

"Can the police track the car?"

"They did."

"And? Where did it go?"

"To an airport. A small private one."

An *airport*? Oh my God.

"Footage there shows them getting out of the car and into a plane."

They're alive. At least they're alive. If there's footage of them boarding a plane—

"They're working on figuring out where the plane went." His voice breaks.

"This is good news, Drew."

"It's not enough."

"No, but it's something," I say. As terrified as I am, I need to project some sort of calm. One of us needs to be strong right now.

"What are we going to do?"

I hate hearing him like this. Scared, hopeless. "You stay in touch with the police. I'm working on things on my end."

"Yeah?" The hope in his voice is unmistakable.

"Yeah." There's a light rap at the door. I start walking toward it. "I gotta go. Let's chat as soon as either of us hears something. Drew, I will find them."

Then I drop the phone back into my bag and look through the peephole. It's Alex. I open the door and she steps inside, closes it behind herself.

"How'd you get in?" she asks quietly, looking around the room.

"Housekeeping." I turn and head to the living room. I need to see what else is here.

There's a couch, the kind that's probably a pullout, with a coffee table in front of it, a television mounted on the wall. A desk against one wall, a rolling chair pushed in under it, a corded hotel phone on top, some papers beside it, held down with a paperweight.

I walk over to the desk. The paperweight is clear, with an inscription engraved on top. Cyrillic writing. Words I don't recognize.

I pull out my phone again, swipe until I reach the screen with my favorite translation app, the one I always suggest my students download. I pick up the paperweight and snap a picture of the inscription, wait for the translation—

"What does it say?" Alex asks, reaching for the papers underneath.

I wait for the words to appear on my screen. " 'What is right is not always easy, and what is easy is not always right.' "

"Deep," Alex says with a roll of her eyes.

I wish it were something else. Something clearer, something that gets me closer to finding my kids. My desperation is growing, and it's taking everything I've got, every ounce of my CIA training, to focus on the mission at hand.

"Look at this," Alex says, holding out a sheet of paper. I take it from her. It's a medical record from the Hart-Schofield Memorial Hospital. Vitals, lab work. The patient name is listed as *Redacted,* followed by an ID number.

"Right here," Alex says, looking up from the paper she's reading, pointing to a spot about three-quarters of the way down on the page in front of me.

Clinical Diagnosis: Acute Anthrax Poisoning.

"Oh my God," I murmur.

"It's on this one, too," she says, holding up the sheet of paper she was just reading.

I take that one from her, too. Another redacted patient name, an ID number just one off sequentially from the last.

Two people dead from anthrax.

Was this the accident Natalia mentioned? Was there an *anthrax* attack at the Farm? How could—

A sound, at the entrance to the room.

The scrape of a key card, the click of a lock disengaging—

I look up, my heart beginning to pound—

And Natalia Ivanova opens the door.

CHAPTER THIRTY

Alex

Natalia locks eyes with me. She's frozen in the doorway. Her gaze shifts to Jill, holds there. Then she steps forward, lets the door close behind her. Reaches for the deadbolt, locks it, all the while looking directly at us.

Shit is an understatement.

I should have turned the deadbolt. But Jill was so sure she wouldn't come back. I was, too. Certainly not so soon.

"Alex Charles," she says. "You found me."

She has the hint of an accent, but just barely.

And she looks calm. Too calm.

The fact that she walked in, locked the door—it's wrong. She should have left. Escaped. Turned us in.

Instead, she entered. Locked herself in a room with us.

Why?

This is dangerous.

It's not like I've never had a dangerous source meet before. I've had tons. Especially abroad. The kinds of sources Beau then went on to recruit—militants, opposition leaders, members of shadow governments.

But this is different.

She wanted to remain anonymous. She didn't *want* to meet. And we just broke into her hotel room.

She looks at Jill, then down at the papers in Jill's hands. "And you're the one who was following me. What are you, CIA? FBI?"

"Neither," Jill says, laying the papers carefully back on the table.

Natalia scoffs.

"Look, we need to know who's behind this," Jill says.

She ignores Jill and focuses on me again. "I made a mistake coming to you."

The words sound bitter. And they sting. I've always prided myself on protecting my sources. I've never had anyone regret coming to me. Never had a source targeted, either, until Jill's kids were nabbed. Everything's falling apart.

"I was trying to do the right thing," she says, her gaze still locked on me. "I thought you'd find the truth."

"I was looking for it," I say. I was. I was trying my damn best to get to the bottom of this.

"You got the *government* involved." Her eyes flash toward Jill. "I did *not* want the government involved."

"I'm not the government," Jill says. "I'm here because they have my kids."

Natalia focuses on Jill. She looks impassive. She's hard to read. Well, she's a spy, isn't she?

"Owen's four. Mia's three," Jill says. "They're my whole life."

Natalia is still wearing that same stone-faced look, but I swear right now I see a flicker of emotion.

"I'm just trying to find my kids."

Natalia's lips are set in a thin line.

"You said this was coming from within the CIA," Jill says.

"Yes."

"I need names."

"What you need to do is publish this story," she says, turning toward me.

"I can't," I say. "Not without—"

"You said you needed to know who I am. What my access is." She throws up her arms. "You *know* now."

She's right.

"Uphold your end of the bargain," she says. "Publish this story."

"*Why?*"

"Because it'll put an end to this."

"To *what?*"

Her gaze shifts to the papers on the desk. The ones from the hospital. "Did you see those?"

She already knows I did, so I nod. I saw them. I just don't know what the hell they mean.

I wait for her to say something else, but she's silent.

"Was that the accident?" I ask. "The one at the Farm?"

"What do you think?"

I think it was. Again, I just don't have a damn clue what it means.

"Who was behind it?" Jill asks.

Natalia turns toward her. "Who do you think?"

"If the reporting's to be believed, Syria."

"And *is* the reporting to be believed?" Natalia asks.

"You've been pretty clear that the answer's no," Jill says.

Natalia is silent. Expressionless.

"If the U.S. is making up the intel," I say, "is it *our* anthrax?"

Natalia faces me. "Yes."

I'm stunned. I wasn't expecting a straight answer. "But that's . . . impossible."

It can't be ours. We destroyed our stockpiles of anthrax ages ago. If we do have any, it's in a lab somewhere. For researching antidotes, or something like that. We don't use anthrax as a *weapon.*

"You don't *want* to find the truth, do you?" she asks.

Of course I do. But it makes no sense—

Or does it?

We can't go to war over unverified intel. Over a source *saying* Syria has a weaponized strain of anthrax.

We need proof.

"You need to leave," she says. "Both of you."

There's an awkward pause. No one moves, no one speaks.

"Natalia, do you have kids?" Jill asks.

"That matters why?"

"You do, don't you? Those boys in the picture." She nods toward the bedroom.

Natalia's jawline tightens.

"Can you try to imagine what it would be like if they were taken from you?"

There's a beat of silence, of hesitation, before she answers. "I suppose I would do absolutely *anything* to be reunited with them."

"Please, I'm begging you. Tell me who's behind this."

She gives her head a firm shake.

"I need to know," Jill says.

"I'm not giving you a name."

"My children's lives are on the line."

"There's far more than that on the line." She looks over at me. "If you don't publish this story, you'll have blood on your hands."

"Natalia—"

"You need to leave," she says again. More firmly this time.

"I'm not leaving," Jill says. "Not without names."

"Then *I'll* leave," Natalia says. She turns toward the door. "And I'll tell the concierge—"

Jill lunges forward, grabs her by the upper arm, spins her back around. Shoves her against the wall. "You're not leaving."

Now I see emotion on Natalia's face. Shock. And fear.

"You're a Russian spy, in the U.S.," Jill says. Her demeanor has completely changed. There's fire in her eyes. "Do you know what happens to Russian spies in the U.S.?"

"Jill, stop," I say. She can't shove my source. She can't threaten my source.

"You get locked away," she says to Natalia, ignoring me. "And you don't get out."

"I'm *aware*," Natalia says coolly.

"Stop," I say again.

"She knows who has my kids," Jill says.

"She's my source," I say.

"And these are my kids' lives we're talking about!"

"I'm not giving you a name," Natalia says.

Jill shoves her against the wall again, harder this time.

I move toward Jill, reach for her arm—

She draws a gun from her waistband, steps back—

And aims it directly at *me*.

CHAPTER THIRTY-ONE

Alex

"What are you *doing*?" I ask.

I'm staring down the barrel of a gun. And it's terrifying. With all the shit I've gotten myself into over the years, I've never had a gun pointed at me.

"This is what they told me to do, you know," Jill says. "They told me to kill you."

What? "Why?"

"To prevent the story from getting out. To save my kids—"

"You can't really believe that."

Her expression falters, just the slightest bit.

"Don't do this," I say. Because I know she'd do damn near anything to get her kids back.

She keeps the gun trained on me. I look from the barrel to her face and back. She looks wild.

Oh my God. What have I gotten myself into? "Jill—"

"Of course I'm not going to do that," she says. "But you"— she swings the gun toward Natalia—"you're a different story. You know who has my kids."

Natalia doesn't move. Doesn't speak. And I don't see any of the fear I felt. Hell, I'm *shaking*.

"Tell me who has them."

Natalia stays silent.

"You think I won't do this? Think again." Jill takes a step closer. The barrel of the gun is level with Natalia's chest. And *close*. If Jill shoots, she's not going to miss.

"*Never* underestimate what a mother will do for her children," Jill says.

"Oh, I don't," Natalia says. She's still too calm.

"Give me a name."

"I have no intention of helping your country—"

"Give me a *name*."

"I'd sooner have you kill me."

What?

"What's the alternative?" she says. "You turn me in? The government makes some bogus claim about how I'm stealing secrets? I'm not about to spend the rest of my life in prison."

Jill's fury reaches a boiling point. I can't blame her, really. Natalia *knows*.

The two of them stare at each other. I can see Jill's finger start to curl around the trigger—

"Jill, look at what you're doing," I say.

She doesn't turn toward me. Her finger doesn't loosen on the trigger. No one even breathes.

The gun shakes ever so slightly—

And then it drops to her side.

CHAPTER THIRTY-TWO

Jill

I can't do it.

I look at the woman in front of me, this person who has the information I so desperately need, the one who holds the key to finding my children, who's staying silent. I hate her. I hate her so much I want to kill her.

But I won't.

Killing her won't help me find Owen and Mia.

It would be revenge, nothing more.

I tuck the gun back into my waistband.

This is the end, isn't it? The best hope I have of finding my children, now quashed.

"You contacted me because you wanted to do what's right," Alex says to Natalia. I almost forgot she was there. "Because you had a moral obligation."

"Are you going to lecture me on morality right after your friend almost kills me?"

Alex seems to be at a loss for words.

"Come on," I say to her. "Let's go."

I want to get out of here, away from that woman. To call Drew, because it really does seem hopeless at this point.

I walk to the door—

"You're asking me to turn on my country," Natalia says.

I swing around. "No. I'm *begging* you to do the right thing."

I look at her a moment longer, but she doesn't say a word, and I'm not in the mood to be toyed with. I unlock the deadbolt, reach for the handle—

"I'm not the enemy, you know."

I go still. I want to hear what she has to say, but I don't want to give her the satisfaction of my attention when it's clear she's not going to give me the information I need.

"*I* reached out," she says. "To Alex. I volunteered information. I didn't have to do that."

I know what she's saying is true. But it doesn't change the fact that she won't tell me what I need to know.

"You Americans think all Russians are the enemy."

At this, I turn. "No we don't. *I* don't." But even as I say it, I wonder if it's true. It's ingrained in us, as intelligence officers, not to trust. *Russia* is not to be trusted.

But the Russians that give us information, our sources, as few and far between as they may be, obviously we trust *them*.

And she's right. She came to us. I wouldn't have this lead to chase if she hadn't reached out in the first place.

"The *Russians* aren't the enemy here," she says. "The Americans are."

"Why can't you tell me who's behind this?" I ask.

"I can't explain why. But I just can't."

I remember what she said a few minutes ago. *You're asking me to turn on my country.* "You think you'd be betraying your country—"

"I wouldn't *just* be betraying my country. I'd be betraying my *family*. That's a line I can't cross."

"What about *mine*?" I don't know what her family has to do with this, and frankly right now I don't care. I care about *my* family. My kids.

"I feel for you. I do. But this is a bridge too far."

I think of that paperweight on the desk. *What is right is not always easy, and what is easy is not always right.* "It would be the right thing to do."

She stares off into the bedroom. At the picture on the bedside table? "If I do this, there's no turning back."

She's considering it, isn't she? "Please, Natalia."

The room is absolutely silent. She's still staring at that picture.

"The two people who died at the Farm. They were involved."

She's talking. She's giving us *something*.

What does that mean? That it *was* our anthrax, that they were moving it, handling it, and there was a mishap?

"They changed their minds, wanted out. Another person . . . he didn't want that to happen."

"Who's the other person?"

"I can't give you that name."

"Who are the two?" Alex asks. "The ones who died?"

"I've said too much already. I just wanted you to find the truth."

"We *will* find the truth. Eventually. Just give us the information that will save two innocent kids."

"I can't."

Why *can't* she? I don't think I've ever felt more desperate than I do in this moment. *We're so close.*

Alex's phone buzzes. Out of the corner of my eye I see her reach for her phone, check the screen.

"Jill, you gotta see this," she says. She holds the phone out.

It's a CNN news alert. Breaking News.

CIA reports that two senior officers, Rosemarie Harris and Gladys Chen, died at a CIA facility in an unidentified incident.

Rosemarie Harris and Gladys Chen.

Harris and Chen. The heads of two directorates. Analysis, and Science and Technology. Two of the Gang of Three—

Natalia's voice rings in my head:

They were involved. . . .

They changed their minds, wanted out. Another person . . . he didn't want that to happen.

At that moment the pieces fall into place, and I know who has my kids.

"Come on," I say to Alex. "We need to go."

CHAPTER THIRTY-THREE

Alex

"It's Langston West," Jill says when we're inside the stairwell, heading down. "The third member of the Gang of Three."

I take the stairs as fast as I can, trying to keep up. Damn, she's fast.

Fast on the stairs, fast with connecting those dots. I still don't know how the hell she knows it's Langston West.

She's at the bottom now. She pushes open the door. Slows her pace as she walks into the lobby.

I'm close behind. I try to look as normal as possible. Try not to look at the people around me. Don't want to draw attention.

I'm still trying to process how she knows it's West. That it's the Gang of Three.

The sliding doors open and Jill walks through, out onto the sidewalk. I'm just behind—

And then it clicks. "Those op-eds," I say.

She doesn't answer. Doesn't look back. Heads right, down the sidewalk. I have to almost jog to keep up.

That's it, the op-eds. Penned by the Gang of Three. They complained about being hamstrung by a need to attribute everything to a specific source. About budget cuts—

"Exactly," Jill finally says. "The three of them thought they didn't have the intelligence they needed. So they *created their own.*"

A car whizzes past us on the street, and a horn sounds in the distance.

What she just said couldn't be more far-fetched—and, strangely, couldn't be more *obvious* at the same time.

They didn't think they could do their jobs, because they didn't have the intelligence they needed. The *specific* intelligence. It wasn't enough to make judgments. Analytic assessments. Policy-makers wanted cold, hard facts. Statements direct from the source.

But those didn't exist, because good sources are hard to find. And expensive to maintain.

So they *created* those sources.

"It probably started out innocently enough—" Jill says.

"You call that *innocent*?"

"I mean it was probably plugging gaps, holes in our report-ing," she says. "I'm not saying it's right. But I know how things work. If they had *almost* enough to take some sort of action, or reach some sort of conclusion, and they just needed a *little* more . . ."

"It's wrong." It's black and white. I can't believe she's trying to defend this.

Another car speeds past.

"Harris and Chen probably came to that conclusion, too," Jill says.

Natalia's words ring in my mind. *They changed their minds, wanted out.*

Maybe Jill's right. Maybe it *did* start out innocently enough—

"*West* was probably the one controlling Falcon's COVCOM," she says. "*West* started sending in that sensational reporting."

"What's the end goal? War in the Middle East?"

"I don't know. Maybe. *Something* Harris and Chen didn't agree with. And they saw what was happening, and they wanted out."

"But there's no way out at that point, is there?" Not when they've been doing something so illegal. So wrong. They were trapped.

And so was West.

"He had them killed," I say. It must have been the only way to protect what he had done. To continue what he was doing.

This is crazy as hell. Langston West is responsible for the deaths of two senior CIA officers. He's probably planning something even more nefarious. Marching us toward war, maybe. Fabricating untold amounts of intelligence.

"He knows where my kids are, Alex. I can feel it."

"Anything from Drew yet?"

"The police tracked them to an airport. They took off on a charter flight."

"Where to?"

"Waiting to find out. They're trying to track down the flight plans."

My phone vibrates in my back pocket, and I pull it out. Incoming call, through Stronghold.

"It's Beau," I say to Jill, still almost jogging to keep up with her pace. I answer the call. "Hi."

"That accident," he says. "Did you see the press release?"

"Saw the victims' names. Haven't seen anything else."

"Nothing else to see. Agency's being really tight-lipped. More so than usual. I don't know what happened."

"Okay. Listen, Beau, I need another favor. Remember when we talked about someone on the inside running a fake source?"

"Of course."

"Well, I know who it is."

"Who?"

"Langston West."

He laughs. He actually *laughs*. "I don't think so, Alex."

"It is. And it's worse than I thought. It's not just about planting fake intelligence."

There's a beat of silence on his end of the line. "Yeah?"

"Beau, he's behind something . . . terrible."

"Alex—"

"And two kids were kidnapped."

He scoffs. "Langston West didn't have anyone kidnapped."

Frustration is bubbling up inside me. I know it sounds crazy, but it's *not*. "Can you just figure out where he is right now?"

"Is this from your source?"

"Yes."

"I want to talk to her."

"I know."

"I'm doing an awful lot of favors for you . . ."

"I know." I'll owe him. I know that. But right now we need this information.

"I'm in my car. Let me head back to my desk. See if I can track him down."

"Thanks, Beau."

The line disconnects, and I turn to Jill. "He's going to see if he can track down Langston West."

"Good."

There's the fish and chips shop. Jill's car, parked in front. She unlocks the doors as we approach. I slide into the passenger seat.

It's hot as hell inside. Jill starts the ignition, cranks the air-conditioning. Then she just sits, makes no move to drive.

"It's the tip of the iceberg, isn't it?" she asks.

"I'm sorry?"

"Langston West. Falcon. This is just one source. But there are others, aren't there?"

I hadn't considered that possibility. But now that she says it, it makes sense. Why just stop at *one* fake source?

"He's ambitious. He's going places. And right now he's laying the groundwork. If he moves up the chain, he's going to produce whatever intelligence he wants."

Maybe that's true. Maybe it's *not* just a march toward military conflict. Maybe there's more. With power like this, with the ability to create intelligence, there's no telling *what* he could do.

"What do we do now?" I ask. A rhetorical question, really. I don't think she has the answer any more than I do.

"We can't do anything. We don't know who else is involved. It's not *just* Langston West. It's Falcon, too, whoever he is. Who else?"

I don't know who else. I don't know how deep this goes. None of us do. And she's right. Her kids aren't safe until we figure that out.

A few minutes later, my phone buzzes. The caller ID says *703,* nothing more. I answer. "Hello?"

"It's me." Beau's voice.

"Did you track him down?"

"Yeah. He's here, Alex. In the office." He's speaking quietly, barely more than a whisper. "There's a messenger app, and he's green. He's logged on, at his desk."

He doesn't say the rest, but I hear it in his tone. *He didn't do anything wrong.*

Jill's phone rings, and I see her practically pounce on it. She answers with a panicked "Drew?"

"Okay," I say to Beau. "Thanks for checking."

"What the hell's going on, Alex?" he asks.

Jill's listening intently to something on her own call.

"I gotta go, Beau. I'll fill you in later."

I end the call and lower the phone.

"What is it?" I say to Jill.

She covers the mouthpiece. "Plane landed at a private airport in rural Virginia."

"Where in Virginia?"

"Near the Shenandoah Mountains."

The Shenandoah Mountains.

The pieces of this puzzle floating around in my brain slide together, snap into place.

"I know where they are," I say.

CHAPTER THIRTY-FOUR

Jill

"**W**here?" I ask, even as I'm yanking the shoulder strap across my body, clicking the lock into place. *How does she know where they are?*

"I'm finding the address," she says, thumbs tapping the screen of her phone.

I shift into reverse, eye the mirror, pull from the spot. Shenandoah. That's where they landed. It's, what, an hour or two from here?

I pull out of the lot, onto the road, try to get my bearings. The mountains are west. I need to head west.

The voice from Alex's phone fills the silence in the car, tells me to take a right—

I take a right.

"How do you know where they are?" I ask again.

"A source."

"Natalia?"

"Different one. A tip. One that didn't make sense until now."

I feel a wave of frustration. She had this information the whole time?

But in a way, didn't *I*, too? How did I not connect that Langston West was behind this? He's the one who streamlined the asset approval process, removed many of the intermediaries. He's the reason it was just A.J., and the Chief of Station, and me, and COPS—and *him*.

Why didn't I see that sooner?

Abruptly Alex reaches for her phone again, places a call. "Hey, Marco," she says. "I'm going to text you an address. Can you tell me who owns the property?"

She lowers the phone and looks over at me. "I just need to verify this tip."

I nod. I'm too wound up right now to press for details. I don't care about the details, not really. I just care about finding my kids.

A moment later her phone chimes. She looks at the screen, then smiles. "Bingo. Langston West."

A surge of adrenaline rushes through me. I press down even harder on the gas. Whatever this tip was, it's good.

There's a big rig ahead of me, driving too slowly. I turn on my blinker, switch lanes—

In the rearview mirror, I see another car switch lanes, too. A dark blue SUV.

I press down on the gas, pass the rig, veer back into my own lane. I watch the mirrors. The SUV stays put, and slower. The distance between our two vehicles is growing.

I'm just being paranoid, aren't I?

We're just crossing into Virginia when Drew calls again, through Stronghold. I fumble for the phone, answer on speaker.

"Hello?" I say. "Drew?"

"Hi."

"What's the latest?"

He hesitates. "Not good. Apparently the police out in Shenandoah just visited the airport, but there's no surveillance footage.

We don't know where they went after they got off the plane." He sounds desperate. "I think it's a dead end, Jill. We've lost them again."

"It's not a dead end," I say. I don't want to get his hopes up by telling him too much. "We're working something on our end."

"You *are*? Oh God, Jill, I hope it works." His voice breaks. "We need to find them."

"I know," I say. "Listen, I gotta go. I'll let you know when we have something."

I lower the phone and focus on the road. I-66 is clear and wide, relatively empty, and I'm driving as fast as I can get away with, checking the mirrors for police, because that'll only slow us down, and I can't be slowed down.

We're just past Gainesville when I catch sight of something in my rearview mirror. In the distance, in my lane, but matching my speed, which is far above the limit. And matching my *route*, because it's here again, far from DC.

It's the dark blue SUV.

We're being followed.

I press down on the gas so hard I hear the engine struggle to respond. Out of the corner of my eye I see Alex look over, brace herself with one hand on her door.

"We're being tailed," I say without turning toward her.

There's an exit just ahead. Just past an incline in the road, one steep enough to block the view of the road from a distance. If I really gun it, if I can put enough space between the SUV and my own car, I can take it, and I can have a chance at losing him.

The dial on the dash points to 90, 95—

I speed past the exit.

I can feel Alex turn toward me, surprised.

There's a flat dirt area in the center of the highway just ahead. A turnaround for official vehicles, the kind of place police would sit for a speed trap, shielded from view by the rise and dip of the highway.

I slam on the brakes, jerk the wheel to the left, go careening into the dirt, spin at a 180, and back into the highway in the opposite direction, gunning the engine once again to increase my speed, blend in with the traffic that's fast approaching. The kind of move I learned ages ago on the Farm: operational security, how to outmaneuver a threat.

There's just enough of a gap in traffic to slide across all the lanes on this side of the highway and come to a stop in the grass on the shoulder of the road.

My seatbelt's locked tight into place. I'm almost dizzy with adrenaline. Cars whiz past. I can't believe that just happened. Alex is breathing hard, leaning back against her seat, holding on to the door handle with a white-knuckled grip.

I scan the highway in the opposite direction, the one from which I came, wait for the SUV to come into view.

Nothing. Other cars appear over the crest of the hill, but not that one. By now it should have come into view.

They must have taken the exit. Whoever's following me thought I went that way. I wish I could see the exit from here, but I can't.

They must be on that other road, trying to pick up my trail, or maybe they've gotten back on the highway ahead and they're gunning it, trying to catch up to where they think I might be. I don't know.

What I know is that they're not here.

I lost them.

There's a gap in traffic behind me, and I pull back onto the road, press down on the gas. I'll turn around at the first opportunity, get back on the path toward Shenandoah.

I'm in the clear. I'm not leading anyone toward my kids. I've escaped whoever's trying to follow me—

And then another thought occurs to me, one that fills me with a sense of dread:

Or they already know where we're heading.

The map brings us deep into the Shenandoah Valley, then up a winding road, one that's densely treed. There are homes here, older ones, spaced far apart, each set back in the woods, off long drives, private and serene.

I slow to a stop on the side of the street as we approach the destination on the map, idle there. The house we're looking for—1457—is up ahead. I can see the bottom of the driveway, the mailbox, but nothing more. And I don't want to get close enough for whoever's inside to see me.

"What now?" Alex asks.

"I don't know."

We decided not to call the police, not yet anyway. We don't know for sure the kids are in that house, and if they're *not,* and we get the authorities involved, and it gets back to *them,* I don't know what they'd do.

"Why don't we—"

My thought's interrupted by the buzz of Alex's phone. She looks at the screen, then answers on speaker.

"Hana. What'd you find?"

"Natalia, she's pretty senior. Works Middle East issues. Or *did,* anyway. She's on a different assignment right now, but we don't have info."

"How senior?"

"Holds the SVR's highest set of clearances."

That's pretty senior. The old CIA officer in me feels a rush of excitement. Nothing better than hearing someone has access like that.

"And her family—it's one hard-core SVR family, Alex."

Natalia's words ring in my head. *I'd be betraying my family. That's a line I can't cross.*

"Tell me," Alex says.

"Her husband is Viktor Ivanov. Senior SVR, arrested five years ago. *In the U.S.* In that big roundup. He's in a supermax in Colorado."

I watch a trail of dry leaves skitter across the street in front of us. The gust of wind whistles around the car.

"And her kids. She has two. They went off to the SVR youth program when they were young."

"Where are they now?"

"I don't know. Can't track them."

"Still SVR?"

"No reason to think otherwise."

There's a swift knock at my window.

I spin toward the sound, and there's a man there. Tall and lanky, about my age, thinning blond hair. He has a goofy grin on his face, and he's waving.

"Gotta go, Hana," Alex says, abruptly ending the call.

"Who's that?" I say.

"That's Timothy Mittens," Alex says.

Who the hell is Timothy Mittens? I roll down the window, and he bends down to look at us through the opening. He's still wearing that grin.

"Alex Charles! You came. I'm so glad."

"Hello, Timothy. Thank you for the tips."

"My pleasure, Ms. Charles. I'm thrilled to see you following up."

Alex nods. "Timothy, have you seen anything unusual in the past day or so?"

Timothy straightens, looks down at the cabin. "Well, yes. In fact I have. I was going to send you a message—"

"What is it?" I ask.

He shifts his focus to me. "A car pulled up late last night. A black Nissan Sentra."

Black Nissan Sentra. Like the car that followed me to the National Mall. The one driven by Falcon.

"DC plates?" I ask.

He looks surprised. "Why, yes." He shifts his gaze to Alex. "It was very late. *Suspiciously* late."

"Did you see who got out?" she asks.

I can just picture this Timothy character at the window of his own cabin, peeking through the curtains—

"No," he says with a frown. "Can't see the top of the driveway from here."

I glance at the house, and I know he's right. I can't tell if the car is there right now.

"But I did find this, in the driveway." He holds up a floppy toy, one that's instantly familiar.

It's Owen's stuffed elephant.

CHAPTER THIRTY-FIVE

Jill

I unbuckle my belt, push open the driver's-side door. Out of the corner of my eye I see Alex doing the same thing.

"Call the police," I say to Timothy. It's time to get them involved, because I know for sure now:

Owen and Mia are in that house.

I bolt out of the car, pull my gun from my bag, and Timothy Mittens steps back, the stuffed elephant at his side, watches me wide-eyed. I head past him at a jog, gun at my side, singular focus on the driveway up ahead.

Another gust of wind whips the branches of the trees, sends more leaves skittering across the road. They crunch under my feet as I pound the pavement. I can hear Alex just behind me.

When I reach the gravel driveway, I can see a car, parked up near the house. The black Sentra. It's still here.

The house itself looks dark, no sign of life. It's a two-story colonial, the blinds on all the windows tightly closed. There's a wide front porch, and two rocking chairs stand empty beside the door. One moves, ever so slightly, as a breeze blows through, almost eerily.

But the car—that car is here. That means my kids are here, doesn't it?

"I'll go this way," I whisper to Alex, nodding to the right. "Can you take the other side? See if there's a way in, or any sign of the kids?"

"Got it."

I creep around the right side of the house, trying my best to use trees as a cover, to stay hidden. I try to peer through the windows, but I don't see a thing through the blinds. Don't see any lights.

There are two small basement windows, down low to the ground. It looks dark down there, too.

I continue on to the back of the house. There's an empty firepit, four Adirondacks around it, covered in a thin film of dirt. A sliding glass door, with vertical blinds tightly closed—

A figure appears from behind the other side of the house, and my heart feels like it momentarily stops. But it's just Alex.

I motion for her to stop, and then I make my way quietly past the back of the house, meet with her.

"Anything?" I ask.

"Don't see a thing."

It's the answer I knew was coming, but it's disheartening nonetheless.

What am I supposed to do? Wait for the police to arrive? Try to get in there immediately?

What's safer for my kids?

That man, Falcon, what will he do if he sees the police arrive? Will he hurt Owen and Mia?

I have to get in there.

I look around this side of the house, so similar to the other. The first-floor windows are too high to reach. The basement windows—I drop to my knees in the dirt, dry leaves crackling under me. Stick my gun into the waistband of my pants. Push on the glass pane. Nothing. I push harder. There's a little bit of give.

I center my right foot on the glass, and kick in as hard as I can. The glass shatters. It feels loud. Was it too loud? I kick out the fragments until there's an opening big enough to climb through. Then I peer down. Nothing but darkness. I don't know what I'll be dropping down into.

"I'm going in," I say to Alex.

"Want me to follow?"

"Probably better if you don't. At least not right away." If anything happens, better that it just happen to one of us.

I put my legs through the opening, lower my body into it, slowly, wary of any last sharp fragments of glass, until I'm just hanging there, until I can't hold on anymore—

I squeeze my eyes shut and drop.

My feet hit solid ground. A floor, concrete. I bend my knees, manage to catch my balance.

I hold my breath. Hold still, crouched down, every nerve on alert.

It's silent, except for a faint drip coming from the other side of the basement. There's no one coming.

I let my eyes adjust to the darkness, and the surroundings gradually come into focus. A stack of cardboard boxes along one wall. Tools on a table along another wall. Furnace, water heater—

There's a thump on the other side of the basement, and without thinking I yank the gun from my waistband, draw down. My heart's pounding. But it's silent again, no other sounds. Must have been the furnace, something kicking on.

I creep forward quietly, carefully, toward the stairway at the far side of the room. The stairs are steep, wooden, with a closed door at the top. I start climbing slowly, gun at the ready. The third stair creaks, and I pause, listening intently for any sounds upstairs. Nothing.

Another step, and another, these thankfully silent. I'm closer to the top now. Another step—

Footsteps, from above. I go still and listen.

More steps, just on the other side of the door.

I aim the weapon at the door—

They're heading away. I listen to each step, the fading sound. Then there's a creak on the stairs. Just one person, I think. Heading upstairs—

A voice, from the other side of the door. Slightly muffled through the door, but high-pitched and sweet and oh so familiar—

"Owen, I'm scared."

It comes out like *Oh-ie, I'm scared.*

I don't even think. I just act. I shift the gun to my right hand and reach for the doorknob with my left. Open the door slowly, quietly, hoping the hinges don't make a sound—

It opens silently, and I take in the sight. A dimly lit kitchen, dark except for the light filtering in from outside. Two chairs in the center of the room. Owen's in one, Mia's in the other. Their hands are bound behind them—

I raise my index finger to my lips in a silent shushing motion.

Owen understands. I can see it in his eyes, big and solemn and scared. He's silent—

"Mommy!" Mia says, and she starts to cry.

"Shhh," I say, heart racing.

That was too loud. Someone's in the house. Falcon, probably. He heard that, didn't he?

Oh God, he's going to be back any minute.

I rush to Mia first, because she's crying. Shove the gun into my waistband, find the knot in the rope behind her back, start working on it, my hands trembling. "You have to stop crying," I whisper. "You have to be silent."

Owen's watching me with those big eyes, so serious.

The knot comes free and I pull the rope off her. "Go hide," I whisper.

"Where?" she whispers back. Her eyes are glassy, her cheeks streaked with tears.

I look around in a panic. "Behind the couch," I say, because isn't that where she loves to hide when we play hide-and-seek at home?

"Okay."

I move over to Owen next. Reach for the knot. This one's tighter—

There's a thump, from the basement. Alex, dropping down? Something else? Some*one* else? Oh God.

Footsteps, upstairs.

I try to work faster, but the knot's too tough—

Steps on the stairs now, the ones leading up from the basement. I let go of the rope and step in front of Owen, draw my gun, just as a figure comes into view—

Alex. She raises her hands, palms forward, mouths the words *It's just me.*

I holster the gun and get back to work on the rope—

Footsteps, upstairs again.

I work frantically, but the knot's stuck, I'll never get it in time.

The steps are on the stairs now, coming down—

I drop the rope and pull out the gun again. Alex takes my place behind Owen, thank God, starts in on the knot—

He's at the bottom of the stairs now. I start walking toward the sound, gun drawn, because I can't let him round that corner, can't let him in the same room as—

"Mommy, I'm scared," Mia cries, and I hear the sound of her little footsteps running toward me, only they're on a path to reach *him* before they reach me—

A scream.

There's Falcon, in my sights—

And my daughter's in his grasp, and he's holding a gun to her head.

CHAPTER THIRTY-SIX

Jill

"Drop the gun," he yells, and I don't, because I have him in my sights. Barely, though, because he's moving, ducking behind Mia, making it so I can't get a clear shot, and he knows it. He knows exactly what he's doing.

"Drop it!" he yells again, louder this time. He digs the barrel of his gun into the hair on the side of her head, and she squeezes her eyes shut, cries harder.

I focus on the sights, because he's *there,* and this is my chance to end it all, to get out of here with my children, to get out of here *alive,* but Mia's in the sights, too. I can't get a clear shot, and I can't pull the trigger, not when I might hit my daughter.

I lower the gun to my side, because if I don't, I know he'll shoot her. "Let her go."

"I said *drop* the gun!"

I open my hand, and it clatters to the floor.

He keeps the gun pressed to my daughter's head. "Kick it this way."

I reach for it with my foot, send it sliding across the floor toward him.

He glances down, ever so briefly. Then in one swift move he lowers his own gun, shoves Mia toward me. I catch her in my arms, wrap her into an embrace, my eyes immediately finding him over her shoulder. He's already picked up my gun, holstered it. And he's aiming his own at me.

It's that face I know so well, the one from the cable, the one that's been in my mind all these years.

Mia's crying, shaking uncontrollably, and I feel the strangest cocktail of relief and fear running through my veins. Relief because she's in *my* arms and not *his*, but fear because I've just lost the only chance I had to take him on, because my gut feeling is that both of us aren't walking out of here alive.

"Let my kids go," I say.

"You don't get to make demands." He nods toward the kitchen, behind me. "Walk."

"Let them go and—"

He levels the gun at my chest. *"Walk."*

He has the upper hand here. I don't think for a moment he wouldn't shoot. I pick up Mia, rest her on my hip, turn and walk toward the kitchen, toward Owen. God, I hope Alex managed to free him, that the two of them have somehow gotten away, or hidden at least.

The chair's empty. They're gone.

"Where's the boy?" he asks.

"I don't know."

"Get him back here."

My heart's pounding. I turn toward Falcon. He's right there in front of us, and he has that gun—

"Get him back here or I kill the girl."

Oh God. This just keeps getting worse and worse. Mia wraps her arms tighter around my neck, buries her face in my shoulder.

"Owen," I call. "Come out here please."

The house is silent, thank God. I realize I'm holding my breath.

"He's not here," I say to Falcon.

"He's here. *Get him.*"

Is he here? I have no idea. The back sliding door looks closed, the blinds still tightly closed. I know they didn't leave through the front. There's the open basement door—could he and Alex be down there? If so, they're trapped, because there's no reaching that window.

Falcon looks deadly serious right now, and I know I have to do something.

"Owen, it's Mommy. I need you to come out, honey. It's okay." I say the words, even though I know it's most certainly *not* okay.

There's no sound in the house, no movement.

"If you don't come out right now," Falcon calls, "I'll kill your sister."

Mia whimpers into my shoulder. I squeeze her tightly, my entire body tense with fear.

Silence. More silence, more stillness, and I'm relieved Owen isn't here but overwhelmed with a wave of terror that Falcon will hurt Mia—

A creak. Movement. The door to the coat closet is opening—

Owen steps out. He looks as scared as I've ever seen him, and my heart breaks for him, for the position he's in.

His gaze lands on me and his eyes fill with tears. He starts walking toward me—

"Were you alone in there?" Falcon asks.

Owen goes still. His eyes are still locked on me, and they widen, like he doesn't know what to say, whether to lie and protect Alex, or tell the truth and give her away.

"Come here," I coax him, crouching down, Mia still on my

hip, because I need them both close to me, and because I don't want him to answer this question, one with no good answer. He walks the rest of the way and falls into my open arm.

He reaches over and tightly touches Mia's back, like he wants to make sure she's okay, and my heart breaks again.

"Were you *alone* in there?" Falcon asks again.

Owen glances back ever so briefly at the closet—

"No," comes a voice from the closet. Alex steps out, hands up.

Relief washes over me, that she didn't put Owen in a position where he had to lie, didn't force him to give up her location, either.

I set Mia down gently on her feet, press Owen closer to her. "Go sit over there," I whisper, pointing to the other end of the kitchen, away from Falcon, away from the coat closet, praying they listen, that they obey, that I can put some space between them and Falcon during this moment of distraction.

Owen reaches for Mia and she silently follows him. Falcon glances at them and I'm filled with fear that he'll object, that he'll try to stop them, but he says nothing, turns back to face Alex. "I had a feeling you weren't far away," he says to her. "Move over there." He nods toward where I'm standing, and Alex walks slowly over, hands still raised, eyes locked on mine.

I can see fear there, but also a quiet strength, a determination.

She comes to a stop beside me, turns around slowly to face Falcon.

I glance over at the kids. Owen is sitting with his back against the cabinets, Mia snuggled into his lap, his arms around her. He's watching me, and he looks far older than his age right now.

"Who else knows about this?" Falcon asks, and I realize why we're standing in front of him, why he hasn't done anything yet.

Because it's not enough to just kill us. He needs to kill the whole story.

"Just us," Alex answers, and I don't know if that was a good move or not. If he thinks it's just us, there's no reason *not* to kill us, is there?

"Bullshit," he says. "How'd you find the story in the first place?"

"A tip," Alex says.

"From who?"

"I don't reveal my sources."

He levels the gun at her. "Who is he?"

Alex gives him a defiant look. "I protect my sources."

"Even if it costs you your life?" He gives her a wry smile. Makes a show of lining up the sights.

It's utterly silent. I'm holding my breath. I wouldn't blame Alex a bit for revealing the name of her source. God, I hope she *does,* because he's going to kill her otherwise, and this is *Natalia* she's protecting, someone who wouldn't protect my own kids by giving us the information we needed.

"Was it the Gang of Three?" I ask. Because I need to distract him, take his focus away from what he's about to do.

"Gang of Three plus me."

"Who are *you?*"

"I'm Falcon." He smiles, a creepy smile.

"Why'd you do it?" Alex asks. I glance over, and she meets my eye. I think she understands what I'm doing, the distraction technique.

"You can't help yourself, can you, Lois Lane? You just have to know the truth."

"What's the harm, at this point?"

"I guess there isn't any." He shrugs, the gun waving ever so slightly.

I glance back at the kids. Mia's lifted her head and is watching now, her thumb in her mouth. She hasn't sucked her thumb in ages.

"We did what needed to be done," he says, and I don't know if he's talking about the fake intelligence, or the attack at the Farm—

"Why Syria? Why *anthrax*?" I ask, and this time it's because I want to know.

"Because the American public is terrified of both. Because as soon as this *threat* becomes public, we'll get all the resources we need. We'll have a decent budget again, be able to afford sources, and technology. Congress will stop demanding specifics, and start *listening* to us."

"Because we'll be at war?" I ask.

"If war's what it takes, so be it. The CIA's never stronger than when we're at war."

So it *was* war, but not for the reasons we thought. Not because someone—or some group of people—would benefit financially. Because an *agency* would benefit, in terms of prestige. Because West would, too. *Power* was the currency, not money.

And the Gang of Three's complaints were key, like we thought. We just underestimated what they'd do to right those wrongs.

"What about Harris and Chen?" I ask.

"We couldn't let them ruin everything."

"Is that what happened with A. J. Graham, too?" Alex asks. "Were you afraid he was going to *ruin everything*?"

"He would have, if we'd let him. He figured out I was a fake."

"So you killed him?"

He shrugs. "West's orders. Ensure success of the operation at all costs."

Something changes in his expression, like he remembers where he is, who's in front of him, what's going on.

He takes a step forward, levels the gun.

He's about to shoot, and I can't let him shoot.

I could lunge at him. I stare down the barrel of the gun. The odds that the bullet *wouldn't* hit me are slim to none, but a slim chance is better than nothing.

I take one last look at my children—

And then there's a shot.

CHAPTER THIRTY-SEVEN

Jill

It's loud, almost deafening in the small space, and terrifying, because Falcon was just pointing that gun directly at me.

I duck, a reflex, a delayed one, since if the bullet was going to hit me, it already would have, and spin toward Falcon. *He's* ducking, as well, and swinging his gun *away* from me, toward the opposite side of the room—

Three more shots, rapid-fire, and I realize they aren't coming from *him,* they're coming from across the room, from the door that leads down to the basement—

I drop to the floor and turn toward the sound, and it's Natalia, standing in front of the open door, gun aimed at Falcon—

Natalia's *here.* In front of the open basement door, the same place Alex and I entered the room. *She* must be the one who was following us—

A burst of gunfire, from Falcon this time, and now it's Natalia who dives out of the way, out of the line of fire.

I crawl on all fours toward the kids, shield them behind me, because who knows if there'll be a stray shot—

Natalia gets off another burst of shots, but they go wide, and Falcon aims—

Nothing.

The room's silent, my ears ringing. His gun's jammed, or he's out of ammo—

I spin toward Natalia, but she's in the corner, reloading—

Falcon drops his gun, reaches into his waistband for mine—

It's not there.

At the same moment, I see it, on the floor, halfway between us. It must have fallen out when he dove.

I don't hesitate. I lunge for it, and just as I start to move I see *him* notice it, too, and I know he's going to go for it, and the only hope I have now of getting out of here alive, of getting *my kids* out of here alive, is to get to that gun first—

He *doesn't* go for it. He turns toward the back door. Pushes the blinds out of the way, yanks it open—

I pick up the gun and aim it in one fluid motion, but he's just barely out the door, and I don't catch him in my sights in time. I follow him outside, search for him in my sights—

But he's *gone.*

There's the firepit, and the Adirondacks, and the giant trees all around, leaves rustling in the breeze—

And no Falcon.

A sound, in the driveway, around the front of the house. An engine, starting. I bolt out into the yard, around the house, toward the driveway—

Tires peel.

I reach the driveway just as the Sentra is speeding out onto the street. I raise my gun, catch the rear of it in my sights—

But it's too far away. The best I could hope for would be a glancing shot, not enough to do real damage, and I can't risk firing a shot when I don't know what else is around.

I lower the gun to my side.

Natalia runs up behind me. The two of us stand at the top of the driveway and watch the taillights disappear into the distance.

"I missed," Natalia finally says. "I can't believe I missed."

"You saved us," I say.

Another breeze blows through, sends a chill through me.

The front door to the house opens, and I see Alex framed in the doorway. I turn and walk back inside, Natalia following behind me, then straight over to my kids.

Mia's face is streaked with tears; Owen's ashen. They're still clutching each other. I drop down to the floor in front of them, wrap my arms around them, pull them into a hug.

I look up, and Alex is turning the deadbolt on the front door. I glance around and see that the sliding door is tightly closed again, and the basement door is shut and locked.

I hug the kids tightly. My God, how close did I come to losing them? Owen's trembling, and I can hear Mia's heartbeat, fluttering away, much too fast. I bury my face in her baby-soft hair. It smells like shampoo, but not the no-tears kind, the hotel variety, maybe.

Natalia's watching us, a strange expression on her face. Wistful, I think. She catches me looking at her. "I should leave."

"Stay," Alex says.

"The police will be here soon."

"Natalia, you helped us," I say. "You don't have to fear the police."

"Oh, but I do. I don't want anyone to *ever* know that I helped you."

"You're afraid it'll get back to Russia?"

It doesn't seem like she hears me. She's still staring at my kids.

"Natalia?" I say.

She blinks, focuses on me. Outside, a gust of wind whips by the house.

"I had two boys, you know," she finally says. "Sacha and Misha."

In my mind I see that picture on her bedside table.

"The service took them into training when they were seven and eight. So when you said your kids were taken . . ." She shakes her head. "I always *felt* like mine were taken. Like I missed out on the chance to raise them."

I hug my kids just a little tighter, feel a pang of sympathy for her.

"My dream was always to one day be together again, with both of them." She says it almost sheepishly, like it's a foolish hope. "Working an operation together, side by side. That's why this was so hard—" Her voice breaks, and she stops. She blinks quickly, like she's trying to maintain her composure. "Doing this . . . it meant giving up on my dreams."

"I'm sorry," I say, and it seems completely inadequate.

"I once thought I'd have it all." She shrugs, again like it's foolish.

Alex and I exchange a glance, an uncomfortable one. I'm not sure either of us knows how to respond.

"Now I have nothing. My kids are gone. I just betrayed my country. My husband is in prison—"

"He's in prison?" I ask, even though I know he is, because I want to hear more.

"Thanks to Langston West," she says bitterly.

"That's why you were watching him," Alex says.

"Like a hawk. I hated him."

"And you found out about Falcon."

She nods. "It was gold. It was *blackmail*. The kind of blackmail that we could have used to convince Langston West to release Viktor."

"It didn't work?" Alex asks.

"We didn't *try*. If it was up to me, we would have. But the higher-ups, they wanted more. They *wanted* West to lead the U.S. into a conflict with Syria, or do something terrible with that anthrax, because the blackmail potential would have been that much greater."

"And you didn't want that to happen."

"Of course not. Innocent people would have perished."

"That's why you wanted me to reveal that Falcon was a fake," Alex says. "To put an end to whatever West had planned."

"Yes."

"But you wanted West's involvement to stay hidden," I say. "To hold on to that blackmail potential. That's why you wouldn't give us his name."

"That blackmail was the one thing that could have gotten Viktor released from prison. Blackmail West into agreeing to a spy swap, you know? *He's* the one who refuses to trade."

It's all making sense now. "You've helped us a great deal, Natalia. We can look into whether anything can be done about Viktor—"

"Absolutely not. If he were released, the SVR would figure things out. They'd know I betrayed them, or worse, they'd think it was Sacha or Misha. Better he stays in prison."

Mia shifts in my arms, burrows down deeper.

Natalia glances at her. "I didn't want anything to happen to your kids. It's just . . . It was so hard to cross that line. To give you that name."

"I understand," I say, and it's the truth. I do.

"I knew where you were headed. I followed you here, and I

didn't know what I was going to do. But then I saw your kids. And I heard you"—she turns toward Alex—"refuse to give up my name. *Protect* me."

"You did the right thing," Alex says.

"Did I? I always thought the right thing would be reuniting my family, protecting my country." She shakes her head. "Those dreams are dead. Now I'm nothing more than a traitor."

The wind outside howls. In the distance I hear the wail of sirens.

"I need to leave," she says.

I don't argue this time, and Alex doesn't either.

"I'd appreciate it if you could continue to protect my identity," she says to Alex.

"Of course," Alex says.

She gives Owen and Mia one last look. "Take care of those kids."

"I will," I say.

She heads for the sliding glass door at the rear of the house, opens it. The wail of the sirens is suddenly louder.

She steps outside and pulls the door closed again without ever looking back.

"Mommy, is that the police?" Owen whispers.

I nod.

"Are we safe?" Mia asks, pulling away, looking at me with those big innocent eyes.

I can see flashing lights out front, through the blinds. Splotches of red and blue color the walls of the kitchen. "We're safe."

I feel absolutely overwhelmed with emotion. I hug Owen and Mia tighter. Then I stand, lift Mia onto my hip, take Owen's small hand in mine, and walk to the front door.

I still need to face what's next. Responsibility for my role in all this, for approving Falcon. But come what may, my kids are safe.

Mia rests her head on my shoulder. Owen squeezes my hand, sidles up closer to me. I look over at Alex, who nods and gives me a smile.

Then I open the door, and I'm met with a bright sea of flashing lights.

And for the first time in as long as I can remember, I feel at peace.

CHAPTER THIRTY-EIGHT

Jill

Things moved fast after that. Less than an hour after we emerged from that cabin, police descended on Langston West's sprawling property on the outskirts of DC, took him into custody. Our claims on their own might not have been enough, but finding my kids at a property he owns? That did him in.

That night Alex's story went live on the *Washington Post* website. She ended up getting her scoop after all. It detailed everything—everything *except* Natalia's involvement, and mine. Nothing about Owen being kidnapped as a baby, or about me approving Falcon. She would have had a stronger story with it, a more sensational one. But she told me it wasn't about that. *Doesn't have to be the biggest story,* she said. *Just has to be a truth that people need to hear.*

And I'm grateful, because it kept my family out of the spotlight. But I came clean about my involvement, because it was the right thing to do. Because you can run from your past, but you can't hide from it. I told Agency investigators everything I did, and why I did it. Maybe they'll keep it in-house, maybe not. Either way, it doesn't matter. The kids are safe. *That's* what matters.

Alex's story made waves around the world, as it should have. The President and the director of the CIA denounced the Gang of Three in the strongest of terms, made it clear they were rogue actors, pledged that the U.S. would never deploy offensive bioweapons, never enter into a military conflict without abundant and unquestionably strong evidence. But the damage was done. Criticism of the U.S. reached an all-time high. The CIA was thrown into disarray. The director won't survive the fallout; her resignation is expected any day now. I'm not sure anyone will ever trust U.S. intelligence again—at home or abroad.

Langston West refuses to divulge details of his activities; he just keeps claiming he wasn't involved. The FBI's investigating, keeping the details out of the public domain, putting a lid on it, just like the CIA would do, but everything will come out eventually. It always does. Natalia says the SVR has intelligence that the anthrax was a research sample stolen from Fort Detrick, and that West was ultimately behind it. The dots are all there; we just need to connect them. And the CIA's hard at work on that, with Hana leading the charge. Alex gave her a tip about Falcon as soon as we were out of that house, and she got her scoop, just like she wanted, and a promotion, to boot.

Alex also called A.J.'s mother before the story went live, told her the truth, said it brought the woman a great deal of peace. I don't blame A.J. for what he did, sending in that cable. I don't blame Jeremy, either, for stepping away, refusing to help. Langston West found their price for silence, just like he found mine. Thankfully, Jeremy's dog Max turned up at a shelter a few days ago—one not far from Langston West's home—and the two were reunited.

Things with Drew are on the mend. He told me that when the kids were taken, he'd have done *anything* to get them back. I think for the first time he understood where I was coming from all those years ago. Why I did what they said, then stayed quiet, didn't tell anyone what had happened. Because it was the way to get Owen back, and then to keep him safe. Because I was doing what I thought was best for our family.

We're together again, the four of us. In temporary housing in Virginia, protected by elite Agency security. Langston West is locked away, no longer a threat, but Falcon is still out there. *Benjamin Goodson* is still out there, I should say. His picture was run through every facial recognition software system in the country. There was a match on a New Jersey driver's license. The Bureau's working to track him down. He'll turn up sometime; everyone does.

You can run, but you can't hide.

Every so often I look at my family—my husband, my two kids—and I think of Natalia. *Her* husband, *her* two kids. Her dream was for them all to be together. And I feel such sadness for her. Who would have ever thought I'd feel sympathy for a Russian spy? But she's so much more than that. She's the reason this all came to light. The reason I can finally find some peace.

I'm looking forward to getting back to regular life. Craving it, much more than I would have ever anticipated. Our home in Florida, my teaching job. It's not the life I envisioned, but I'm realizing that doesn't really matter. It's okay that life doesn't look the way I thought it would. I'm content. I have my family, and we're together. We're safe.

This nightmare is finally over.

CHAPTER THIRTY-NINE

Alex

I open the shipping box and carefully move aside sheets of packing paper, revealing the item nestled within: a large framed copy of the front page of *The Washington Post*. The one that features my headline, front and center and so damn *big*. I carefully pull it out and smile. A gift from my colleagues at the *Post*. They'd all chipped in when they learned I hadn't put this in a frame. *Unacceptable,* Marco had said in mock horror.

I zero in on the byline. *Alexandra Charles.* My full name, for the first time. And I finally let the *Post* attach a picture to my online profile. Added one to Twitter, too. Sure, life as a journalist might be easier as a faceless Alex. But I'm ready to tackle it as *me*.

I walk over to the built-in shelves. My gaze settles on the framed wedding picture of Miles and me. Still there. The last visible reminder of our old life together. I reach for it, remove it from the shelf. It's not nearly as hard as I always thought it would be. There's a quick pang of sadness. Of nostalgia, really. It was a time in my life that was happy, but it's in the past. I'm ready to move on.

I put the framed article in its place and nod approvingly. Looks a hell of a lot better, I have to say.

My eyes drift to the picture of my mom. Rumor around the journalism community is that I'm a shoo-in for a Pulitzer. My ultimate goal, for so long.

Black women *do* win journalism Pulitzers.

But now that I'm on the cusp of it, I realize it matters a lot less than I thought it did. My mom would be more proud of the *story* than the award. That I found the truth, exposed it. Informed people, protected people. Made a difference.

Those are the things that brought me to journalism in the first place. *That's* why I'm in this career. *That's* what makes me proud. It was far more rewarding to see Langston West in handcuffs than it was to see my byline on the front page.

I still wish my mom had seen her own byline on a story like this. But I've stopped worrying that deep down she secretly blamed me for missing out. After watching Jill and her kids, I find that my perspective has changed. Jill would have sacrificed anything for those kids. Because they were what mattered most to her. And I was what mattered most to my mom. I don't doubt that for a minute.

I scan the rest of the room. It looks so different than it did a couple of weeks ago. So much better. Gone are the neutrals, all the décor I agreed to in an attempt to compromise. I've replaced them with things that are *me*. A sunny yellow rug, teal throw pillows, fresh lilies in a vase. There's a stack of travel books on the table in the center of the room. I booked flights last week: three weeks in Southeast Asia. I can't wait.

There are many different paths to happiness. I'm finding mine. And I know one thing for sure: Miles isn't part of it. I don't need a spouse who brings me down.

I check my watch, then grab my bag and keys. Time to go. As I open the door, I take one last look around the loft—this loft that finally feels like mine—and smile. Life has never felt so damn perfect.

Thirty minutes later I'm at the Lincoln Memorial. Sitting on the steps, looking out over the Reflecting Pool. Jill's on one side of me. Natalia's just sat down on the other. It's a beautiful day. The sun's sparkling on water, tourists are milling about. Jill's plainclothes security detail is hovering nearby somewhere, blending into the crowd.

The *Post* had offered to cover a detail for me, too. At least for a short time. I declined. I'm sure I'd have thought differently if the threat was to someone I loved. It's one thing to accept risk to myself; it's another to accept it on behalf of someone else. In fact, if they'd have attacked someone I loved instead of me, I might have let the story go. I might have stayed quiet. I might never have found the truth.

I'd reached out to thank Natalia when it was all over and done with. Sent her a message on ClandestineTips. *Thank you again for all you did.*

Thank YOU, she'd written back. *For sharing the truth. And for protecting my identity.*

We made plans to meet here at the memorial, just before she flies back home to Moscow. It's a place she said she'd always wanted to visit. A place I knew would be teeming with oblivious tourists, where I could comfortably hide behind dark glasses and a hat. My picture hasn't been bandied about nearly as much as my name, but I don't want to take any chances, meeting in public with my source.

I look over and smile at her. "It's nice to see you again."

"Likewise." She leans forward to look at Jill. "And nice to see *you.*"

"It's really good to see you, Natalia," Jill says.

"How are your kids?" Natalia asks.

"They're doing really well."

She smiles. "I'm glad."

I can't help but think of her own kids. Those two little boys in the picture.

"Have you heard anything from your own?" Jill asks. We're clearly on the same wavelength.

"No." She stares out at the Reflecting Pool. It takes her several moments before she speaks again. "I just hope they're happy. And safe. That's what matters in the long run, isn't it?"

"You seem at peace," Jill says.

"I'm getting there. This is a process, you know?"

I know. Or at least it is for me. Finding my own peace.

"It wasn't our government," I say. I hope it didn't come across like an *I told you so*. "It was some people gone rogue."

"I see that now. And I'm pleased with your government's response. My own government would have done things differently."

I turn the words over in my mind, and I can feel Jill's eyes on me. Beau has been begging to meet with Natalia ever since the story broke. Hell, even before it broke. *She could be an asset, Alex,* he said. *We could have a penetration deep in the Russian intelligence services.* He told me they need it more than ever. That they're desperate. That after the Falcon debacle, all of the Agency's sources have been thrown into question.

I know he's right. She'd be an excellent source. She's willing to betray her country to do what's right. And her access is unparalleled.

"You know, you could continue to make a difference," Jill says cautiously.

Natalia replies almost instantly. "I'm not going to work for your government."

There's a beat of silence. I look down at my hands. I'd agreed to let Jill handle this part; it was the deal we reached with Beau.

"Maybe you don't need to look at it like that," Jill says. "Maybe you just look at it as doing the right thing. If there's ever information you feel needs to get into different hands, or if there's any critical information we need to ask for—"

"I don't want any part of this. It's dangerous. I'm not going to be in Moscow, meeting with a CIA officer."

Jill and I exchange a glance, and then she speaks again. "Well, here's the thing. You wouldn't have to. We have technology—covert communications—that would allow you to communicate remotely. Discreetly."

"I know what COVCOM is. And I know you're not just going to send me on my way with it. I would have to be vetted."

"You've proven yourself. What you've done, what you've given us, you've gone above and beyond."

It's true; I heard the conversation between Jill and Beau. Natalia gave us sensitive information. The kind that could have given her country blackmail, and leverage. She put herself in a precarious position, because they'd never forgive those actions. She didn't have to intervene in that house. She could have let Falcon take us out and just reached out to another journalist. She saved our lives and risked her own in the process.

The only thing that's missing, really, is a polygraph. And a polygraph would be pointless; she works counterintelligence for the SVR. She knows how to beat a poly.

"So you're saying . . ." She trails off.

"We're willing to make an exception. This is highly unusual. But extreme circumstances call for extreme measures."

She's quiet. "Your COVCOM, it's not exactly the best. I know it's been used to uncover other sources—"

"We have a new system. Best system we've ever created. It's

secure. No one's penetrated it. It's only gone out to our absolute most trusted sources, the ones in the most sensitive positions, with the very best access to information, the most important sources. You'll get one of those, Natalia."

"You're speaking like a CIA officer."

She smiles. "*Former* officer. But we've talked to a colleague. He's nearby, actually."

Natalia looks around, spooked. She doesn't spot Beau, but I know he's just a few steps up and over, COVCOM system in hand, waiting. Ready to deliver it and provide a quick training before she flies back to Moscow.

"No pressure, Natalia. We understand if you don't want to. But we also think you could be of great service to . . . well, to the world. A check on abuse of power. A back channel to help ensure stability between Russia and the U.S. You could truly make a difference."

She looks conflicted.

"We can discuss compensation—"

"I don't want to be paid."

Jill holds up her hands. "Okay."

Way in the distance, I can see a pair of ducks floating toward the center of the Reflecting Pool.

"So I'd just hold on to it. I don't *have* to do anything. But if I ever have information . . ."

"If you ever have information, you can get it directly to the CIA. No more anonymous tips to a reporter." She smiles.

"And what will you ask of me?"

"You'll never be required to share more than you're comfortable sharing."

I watch Jill with a sense of awe. She's damn good at this. She looks completely in her element, and she looks happy. She told me before Natalia arrived that she was excited to do this, recruit a source, a critical one at that. She said it felt like a last hurrah, and a way to atone for what she did wrong all those years ago. One last thrill before returning to normal life—something she said she now realizes she wants more than anything. And the CIA's letting her; so far there's no appetite for punishing her. The Agency agrees she's the best positioned to attempt this recruitment, given how skittish Natalia is.

"Natalia, you once said you didn't think there was any such thing as having it all. But maybe you *can*. Maybe this is a way to continue leading the life you're comfortable leading—but doing the right thing at the same time."

She raises her eyebrows, but says nothing.

"For me, it was about changing my perspective," Jill says. "Letting go of how I thought my life would look. It took almost *losing* it all to realize that I actually *have* it all."

I feel compelled to talk. "You know, a different perspective was what I needed, too. My mom used to say there are many different paths to happiness. I really think that's true. For the first time since I lost her, I feel content. I want you to find *your* path, Natalia."

She examines her hands. Then she looks up at me. "I'm glad you're both happy. But it's not that easy for me."

"You'd be doing what's right," Jill says. "And that will bring you more peace than you'd guess. Trust me: I know."

"It's why you joined the intelligence service in the beginning, isn't it?" I say. "To make a difference? This is your chance."

Natalia searches my face, then Jill's. I try to read her expression, determine what she's thinking, but I can't.

"I always imagined making a difference," she says.

A couple of young girls in pigtails skip by beside us, darting from step to step. She watches them, then turns and faces the Reflecting Pool. Sits quietly, deep in thought.

Losing everything changes you. Those words that A.J.'s mother spoke float through my mind.

Life doesn't always turn out the way we expect, that's for sure. If we're lucky, it's just as sweet. Sweeter, even.

I don't know if it will be for Natalia. But I didn't think it would be for me, either, and I'm more content than I've ever been.

She might have lost her dreams, but maybe, just maybe, she'll grab on to this new one.

"Okay," she says at last. She gives us a resolute nod. "I'll do it."

EPILOGUE

The woman now known to the U.S. government as Python boards a United flight to Beijing, where she'll catch a connection to Moscow. She slides into the last row of business class, past two empty seats to the one by the window, sets her carry-on down by her feet. Then she reaches in, pulls out a slim black case, barely bigger than a notebook. Places it on her lap, clasps her hands over it, and waits.

A few minutes later the man once known as Falcon stops at the same row. He lifts a carry-on into the overhead bin, slides into the middle seat beside her. He removes his baseball cap, runs a hand through his newly shorn hair, over his freshly smooth cheeks. Even his once-bushy eyebrows have been plucked; he looks like a completely different person.

Wordlessly she hands him the slim black case. He unzips it, pulls out a laptop barely bigger than a sheet of paper. "Quite a bit smaller this time."

"Technology has improved."

He smiles. "If it hadn't, none of this would have been necessary."

Another man hustles down the aisle, like he's running late. He's awkwardly carrying a large duffel bag, bumping people as he goes, apologizing hurriedly. He stops at their row, hoists the bag into the overhead bin, plunks himself down in the empty seat. Then he leans into the aisle, hails a flight attendant. "Vodka rocks please. Double."

The attendant heads toward the galley, and the man leans back in his seat, lets out an exaggerated sigh. Then he looks at the two passengers beside him, plasters on a fake cheery smile, and extends a hand as though offering a handshake. "Mittens. Timothy Mittens."

"How did you come up with that ridiculous name, anyway?" the woman asks.

He leans back theatrically, hand over his heart, as though offended. "Thought it had a nice ring to it."

The woman seated in the window seat in front of them stands up, and the three fall silent. She steps out of the row, reaches into the overhead bin for her handbag, then makes her way back to her seat, never giving the passengers behind her so much as a glance.

"You had it easy, you know," says the man once known as Falcon, quietly, to the man beside him. "One infant. Now it's two *children*."

"The *infant* did nothing but cry," he replies in Russian. "I wanted to smother him."

The flight attendant approaches, deposits a drink on his tray, continues on down the aisle. He flashes her a fake smile, one that disappears as soon as she does, grabs the drink, downs it.

"And *you*," says the man once known as Falcon to the woman beside him. "You nearly took me out with that first shot. I think the bullet grazed the hair on my arm."

She smiles. "Exactly. Had to look convincing. And come on, when have I ever missed a shot?"

"Is this it?" asks the man known as Timothy, nodding toward the device, switching back to English.

"Yes," replies the woman, reaching for the case, taking possession of it once again.

"Better be worth it."

"It was before, wasn't it? And they're even more confident now that they're getting this new technology into the right hands."

She smirks, and the man once known as Falcon snorts.

The flight attendant hurries back down the aisle, and the man known as Timothy flags her down. "Ma'am?"

She turns, her expression harried. "Yes?"

"Another vodka, please." He flashes her a grin. "Whenever you get a chance."

Her expression softens. "Certainly, sir," she says, and heads on toward the galley.

He watches her go, then turns to his seatmates. "International opinion of the U.S. has reached an all-time low, you know."

"Their loss is our gain," the woman replies, in Russian.

"No one's losing more than Mr. West," he replies, effortlessly shifting to Russian.

"Divine justice. He's going to rot in prison. And what about Chen and Harris?"

"Ah, the collateral damage. It was quick, at least. Where'd you get that strain, anyway?"

A smile pulls at the corner of her lips. "Just a little something we've been working on. Might be useful in the future."

The flight attendant approaches from the galley, sets down three small bottles of vodka on the open tray. "Thought you might want extra." She puts a finger to her lips and winks.

"Oh, don't worry," the man known as Timothy says to her, his tone conspiratorial. "I can keep a secret."

She continues on down the aisle, and he hands one of the mini bottles to each of his seatmates. "Cheers," he says, twisting the cap off his bottle and raising it in a toast.

"To you, boss," says the other man, clinking his bottle against the woman's. "To a successful operation."

"Hear, hear," agrees the man called Timothy. "To our fearless leader."

The woman clinks her bottle against his. She unscrews the cap and takes a sip, her nose scrunching ever so slightly. Then she settles back into her seat, rests her hands gently on the black case.

Success. She's had it before, sure. Especially four years ago, when they got access to the first COVCOM system. But *now* . . . Now it's even sweeter. The accolades are sure to roll in. This is the pinnacle of her career, if she wants it to be. Otherwise, the sky's the limit.

Those women, they were wrong. She doesn't have to change her perspective. She doesn't have to let go of what she thought she'd have, of how she thought her life would look. And she certainly doesn't need their pity. It was a useful distraction, kept their minds off the truth. But it's *she* who pities *them*. Because they abandoned their dreams. She made hers a reality.

She watches the flight attendant close the cabin door, push the lever into the locked position. There's something very final about it. Like they're putting this all behind them—America, those people—once and for all. They're almost home.

Viktor will be home soon, too. Once her country starts nabbing some very important American agents—something that's inevitable once they exploit the new COVCOM—spy swaps are sure to resume. Viktor will be free, and the man who arrested him will spend the rest of his life behind bars.

She lays a hand on the arm of the man once known as Falcon, and looks over at the man known as Timothy.

Then she leans back in her seat, and a smile spreads to her face—the deep, contented smile of a woman whose dreams have come true. "I'm glad we're together again, my sons."

ACKNOWLEDGMENTS

Thank you to *you*, readers, and to all the booksellers, librarians, bloggers, and reviewers who help us find books to love.

Thank you to everyone at Ballantine, especially Kara Cesare, Jesse Shuman, Kelly Chian, Karen Fink, and Taylor Noel. And my gratitude, as always, to David Gernert, Ellen Coughtrey, Anna Worrall, and Rebecca Gardner at The Gernert Company.

Much appreciation goes out to my friend and trusted test reader Karen Boyer, the CIA's Prepublication Classification Review Board, and all the foreign publishing teams I've been fortunate to work with.

To my wonderful family members in Florida, Costa Rica, Massachusetts, Connecticut, and Colorado: I'm grateful for all of you.

To Barry: Thanks for being the best husband and dad, hands down. And to our kids, James, William, and Emma: I love you so much, and I feel lucky every day to be your mom.

ABOUT THE AUTHOR

KAREN CLEVELAND is a former CIA counterterrorism analyst and the *New York Times* bestselling author of *Need to Know* and *Keep You Close*. She has master's degrees from Trinity College Dublin and Harvard University. Cleveland lives in North Carolina with her husband and three children.

karen-cleveland.com
Facebook.com/KarenClevelandAuthor
Twitter: @karecleve

ABOUT THE TYPE

This book was set in Sabon, a typeface designed by the well-known German typographer Jan Tschichold (1902–74). Sabon's design is based upon the original letterforms of sixteenth-century French type designer Claude Garamond and was created specifically to be used for three sources: foundry type for hand composition, Linotype, and Monotype. Tschichold named his typeface for the famous Frankfurt typefounder Jacques Sabon (c. 1520–80).